Jaci Burton i̶ ... lives in
Oklahoma w̶ ... wn chil-
dren, who are ... of their
own. A lover of spo̶... it is by what
sport is being played. She watches entirely too much television,
including an unhealthy amount of reality TV. When s̶h̶... n't on
deadline, Jaci can be found at her local casino, trying ... ̶me a
... ̶story
... ̶ppily ever after, which you'll find in all her books.

Find the latest news on Jaci's books at www.jaciburton.com, and
connect with her online at www.facebook.com/AuthorJaciBurton
or via Twitter @jaciburton.

Praise for Jaci Burton:

'A wild ride' Lora Leigh, No. 1 *New York Times* bestselling author

'It's the perfect combination of heat and romance that makes this
series a must-read' *Heroes and Heartbreakers*

'Plenty of emotion and conflict in a memorable relationship-
driven story' *USA Today*

'Strong characters, an exhilarating plot, and scorching sex . . .
You'll be drawn so fully into her characters' world that you won't
want to return to your own' *Romantic Times*

'A beautiful romance that is smooth as silk . . . leaves us begging
for more' *Joyfully Reviewed*

'A strong plot, complex characters, sexy athletes, and non-stop
passion make this book a must-read' *Fresh Fiction*

'Hot, hot, hot! . . . Romance at its best! Highly recommended!'
Coffee Table Reviews

'Ms Burton has a way of writing intense scenes that are both
sensual and raw . . . Plenty of romance, sexy men, hot steamy
loving and humor' *Smexy Books*

'The characters are incredible. They are human and complex and
real and perfect' *Night Owl Reviews*

'Spy the name Jaci Burton on the spine of a novel, and you're guaranteed not just a sexy, get-the-body-humming read, but also one that melds the sensual with the all-important building of intimacy and relational dynamics between partners' *Romance: B(u)y the Book*

'As usual, Jaci Burton delivers flawed but endearing characters, a strong romance and an engaging plot all wrapped up in one sexy package' *Romance Novel News*

By Jaci Burton

Brotherhood by Fire Series

Hot to the Touch
Ignite on Contact
All Consuming

Boots and Bouquets

The Matchmaker's Mistletoe Mission (e-novella)
The Best Man Plan

Hope Series

Hope Smoulders (e-novella)
Hope Flames
Hope Ignites
Hope Burns
Love After All

Make Me Stay
Don't Let Go
Love Me Again
One Perfect Kiss

Play-by-Play Series

The Perfect Play
Changing The Game
Taking A Shot
Playing To Win
Thrown By A Curve
One Sweet Ride
Holiday Games (e-novella)
Melting The Ice
Straddling The Line

Holiday On Ice (e-novella)
Quarterback Draw
All Wound Up
Hot Holiday Nights (e-novella)
Unexpected Rush
Rules of Contact
The Final Score
Shot On Gold

ALL
CONSUMING

Jaci **BURTON**

HEADLINE
ETERNAL

Published by arrangement with Berkley.
An imprint of Penguin Publishing Group,
a division of Penguin Random House LLC.
First published in the United States in 2021

First published in Great Britain in 2021
by HEADLINE ETERNAL
An imprint of HEADLINE PUBLISHING GROUP

1

Cataloguing in Publication Data is available from the British Library

ISBN 978 1 4722 7086 3

Offset in 10.5/14.5 pt Sabon LT Std by Jouve (UK), Milton Keynes

Printed and bound in Great Britain by Clays Ltd, Elcograf S.p.A.

Headline's policy is to use papers that are natural, renewable and recyclable
products and made from wood grown in well-managed forests and other
controlled sources. The logging and manufacturing processes are expected
to conform to the environmental regulations of the country of origin.

HEADLINE PUBLISHING GROUP
An Hachette UK Company
Carmelite House
50 Victoria Embankment
London EC4Y 0DZ

www.headlineeternal.com
www.headline.co.uk
www.hachette.co.uk

For my husband, who puts up with my moods,
brings me food and makes me pie.
You're a true romance hero. I love you.

ALL
CONSUMING

CHAPTER 1

EVEN WITH SWEAT POURING DOWN HIS FACE AND MUS-cles straining until they hurt, Kal Donovan was deliriously happy to be doing his job as he made his way through the rope rescue skills activity. He was adept, sure with his hands, balanced twenty feet above the beams in the Technical Rescue Team training room as if he'd been made for this.

Because he had and he knew it. He didn't falter once as he snaked his way down the rope, using his hands to carefully maneuver toward the rescue dummy dangling precariously off the platform below him. Kal was secured by his harness, his teammates above him holding on to his rope and making sure he was safe. In a real-life scenario, this would be a lot scarier. Instead of swinging twenty feet off the ground, it could potentially be twenty stories or more. He made every connection, then rescued the dangling dummy and brought it to safety, his muscles screaming in pain. He was drenched in sweat, but he'd gotten the job done.

And when he finished, everyone on the team applauded. Well, almost everyone. He felt the eyes of a couple of his team members glaring at him in judgement, as if what he'd done wasn't good enough. Even though his lieutenant nodded in satisfaction, there were still a couple of members on his team who felt he didn't belong.

Sure, it had only been four months since he joined the TRT, but in that time he'd more than proved himself, both in training and on calls. He had no idea what the issue was with Phil Beckwith and Dean Starling.

He pulled off his gloves and returned them to his bag, the feel of their eyes still burning on his back.

"Good job, Donovan."

He straightened and smiled at Micah Brown. "Thanks."

Meg Garcia joined Micah, leaning an arm on his shoulder. "You'll never be as good as me, of course. I'm the best here. But still, you're not too bad."

Micah shoved her off. "What're you talking about? I'm better than you'll ever be, Garcia."

"Wanna put those words to action? I'll rope climb you for bragging rights."

"You're on."

And they were, climbing the rope side by side, using only their hands and arms to bring them up. Kal had to admire the effort it took to do it without gloves. That had to hurt like hell.

Meg won by a hand. She slid down to the applause of the squad, including Starling and Beckwith.

Micah and Meg shook hands.

"You're pretty good for a—"

Meg pointed a finger at Micah. "If you say 'for a girl,' you're gonna lose your balls."

"I was gonna say . . . uh . . . for a . . . uh . . ."

"Better quit while you're already behind, Brown," Lieutenant Anderson said. "Clean up in here. Irish said lunch is ready."

"Yes, sir," Micah said, the first to make his exit from Meg.

"Good thing he's a fast runner," Andy Redmond said.

"Yeah, he needed to run," Meg said, then turned to Kal. "And what about you?"

He held out his hands. "I'm no match for you. I already know that."

She grinned. "Smart answer. Let's clean this up. I'm hungry."

They put the training room back in order, then everyone hustled into the kitchen.

Kal loved this station. The TRT shared space with Station 38 since it was a large fire station, with plenty of room for all of TRT's gear and vehicles. Though they often went on calls with all of Ft. Lauderdale's fire stations, depending on who needed their expertise. And sometimes they went out on their own.

Station 38 was out on a call, which meant the TRT could spread out at the large table.

Irish Smith had made amazing Cubano sandwiches for lunch. The smell of the pork cooking had been driving Kal crazy all morning, so when Irish handed him one, his mouth watered. Gooey cheese hung out the sides of the sandwich.

"Irish, you missed your calling," Kal said. "You should have been a chef."

"Nah," the big, burly firefighter said. "Cooking is just for fun. Firefighting is the real job."

"Amen to that," Starling said. "A real firefighter knows that firefighting is the blood, sweat and tears of what we do."

Starling made sure to give Kal a direct look when he said it. And Beckwith, right behind him, offered up a smirk.

Whatever. Kal had given up trying to figure out why those guys had it out for him. He knew it wasn't the color of his skin, because Starling was black like him. So it had to be something else.

He made his way to the table and took a seat, diving into

his sandwich, enjoying the flavor of the pork, ham and all the spices.

"Heard you did good on the ropes, Kal," Irish said, coming to sit down across from them.

"Thanks," Kal said.

"Yeah?" Phil Beckwith asked. "Who told you that? He ain't that good."

Irish pinned Beckwith with a hard stare. "Yeah? Who died and made you the judge of this team?"

The one thing Kal had learned straight off was never to argue with Irish Smith. He was mean as fuck when crossed.

Beckwith didn't answer, just shoved his sandwich in his mouth, which was a smart move.

Kal had just finished the last bite of his lunch when the alarm sounded for the TRT.

They climbed into their turnout gear and headed to their trucks.

"Two tractor trailers collided on I-95," their lieutenant relayed to them. "One on fire on the overpass, one dangling over the overpass, the driver trapped inside. Station 17 is on scene working the fire. We need to rescue the driver and secure the trailer before it falls."

Kal closed his eyes and got a mental picture of what the scene looked like, what they'd need to do once they got there.

Fortunately, it didn't take long to get to the area, which looked like a disaster. At least it was still daylight, which meant it would be easier to assess the situation. Lieutenant Anderson met with the lieutenant of Station 17 to get a sitrep.

Kal studied the scene. They could rappel down and get to the cab of the truck. Wouldn't be easy, but it was doable.

"All right, everyone," the lieutenant said, grabbing their attention. "Brown, Donovan, Starling, I want you all harnessed up to rescue that driver. Be ready to go as soon as the rig is shored up."

They all nodded.

"The rest of you get rigging in place to shore up that semi right now. We've got two heavy-duty wreckers on the way to pull that semi up, but I want that driver out of there in case something goes wrong. Ladder 24 is arriving on scene below to provide assistance."

Kal had gotten into his harness, grabbed his ropes and was ready to anchor and rappel down with his team. They met at the guardrail, and once the rest of the team secured the load and the rig, they started to rappel. Regardless of what Starling thought about him, they worked together to make their way down to the semi cab.

They tossed their ropes over the side of the concrete, Beckwith and Redmond providing anchor support.

Since Micah Brown was the senior firefighter of the three of them, he was lead on this.

"Swing around, Donovan, and make your way to the door."

"You got it," Kal said, inching his way across the cab, trying to do it as lightly as possible so the cab wouldn't sway. Fortunately, there was no wind today, which helped.

He peeked his head inside the door.

"You okay?" he asked the driver.

"Scared shitless. Get me out of here."

"Are you hurt anywhere?"

The guy shook his head. "I'm fine. I just want out."

"Try to stay calm. Don't move. We'll get you out soon. What's your name?"

"Larry."

"All right, Larry. I'm Kal. Keep your seat belt on and stay still. I'm going to open the door. You'll feel like you're falling, but I'm not gonna let that happen."

Larry looked out the window. "Okay."

Starling had made his way next to Kal, and looked over at him.

"Turn around so I can get the harness," Starling said.

Kal pivoted, and Starling unhooked the harness from his belt.

"Hey, buddy," Starling said. "My name's Dean, and when Kal here opens the door, I'm gonna grab hold of you and slip this harness on you. Then I'll hook it to my harness, and we'll head out of here."

Larry nodded. "Yeah, sounds great."

Micah hovered just to the side, helping to provide rope support.

"You ready, Larry?" Kal asked.

"No, but let's do it."

"Okay, Larry," Kal said, keeping his voice calm and even so the guy wouldn't freak out. "You hang tight to the steering wheel, and don't lean toward the open door. We'll handle the rest."

Kal looked at Starling, who nodded. Kal opened the door, and Starling slipped inside, grabbing hold of the driver. Kal made his way around to support both Starling and Larry, and before long they had secured the driver with the harness and unhooked his seat belt. Then it was a matter of getting him to Station 27's ladder team, which was already in place. Kal, Starling and Micah all followed the ladder team down.

Once Larry was securely on the ground, the two wreckers could start the job of pulling the semi off the side of the overpass.

Lieutenant Davenport of Ladder 27 came over to them. "Good save today, guys."

"Thanks," Kal said.

Micah followed the lieutenant over to make sure Larry was okay. Kal turned to Starling.

"We did good today."

"You were lax on the rope. And you didn't back me up fast enough once I reached the driver. If I wasn't as fast as I am, both he and I could have fallen. Next time, step it up."

Starling walked away, and Kal just stared after him.

What the fuck? Kal knew he'd done that job clean and perfect. So what the hell was Starling's problem?

He shook his head and went over to talk to the ladder team, because there was no point in having a conversation with someone who completely disagreed with you.

Ladder 27 gave them a ride back up to the top of the overpass, reuniting them with their team. They did cleanup and returned to the station. Fortunately, the rest of the day was uneventful, and Kal was damn glad when shift was over the next morning. He was frustrated and tired, hadn't slept well the night before and was grouchy when he got home.

He pulled into the driveway at the same time as his brother Jackson.

"How was shift?" Jackson asked.

Kal shrugged. "Saw some action. The two semis on I-95. Rappelled down and helped get the stranded driver out."

"Heard about that. Good rescue."

They went through the garage and inside the house, putting their gear away in the laundry room.

"Not a good rescue on my part if you ask one of my team members."

Jackson tucked his head in the fridge and grabbed some orange juice, then pulled glasses from the cabinet and poured. "Still having issues with those two guys?"

"Apparently. I don't know what it is with them, but I can't seem to do anything right."

Kal went to the sink to wash his hands, dried them, then got eggs and bacon out of the fridge.

Kal and his brother stood side by side making breakfast.

"What do you think it is?" Jackson asked. "Just a personality clash?"

Kal pulled the bacon from the pan and laid it on a plate, then started on toast. "I don't know. Maybe. I've tried to be nice, I've tried hard to get to know them, but they won't give me anything."

"What does your lieutenant say about the job you're doing?"

"Nothing but good things."

"Fuck 'em," Jackson said. "They've obviously got it out for you for no good reason. Or maybe they're jealous that you're doing so well after such a short period of time on the team."

Kal shrugged. "I've tried everything I can, and all I get is shit from them."

They carried their plates to the table and sat.

"Then stop trying," Jackson said. "You don't need their approval. They don't evaluate your performance—your lieutenant does. And as long as he says you're getting it done, that's all that counts."

Kal knew Jackson was right. He didn't need everyone on his team to like him. But, damn, he'd never had a conflict like this with anyone he'd worked with before. He and his fellow firefighters had always gotten along. When he'd worked at the same station with his brothers Jackson and Rafe, the entire group had been like a family. There had been no personality clashes.

He was an easygoing guy. He was friendly.

Then again, maybe Jackson was right and he needed to let it go. As long as they could work together, nothing else mattered.

"I smell bacon."

Kal looked up to see Becks, Jackson's fiancée, coming down the stairs.

Jackson grinned. "I knew the smell of bacon would wake you up."

"And we made extra," Kal said.

"Which is why I love you both—in different ways."

Kal laughed.

She came over and kissed Jackson, went over to fix herself

coffee and filled her plate with bacon and eggs. Then she took a seat.

"How were your shifts?" she asked.

"Kal had mean boys, so his was shitty," Jackson said. "Mine was good. Nothing eventful."

Becks looked over at Kal. "What? You have mean boys on your team?"

"I don't want to talk about it. How's tattooing?"

"Fabulous," she said. "And you know you can talk to me about anything."

"Thanks. If I need to, I will." He'd practically grown up with Becks. They'd all been homeless together, so she was like a sister to him. Finding her again and Jackson and Becks falling in love had been the greatest thing to ever happen to their family. And now that Jackson had finally proposed to Becks, they were getting married. Hell, both of his brothers were getting married. His brother Rafe and his fiancée, Carmen, were tying the knot next month.

They were all growing up. It was kind of surreal.

"So, you guys have a weekend off, which is rare," Becks said. "What's on your agenda this weekend, Kal?"

"My ten-year high school reunion is tomorrow night."

Becks's eyes widened. "How fun. You're going, aren't you?"

"I thought I might. Hang out with a few of my friends, and hopefully catch up with other friends who don't live close by that I haven't seen in a while."

"Totally worth it," Jackson said. "You'll have a good time."

He was looking forward to it. Even though some of the people he wanted to see—or at least one particular person who he hadn't seen in almost ten years—likely wouldn't be there.

They'd broken up after graduation. Then she'd moved out of state. Gotten married, or so he'd heard.

Anyway, that was all in the past. She was his past. And as he knew, the past should stay where it was.

But he'd still hang out with his friends, and after today's shift, he could use a good time.

So he'd go to his high school reunion and have some damn fun.

CHAPTER 2

HANNAH CLARK BARELY HAD ENOUGH TIME TO DASH home, take a shower and get ready for tonight's reunion, one she'd been undecided about attending ever since she'd first read about it on social media.

"I still don't think this is a good idea," she said in the bathroom while she pulled the straight iron through her hair.

"Why not?" her mother asked. "You've been back for months and have hardly connected with any of your friends from high school."

"You know I've been busy setting the shop up, hiring stylists for the chairs, getting clientele."

"And some of your high school girlfriends are potential clientele."

She was not wrong. "Fine. I'm going to the reunion. I'll make connections."

A cute brown-haired boy with the sweetest brown eyes peeked his head around the doorway. "Where you goin', Momma?"

"I have a party tonight, honey."

"Can I go?"

Her mother smiled at Hannah's son, Oliver. "No, sweet boy. Tonight we're going to Aunt Heather's house, so you can play with Isaiah."

Oliver's eyes sparkled with excitement. "I'll go pack up some toys."

Hannah looked up at her mom and smiled. "Clearly hanging out with Isaiah trumps going to a party with his mom."

"Hey, you're not a match for a much more sophisticated nine-year-old boy."

She laughed. "True. Thanks for taking care of Oliver tonight. And tell Aunt Heather hello for me."

Heather was one of her mother's coworkers and best friends who just so happened to be only five years older than Hannah. Since Hannah had lived out of state for so many years, her mom had sort of adopted Heather as one of her own.

"She says you're welcome to come. You're missing lasagna night at her house."

"Damn." She loved Heather's lasagna. She'd make a point to stop by there with Oliver sometime next week.

Since her divorce, she'd felt so unsettled. And so damn scattered and busy. Moving back to Ft. Lauderdale had been the right decision; she knew that. She needed her family after that mess with her ex-husband, Landon. And since he'd never cared about Oliver anyway, she hadn't forced the child support issue and he hadn't contested the move out of state. Sure, money would be tight, but at least she was free of him, and so was Oliver.

Now she and her baby boy could both start fresh. That's what really mattered.

After finishing her hair and makeup, she went into the small bedroom that was now hers, the same one that had been hers when she was a child. When she was little, it had seemed enormous. Now she realized how small it was. Still, it represented freedom to her, and she'd been so grateful to her mother for letting Oliver and her stay here until she could save up enough money to get her own place. The tiny bedroom was fine. And Oliver loved his room, which was larger than the one they'd had at their house in Georgia. Plus, he had her mom, who doted on him.

She pulled out the awesome dress she'd found on sale at the discount store. It was a gorgeous black party dress, still had the tags on it, and she'd only paid ten dollars for it. Such a bargain.

It was a simple design, but it was her size and clung to her body as if it had been made especially for her. She added a long silver chain and her hoop earrings, and the silver heels she'd borrowed from her mom.

She turned around and looked at herself in the full-length mirror.

How long had it been since she'd dressed up like this? Years, probably. She couldn't remember. Landon had never wanted to go out anywhere except the local bar, and he'd mostly done that alone or with his buddies. A nice dinner to him had been the buffet in town. Which was fine, but occasionally it would have been fun to dress up and go out.

But he'd never thought about her desires, or her needs. Only his own.

She shrugged and tossed thoughts of Landon aside. That part of her life was over, had been for a while, actually. Now she had a clean slate.

Tonight, she'd see old friends and have a good time. She sat on the bed and opened up her old yearbook from senior year. Her mom had dredged that dusty thing out from who knows where. The attic, probably. She flipped through the pages, smiling at photos of her friends, horrified by some of the shots of herself and her goofy faces. Still, she laughed because she'd just been a kid.

Her heart thudded when she landed on a picture of her and Kal Donovan. Underneath, the caption read, "Cutest Couple."

Kal was behind her in the picture, his arms wrapped around her, her body resting against his. She looked so happy, so in love. She traced the picture with her fingers, remembering how sweet Kal had been, what that first love had felt like. The butterflies in her stomach whenever she saw him walking down the hall toward her. The sensation of his hand resting on the small of her back, the little shivers she always felt along her spine.

And his smile. She'd always loved his smile.

She shook herself away from the past. Again, she'd just been a kid—a silly teenager. What had she known about love back then?

Or even a few years later when she'd married Landon?

Oliver burst into her room and threw himself on the bed. "Grandma and I are gonna leave soon."

She put her arm around him. "You have fun with Isaiah tonight. Eat some lasagna for me."

He laughed. "I will." He looked down at the picture. "Who's this guy?"

"This is Kal. He was my boyfriend in high school, when I was a teenager."

Oliver studied the picture. "Before Daddy?"

"Yes. Before Daddy."

He scrunched his nose. "Did you like him a lot?"

"I did. But then we broke up after I graduated from high school. Then I met your daddy, we got married and we had you, my shining star." She cuddled him close to her.

"Momma. Too much hugging."

"Oh, right. Sorry."

Oliver hopped off the bed. "See you later."

"I love you."

He waved on his way out of her room. "Love you, too!"

She sighed, realizing her sweet, warm, cuddly baby boy was growing up, becoming independent. A good thing for him. But she missed all the cuddling they used to do when he was little.

So much change in her life. So much failure. The end of her marriage, closing her shop in Georgia, moving back home. She was starting all over again. She sighed once more, closed the yearbook and got off the bed, determined to blow off these feelings.

Starting over wasn't a bad thing. In her case, it was definitely the right choice. The right choice for Oliver, too.

And tonight wasn't the night to think heavy thoughts. She'd already done enough of that.

Tonight she was going to have some fun.

CHAPTER 3

MUSIC WAS PUMPING WHEN KAL WALKED INTO THE HOTEL lobby. He could hear the loud beat all the way out here, which meant there was a definite party atmosphere inside. He was so ready.

There was a table outside the ballroom. He recognized Vicky Hayward and Tom Hart right away.

Tom stood and shook his hand. "Kal Donovan. How long has it been?"

"I'd say around ten years or so?"

Tom laughed. "You got that right. How's it going?"

"Good."

Vicky handed him a sticker with his high school photo. "Wear it proudly, dude."

Kal looked at the photo and winced. He looked like a dork in his senior photo. His hair was wild and unkempt. He'd tried to look oh so cool for the photo and failed miserably.

"Thanks, Vicky."

"Hey, don't worry, man," Tom said. "None of us looked all that awesome ten years ago."

"But he sure looks fine now," he heard Vicky murmur as he walked away.

That made him smile as he strode through the ballroom doors.

It was dark and atmospheric, with balloons in purple and gold school colors attached to every table and around the room. Music from their graduation year pumped into the room, and there was a bar at the far end, which was where Kal headed.

He knew he'd find Eddie there.

"Buddy," Eddie said, wrapping his arms around him and giving him a bear hug. "Knew you'd show up."

Kal ordered a beer and leaned against the bar. "Where's Veronica?"

Eddie swiveled and pointed to a table by the wall. "Over there with Tina and Jess."

"The cheerleader table still going strong, I see."

"Inseparable since high school. You know how it is. Kind of like you, me and Jorge."

"Where is Jorge?"

"Texted me last night. Said he had a late flight from San Antonio, but he should be here."

"I can't wait to see him."

"Me, too, man. It's been too long. Come on, let's go grab a chair and catch up. I keep missing you at the gym."

They headed over to the table. "I go early. You go late."

"Hey, some of us keep regular business hours, not like you firefighters. I start work at seven. My workouts have to wait until after five."

"I get it."

"Kal," Eddie's wife, Veronica, said with a smile. "I'm so glad you're here."

He hugged Veronica, as well as Tina and Jess, who introduced him to their husbands.

Then he took a seat, looking around the room to see if he

recognized people. Everyone was older, of course, and some people had changed so much he had no idea who they were. He had to ask Eddie, and even Eddie didn't know a few. Whereas some people hadn't changed at all.

"Hannah's here," Veronica said, looking down at her phone. She got up from the table. "I promised her I'd meet her at the entrance. Be right back."

"I'm coming with you," Jess said.

"Me, too." Tina followed them.

Kal's heart did a little jump at the mention of Hannah's name. His high school girlfriend. His first love. Hell, the only woman he'd ever been in love with.

Eddie nudged him. "Hey, your girl is here."

Kal managed a tight smile. "She hasn't been my girl in a long time."

"True. Did you know she's divorced now? And living back here in Ft. Lauderdale? I heard Veronica talking to her a few times on the phone."

Oh, shit. "No, didn't know that."

"Yeah, she's been back a few months now."

Apparently, there was a lot he didn't know. Then again, why should he know anything about Hannah? They hadn't been in touch since they broke up. Since he'd gone away to college, leaving her behind.

Was she still angry with him? Did she still hate him? Or had enough time passed that she didn't care anymore?

He watched the door, and it was a long few minutes before he saw Veronica and the other women come through. But then his attention shifted at the sight of a beautiful, raven-haired woman in a black dress.

He had to feel his tongue with his teeth to make sure he hadn't swallowed it when he caught sight of Hannah. The dress clung to her curves, and she had plenty of those. Ten years had added to them, making her even more beautiful than she'd been before. Her hair hung in long, straight lines across her shoulders, looking like midnight silk, making him want to reach out and run his fingers through it to see if it felt as silky as it looked. And her lips were painted a shocking red that just dared some guy to kiss that lipstick right off her mouth.

Fuck. Me. He was in deep trouble, because every memory he'd ever had of Hannah McKenzie had just come rushing back to him, making him wonder what kind of dumbass he'd been to ever let this woman go. And as she approached the table, their gazes locked, and she shot him a look that was just as uncertain as he felt right now.

"Hey, Hannah," Eddie said, going over to give her a quick hug. "Glad you could make it."

"Me, too."

She said hello to Tina's and Jess's husbands, then turned to face him.

Kal didn't know what to say, but he couldn't very well stand there like some jackass and say nothing, so he went over and gave her the most awkward side hug ever. "Hey, Hannah."

She felt stiff as a board as she returned the same awkward hug. "Hi, Kal."

"I just heard you moved back."

"Yes. Not too long ago."

Veronica put her arm around Hannah. "She's getting settled in. She already has a new salon, and she's hired two stylists. She's doing great, aren't you, Hannah?"

Hannah managed a smile. "Yes. Great."

Kal could tell Hannah was uncomfortable, which was probably his fault.

"I think I'll wander and visit with some people," Kal said. "Good to see you, Hannah."

She nodded. "You, too, Kal."

"Hey, you'll be back, won't you?" Eddie asked.

"Sure."

But he wouldn't, because Hannah had the right to have some fun tonight, and it was obvious she couldn't do that with him there.

So he'd go find some of his other friends and leave Hannah alone.

CATCHING UP WITH HER FRIENDS AND SEEING PEOPLE SHE hadn't seen in years had been more fun than Hannah had anticipated. She was glad she'd come to the reunion.

Except for the part when she'd seen Kal. She figured she'd have at least a glass of wine or two in her first, maybe mellow out a little before they ran into each other. Being blindsided right out of the gate had been unexpected, and she hadn't been prepared to see him. Her throat had gone dry, and she'd fumbled for something to say. So, instead, she'd said nothing. He probably thought she hated him, when in fact she'd been dumbfounded at how utterly gorgeous he looked in his white button-down shirt and his black slacks and wow, had he gotten even taller since high school? The sharp edges of his cheekbones seemed even sharper, and he'd gained a lot of muscle.

She'd barely been able to breathe when she'd seen him, let alone form a coherent sentence. Kal Donovan had turned into one incredible specimen of the male species.

"Are you even listening to anything I'm saying?"

She blinked and turned her attention back to Veronica. "What? I'm sorry. It was a long day at the salon today, and I'm a little tired."

Veronica rubbed her arm. "I'm sorry, honey. It must be rough having to work on a Saturday."

"It's okay. It's our busiest day at the salon. And I have the next two days off."

"Good. In the meantime, let's perk you up and get you on the dance floor."

Hannah shook her head. "Oh, I don't think—"

Before she could finish her sentence, Veronica had dragged her out of the chair and onto the dance floor. Suddenly, their entire group was there, swaying and rocking their hips to a hot Rihanna song. Hannah felt her body get into the music and finally let herself relax. The dance floor was crowded with people, all laughing and having a good time.

She spotted Kal standing over by himself at the bar.

"I'll be back," she hollered at Veronica, who nodded and turned away to dance with the other women. Hannah wriggled free of the crowd and made her way toward the bar—toward Kal.

"Hey," he said, offering up an easy smile.

"Hey, yourself."

"Want a beer or some wine?" he asked.

"I'll take a pinot grigio."

He ordered one from the bartender, then handed it to her.

"Thanks," she said, taking a sip to let the liquid cool her body down. "Why aren't you out there dancing?"

"I was enjoying watching all of you."

"So, you're a voyeur now, huh?"

He laughed, and the sound of it sent her straight back to high school, to the two of them sitting on the bleachers after Kal finished basketball practice. They'd talk, make out and laugh. It had been so easy back then. The look he gave her now was just as easy, so maybe it was her that needed to relax.

"Or maybe it's that you're a bad dancer."

He gave her a look. "Please. You know that's not the case. I took you to two proms, and we danced our asses off."

"This is true. So why hasn't one of the single women here dragged you out there?"

He shrugged. "Not interested."

Interesting. "I see. So if I ask you to dance you'll turn me down, too?"

"I'd never turn you down, Hannah."

Ten years hadn't eradicated that flutter in her stomach whenever he said something sweet to her. But he was just being polite, and she shouldn't read anything into that.

"Okay, then," she said, laying her glass of wine on the bar top. "Let's dance."

He put his beer next to her glass. "Sure."

The music was still hopping, and Kal was right about having moves. How could she have forgotten that? Eddie jumped onto the dance floor and twirled Veronica around, and then the whole group danced together, and she forgot all about being awkward around Kal. It was just like the old days, their crowd dancing and singing together and having an absolute blast.

When a slow song came on, her friends coupled up with their husbands.

Kal held his hand out to her. It was as if time had washed away and it was prom again. Only it wasn't. It was now, and they were two different people. Still, what harm would one dance with him be?

She grasped his hand and stepped in. When his arm wound around her and he pulled her close, she felt a zap of electricity. Her eyes met his, and he gave her a slow, easy smile.

"Just like old times, right?" he asked.

She gave a quick nod. Right. Just like old times. Except it wasn't.

She took in a deep breath and let him lead her around the floor.

His body felt different against hers. Broader, more solid. He'd always been an athlete, but there was a lot more muscle now. And as she tilted her head back to look at him, she realized her initial assessment of him had been right—he was definitely taller.

"What is it?"

"You're taller than you were in high school."

"Am I? Good to know."

She squeezed his biceps. "And . . . more muscley."

He laughed. "Thanks. And you're more beautiful now. Which is hard to believe, because you were always the most beautiful girl I ever knew."

Those flutters again. "Does that come naturally to you, or is it something you have to practice at?"

He frowned. "What?"

"Those lines."

"I don't know what you're talking about, Hannah."

"Compliments. The right words to make a woman feel good."

"I don't use lines. I don't practice anything. I just say what I feel in the moment. I'm kind of insulted you'd think that I would."

She shrugged. "Sorry. It just feels, I don't know, kind of disingenuous."

"Really? I'll try not to compliment you again or say anything nice."

She was screwing this up because he made her feel good, because she thought she could waltz in here tonight and maybe run into him and feel nothing at all, when just the opposite had happened. And now she had insulted him. But he hadn't walked away, hadn't tensed up. Instead, he still glided her around the dance floor as if what she'd said hadn't affected him at all.

But she knew better, because Kal had a tell—a small tic on the side of his mouth that let her know when he was irritated. *That* hadn't changed in ten years.

"I'm sorry," she said. "I guess I hadn't expected to see you. Or maybe I had expected to see you and I hadn't expected my reaction to seeing you."

"What reaction is that?"

She inhaled, then let it out. "I'm really happy to see you, Kal."

The song ended, but he still held on to her. "Yeah? I felt the same way. Seeing you again blew me away, Hannah. I couldn't form coherent words."

It made her feel so much better to hear him say that. She smiled at him. "I'd really like to catch up with you sometime soon."

"Same. How about breakfast tomorrow morning?"

"That would be great. But could we make it lunch instead? I have some things I need to take care of in the morning."

"Sure."

They walked over to the buffet table to grab some food, since all that dancing had worked up an appetite. Or it had worked up her appetite, since she hadn't had time to eat dinner.

She piled her plate with salad, pasta and veggies, and it all looked so good.

"Meatballs?" Kal asked.

She shook her head. "I don't eat a lot of meat."

"Are you a vegetarian now?"

"No, I'm not that strict. I can't quite give up a good steak."

He laughed. "Oh, got it. I'll take your portion of the meatballs, then."

"You do that."

They carried their food to the table and sat.

Hannah looked over at Veronica. "I haven't seen Mary tonight."

"She's due with her second baby any day now, and she's huge and uncomfortable and said she had nothing pretty that fit her. She was sad she couldn't make it."

"Oh, that's too bad. She must be so excited about the baby."

Veronica grinned. "She is. Her first, Jacob, is four, and this one's a girl. She's been decorating the nursery for weeks."

"Aww. How sweet. I need to go see her. I'll text her tomorrow."

Hannah dug into her food, which was fairly decent for a catered buffet. The squash salad was delicious, and the pasta was good, too. She was full by the time she'd eaten half of it.

Kal, on the other hand, devoured all the food on his plate, then went back for more. The dude could eat. But it sure didn't show on his body.

After they ate, they refilled drinks, chatted some more and then went out and danced until Hannah's feet were sore and she needed to sit down. It was nice to see her girls hadn't lost a step in ten years. She couldn't remember enjoying herself so much in . . . well, years.

She went to the table to take a breather. Kal was there talking with Eddie and the other guys. They'd been joined by Jorge Rocha, one of their crowd from high school. Jorge lived in Austin now, so she was happy to see he'd made the reunion, along with his wife.

While everyone chatted, Hannah took the opportunity to grab the glass of ice water sitting in front of her, long ago having given up on wine, since she was driving.

Kal leaned over. "Having fun?"

"A great time. How about you?"

"More fun than I thought I'd have. It's good to catch up with people we haven't seen in a long time."

"Yes, it is."

"Speaking of catching up, I need your number so we can get together for lunch."

"Oh, right." She grabbed her phone out of her bag, got his number and gave him hers.

"I'll text you in the morning to let you know when I'm available, and where we should meet," Hannah said.

"I can come pick you up."

"Oh, uh, if you don't mind, I'd rather meet you."

He gave her a curious look but nodded. "Sure. Just text me tomorrow."

"I will."

She was being wary, which was stupid since she knew Kal. But she was also protective of Oliver and didn't want Kal to meet him. Not yet. Or maybe ever. They were only having lunch to catch up, and meeting a guy her son would likely see just one time would only confuse him. So it was best she meet Kal at the restaurant.

The party started to wind down around midnight, which suited Hannah just fine. She'd been on her feet the entire day. Add in dancing in heels, and she was more than ready to go home and fall into bed. Oliver was an early riser, and while she knew her mom was more than happy to get up with him, he was her responsibility.

She hugged her friends, then gathered up her bag and the heels she couldn't stand to wear for one more second.

Kal looked down at her feet. "Walking out to the parking lot barefoot?"

"I guess I'll have to put those evil things on to walk outside."

"I could carry you to your car."

She laughed. "I don't think so. I weigh a little bit more now than I did in high school."

"Oh, come on. You're like a feather."

She shot him a look as they made their way to the door. "A steel feather."

"That's you. Soft on the outside, strong on the inside."

And again, that flutter. What was it with this man?

She was just about to slip the offending heels back on when she was scooped up in his arms.

"Kal. Seriously."

Eddie held the door for them, and Veronica slanted a sly grin in her direction. "Good night, you two," Veronica said.

"Which way?"

"You could put me down."

"Where's your car?"

"All the way in the back of the parking lot. Now put me down."

"There's gravel." He walked toward the end of the lot. Most everyone had left, but she felt ridiculous being carried. It also felt nice. Kal wasn't struggling in the least, which proved to her that all that muscle she felt was genuine.

"The black Acura over there," she said.

He set her down at the driver's door. He wasn't even breathing heavily.

She lifted her gaze to his while simultaneously digging through her bag for her keys. "Thank you."

"My pleasure."

The way he looked at her, the heat in his eyes, made her want to lean into him, to press her lips to his.

Instead, she pressed the button on her remote and unlocked her car. Kal took a step back, and she slid inside. He leaned in and smiled.

"See you tomorrow, Hannah."

"Good night, Kal."

He shut the door and stepped away. She started her car and drove off, watching him in her rearview mirror.

She didn't know whether to look forward to or dread lunch with him tomorrow.

Was it a good or bad idea to reopen the past?

As she turned onto the highway, she didn't have an answer. She supposed she'd figure that out tomorrow.

CHAPTER 4

"DUDE," JACKSON SAID THE NEXT DAY AS HE CAME DOWN-stairs. "You always have an epic grooming routine. But how long did you take getting ready today? Like, an hour?"

Becks elbowed him. "Knock it off. He has a date."

"Not a date," Kal said as he made his way into the kitchen where Becks and Jackson were sitting at the table together. "Just lunch with an old friend."

Jackson leaned back in the chair. "Someone from high school?"

"Hannah McKenzie."

"No shit."

"Who's Hannah McKenzie?" Becks asked.

"His high school girlfriend."

"Oh, really?" Becks said. "You reconnected with her at the reunion last night?"

"Yeah. But nothing happened. We broke up after high school because I was going away to college and we both knew it wasn't going to last. And then she got married and moved out of state, so I haven't seen her in ten years. She's divorced now and back in Ft. Lauderdale."

"Ooh, how interesting. So you reconnected last night and, then what?" Becks asked. "Sparks flew?"

He wasn't going to admit to that, even if it was true. "Nah. We're just going to have lunch and catch up."

"Tell her I said hey," Jackson said, returning to scrolling through his phone.

Becks, on the other hand, continued to stare at him as if she expected more.

He laughed. "There's nothing going on. We just hung out with our group of friends. We had fun. But there was no time to talk, so we decided to have lunch together and catch up. That's all. Really."

"Okay," she said. "Have fun."

"Thanks."

He drove to the restaurant and parked, then waited out front for Hannah to arrive. She'd texted him this morning to tell him she could meet him around twelve thirty, and they discussed where. Since he didn't know where she currently lived, he asked her to name a location that was convenient for her, or some restaurants that she liked. She suggested a place she'd wanted to try called American Social Bar, which was known for its brunch menu. He was all for it since he liked the food there.

Hannah pulled into the parking lot and got out of her car. He watched her walk toward him, the ends of her hair flying in the breeze. She had on a short-sleeved sundress and sandals and damn, she looked fine.

She pulled off her sunglasses when she got to the entrance. "Hi."

"Hi, yourself. I hope you're hungry."

"So hungry."

He was happy she had an appetite, because he was ready to eat. "Let's go."

He'd already put his name in when he'd arrived, so they didn't have to wait too long before they were seated at a table. This place got crowded during brunch hours, and there was a good reason for it—the food was great.

"This menu looks amazing," Hannah said, then looked up at him. "You've eaten here before?"

He nodded. "A few times. There's nothing bad here."

"Good to know."

Their server came with coffee, took their orders and disappeared.

"So, Hannah McKenzie—or what's your name now?"

"Clark."

"Okay, Hannah Clark. Tell me what you've been doing for the past ten years."

She blinked, stared at him for a few seconds, then added cream to her coffee. "Oh, you probably know it all already."

He could tell she was nervous, though he didn't know why. It wasn't like this was a first date, or even a date at all. And she knew him—they'd dated all through high school. It wasn't like they were strangers.

Then again, maybe they were. People changed a lot in ten years.

Had he changed? He didn't think he had.

"No, really, I don't know it all," he said. "I know you moved away and got married. That's it."

"I see." She stirred the cream into her coffee. "Like you said, I got married, moved to Georgia. Got a divorce a year ago, then moved back here a few months ago."

"I'm sorry about the divorce."

"I'm not," she said with a shrug. "It was past time."

"Oh yeah?"

"Let's just say it was a mistake from the start."

That didn't sound good. "Sometimes that happens. Carmen, my brother Rafe's fiancée, is divorced, and she talks to me a lot about her first marriage, about how she married too young, and she didn't see the signs like she should have."

Hannah nodded. "Pretty much like that. But I got a great kid out of the marriage, so I have no regrets."

Kal's eyes widened. Now that he didn't know. "You have a kid?"

She smiled. "Yes. Oliver. He's seven, and the light of my life."

"That's awesome, Hannah. I'll bet you're an amazing mom." He couldn't imagine Hannah as a mother. But they were both adults now. Still, she was so young to have a seven-year-old son. That must have been so tough.

"Thank you. I try to do what's best for him. Which is why I'm back home."

"How did your ex feel about you moving away with your son?"

Hannah inhaled a deep breath, and Kal could tell she was trying to avoid the question.

Their food arrived, so he let the topic drop—for now—and dug into his huevos rancheros. Hannah seemed to relax after that and settled in to eat her avocado toast and eggs.

She took a sip of her juice and swallowed, then asked, "What about you? Did you become a firefighter?"

He nodded. "Yeah. I've been a firefighter for five years, then I transferred to the Technical Rescue Team a few months ago."

"What's that?"

"Typically high-angle or confined space rescue, but there's a lot more that goes into it."

"So you don't fight fires anymore?"

"Sometimes, if we're needed, but mostly it's high-risk rescue situations where the firefighters need our assistance."

"Wow. Sounds dangerous."

He gave her a smile. "All firefighting is dangerous."

"Of course. And you love it, don't you?"

"Yeah. Always have."

She rested her chin in her hand and studied him. "I knew this is where you'd end up. It's been in your blood, ever since your dad rescued you and your brothers when you were kids. And Jackson and Rafe?"

"Also firefighters. Jackson's a lieutenant now. He and Rafe work in the same firehouse. Our dad's the battalion chief there. Same place I worked until I transferred to the TRT."

She gave him a genuine smile. "Wow. I'm so happy for all of you."

"Thanks."

"And how are your parents?"

"They're doing great. They moved into a new house last year. A bigger place, with an office for my mom. And a pool."

Hannah nodded. "She always wanted a pool."

He smiled. "You remember that."

"Of course I do. She hated the hot Ft. Lauderdale summers. She always said if she had a nice pool in the backyard, it would be more tolerable."

"What about your mom? Does she still live in the same house?"

"Same one."

"It's a pretty great house."

"It is. That's where Oliver and I are living right now. At least until I get more settled and I can get my own place."

"That's a good idea. I'm sure she's helpful, and she probably loves having you and Oliver there."

"She does. She's been there by herself all those years since my dad died."

"No guy friends yet, huh?"

"She's dated here and there over the years, but no one has

stuck. I just don't think she'll ever find anyone she'll love as much as she loved my dad."

Kal remembered Hannah's dad well. They'd all hung out a lot when he was dating her. "I understand. He was a great guy."

"He was. But it's been twelve years since he died. I'd hate for her to be alone for the rest of her life."

"She's not alone right now. She has you."

She waved her fork at him. "Which is the exact reason I'm not making my stay permanent. It would just be another excuse for her not to go out and find love again."

"That makes sense, though maybe you shouldn't be in a huge hurry to make your exit."

"Why not?"

"Get your bearings again. Settle in, you know? Take your time before you go rushing off on your own. I'm sure your mom loves having you and Oliver there after you were gone for so long."

She picked up her coffee cup. "Now you sound like my mother."

"Hey."

She laughed. "Sorry. But you're probably right. I just don't want to get in her way."

"I don't think parents ever think we're in the way. If I wanted to bunk at my parents' place I'm sure my mom would be so happy she'd probably cry. You know how they are."

"Yes. Happy when we leave, even happier when we come home again."

"Exactly right."

He finished eating and set his plate aside.

"What about you?" she asked. "Do you have your own place?"

"Sort of. My brothers and I have been living in my grandparents' house that we renovated. Though Rafe moved out several months ago after he bought a house with his fiancée. Now it's just me and Jackson and his fiancée."

"Ooh, cozy."

He cocked his head to the side. "It's a four-bedroom house. They get plenty of privacy."

"But they're getting married, right?"

"They just got engaged so they're wedding planning."

"And what's the plan, if you don't mind me being nosy? Are they going to stay at the house after they get married? Do you have to move out?"

"I . . . haven't given that much thought. I doubt they have, either." But now he was thinking about it.

"I'm sure it will all work out. Like you said, it's a big house."

He took a swig of his coffee, then set it down. "Well, you know, it's something I hadn't considered before now. Newlyweds will want privacy. Jackson and Becks and I just haven't talked about who's going to keep living at the house, who's going to move out."

She frowned. "I didn't mean to interject an opinion there. It's really not my business. That's your family's home."

"No, but you bring up a valid point. The home passed to my mom after my grandmother died. My brothers and I renovated it, so none of us own it. It makes sense for Becks and Jackson to live there after they get married. Then again, they might want to get their own place. With Rafe and Carmen in their own house . . ."

Now that Hannah had brought it up, he wasn't sure what to do about the living arrangement. He was going to have to talk to Jackson.

"Look, I'm sorry I said anything."

He popped his head up. "Why?"

"Because I feel bad. I wasn't suggesting you should move out."

He smiled at her. "I know you weren't. But it's not a bad idea. It's something Jackson and I need to talk about."

"Which is none of my business. I don't even know—"

"Me? You don't even know me? Come on, Hannah. It's not like that. We know each other."

"But really, we don't. We're not high school kids anymore.

You're not the boy who left for college, and I'm not the girl who cried over losing you. We both moved on a long time ago. We're adults, with jobs and responsibilities. We've lived ten years of our lives without each other. We've had experiences and losses and triumphs."

He leaned back in his chair. "Uh-huh. That's true. But did your entire personality change in those ten years?"

She frowned. "Well, no."

"Neither did mine. I might be older, and maybe I bulked up a little in muscle, but I'm still that same funny guy who used to lean against your locker in between classes."

She studied him for a few seconds before answering. "Maybe. Maybe not. I just think life experiences change us. That we get a chance to mature, make choices that we might not have made ten years earlier."

"You're probably right." Now it was his turn to study her while he finished his coffee. Physically, she'd definitely matured. Her body had filled out. She'd gotten curves, her face was fuller and she bore the look of maturity in her eyes that only painful life experience could give someone. That part he understood. But the underlying characteristics of who she was as a person? That part he didn't think had changed. She was still Hannah, the girl he'd known since she was fourteen years old, the one he'd met because their lockers had been next to each other. They'd shared English, history and math classes freshman year. They'd connected right away because they'd both been smart and athletic and they'd both liked to laugh. He didn't think those parts of her had changed.

"How about we find out if we're still the same people?" he asked.

"What?"

"Go out with me, Hannah."

She tucked her bottom lip between her teeth, considering before she answered. "I don't think that's a good idea."

"Why not?"

"Because you can't ever go back."

"I'm not talking about going back. I'm talking about going forward. You're single, I'm single, we already know we liked each other in high school. So let's see if we still have the same things in common, if that chemistry is still there." He already knew the chemistry was still there. He'd felt it last night.

"I don't know, Kal. We're different people now."

"So you keep saying. I say we're the same."

"And I have a child."

He grinned. "I like kids."

She sighed. "You're making this difficult."

"When it should be easy. You want to have fun, right?"

"I guess. Though I don't really have a lot of time for fun things. I work a lot, sometimes late. And then I have Oliver to take care of."

"Okay. So when you can carve out a little time, let me take you out. I'll bet your mom wouldn't mind watching Oliver while we go to dinner or a movie. Or we'll bring him along."

"On our dates."

"Sure. I like doing kid things."

She squinted, as if she didn't quite believe him. "You make me really want to test this theory, see if even you believe what you're saying. Having a child around isn't always fun and games."

He laughed. "I realize that. And if you don't want me to meet Oliver right away, I'll respect that."

"Let me think about it."

"Okay. You let me know what you decide."

"I'll do that."

"In the meantime, it's a beautiful day. What would you like to do?"

"What would I *like* to do? I'd like to spend the day at the beach. What do I *have* to do? Laundry. And cleaning. And grocery shopping. And Oliver's friend is having a birthday party this afternoon, so we have to shop for a present, then I have to drop him off. I have responsibilities, and I don't have time to play with you today."

He could tell Hannah's plate was full and she was stressed. "I understand. We'll do it some other time."

"Sure."

He paid the bill and they walked outside. She turned to face him.

"Hey, thanks for lunch. It was fun to catch up."

This felt a lot like a permanent goodbye. He wasn't about to let that happen.

"How about we go out Friday night?"

"I work Saturday and it's my longest day."

"Then let me take you out Saturday night."

She sighed. "Kal, I'd like to but—"

"We'll do something simple and easy. Nothing fancy."

It took her a few seconds to answer, and he thought during those seconds she was going to say no. If she did, that would be it. He wouldn't press her.

"Fine. We'll go out Saturday night."

He couldn't hold back his smile. "Great. I'll text you."

"Okay." She started to turn away, then stopped. "Thanks for asking me."

"Thanks for saying yes."

She smiled at him in a way that made his gut feel like he'd been punched. Hannah had the kind of a smile that could stop traffic. Bright and beautiful, making her eyes sparkle.

He'd always known when she was happy, because he could see it in her eyes. Like now.

"See you Saturday, Kal."

She walked away, and he stood there watching her, feeling stupid happy.

It was just a date. Nothing to get excited about. But there he was, excited as hell because he had a date with Hannah on Saturday.

He grinned, grabbed his keys out of his pocket and headed for his truck.

CHAPTER 5

HANNAH FINISHED APPLYING THE LAST FOIL ON A PARTIC-
ularly difficult double color on a client, so all she had to do was
wait for that to process. While the client sat under the dryer, she
updated some appointments for next week and returned a phone
call for a client who wanted to change the time for her haircut.

Then she went into the back of the salon to rest her feet and
catch up on how this week's sales had looked.

She rented out space to other stylists, which was going well.

Delilah Watson was the reason Hannah had ended up opening
up this salon when she'd returned to Ft. Lauderdale. Having to
close her salon in Georgia had hurt Hannah, both emotionally
and financially. She figured she'd wait to open a salon once she got
back here, maybe work for someone else until she could get back
on track.

And then she'd reconnected with Delilah, and Hannah had
been thrilled to find out that Delilah was doing hair in another
salon. Getting stylists was one of the biggest problems for a salon
owner. Delilah had been awesome with hair in high school before
she'd ever gotten her license, and when she told Hannah she

worked six full days a week, Hannah asked if she'd be willing to come with her.

Delilah hadn't hesitated. She said the owner of the salon she worked at was a total bitch and she'd leave in a heartbeat. Having an incredible stylist ready to go meant she could get her business up and running. She'd found the location, and they had clients the first week.

Hannah had since added another stylist, and a manicurist was starting next week, which made her very happy.

Her friend Delilah came into the back room.

"You and me both, girl," Delilah said, pulling up the chair next to her. "I was about to die if I didn't sit down."

Delilah was a force. Beautiful, with short spiky blond hair and tattoos down one arm, she was petite but talked with a loud voice, and where Hannah was introverted, Delilah was super outgoing. But they'd bonded over their love of the world of Harry Potter in middle school and had been friends ever since. They'd lost touch for a while after Hannah left Ft. Lauderdale, but once she moved back, she'd run into Delilah at the grocery store and their friendship had kicked right in once again.

"It's been a long day, for sure. But a good day. I've been busy."

Delilah nodded. "Same here. You've got a killer location. Much better than that last shop I was at."

Marguerite, the other stylist, came in to grab a drink from the fridge. "I agree. This is the best spot. Easy to get to, and traffic brings in walk-ins. I love it here and so do my clients."

Hannah smiled. "I'm so glad. We love having you here."

"Thank you. And you're much nicer than the last salon owner I worked with. She was terrible. Always giving me orders like she was my boss, telling me I had to work late, clean up, wash all the towels."

Hannah frowned. "You just rented booth space, didn't you?"

"Yes. But that woman, she didn't seem to understand that all her stylists were independent. I was happy when Delilah told me you were looking for people."

"Hey, I was glad to get you out of there," Delilah said. "Maybe once she loses all her stylists she'll figure out she's the problem."

Marguerite laughed. "I doubt it. She's not what I would call self-aware."

Hannah shook her head. "I ran into that problem with salon owners before I bought my own shop. They think stylists work for them. If you're not paying them a salary, they don't."

"Either way, we're happy to be here with you, where you treat us like equals," Delilah said. "And where we all pitch in to keep the place clean."

Hannah smiled. "You're both so great. I'm so thrilled to have you here with me."

"And we get Josephine on Tuesday," Marguerite said. "You're going to love working with her."

Their new manicurist was Marguerite's cousin. Hannah had interviewed Josephine and even had her do a mani/pedi on her. She'd done a thorough and beautiful job. Delilah knew her as well and had used her services before. It was important to Hannah that all the stylists got along, because she'd worked in shops before where personality clashes caused conflict and tension, and clients always picked up on that. She didn't want that in her shop.

She was confident that wasn't going to happen here.

When her client was done, Hannah rinsed and styled her hair. It turned out great, shades of blond highlights in her beautiful light brown hair. The client was delighted, and Hannah was satisfied it had turned out well. And the client booked a follow-up appointment, which was even better.

Since that was her last client for the day, and both Delilah and Marguerite had finished up as well, they put towels in the laundry and cleaned up the shop. After the women had left, Hannah waited for the towels to finish, then turned out the lights and locked up, happy to be finished earlier than she expected. She called her mom to see if she wanted Hannah to pick up dinner for Oliver and her. She told Hannah she already had dinner planned, so Hannah drove home.

When she got inside, Oliver was watching TV. She went over to plant a kiss on the top of his head.

"Hi, Momma," he said, his gaze focused on whatever cartoon show he was watching.

"Hey, kiddo. Good day?"

"Yup."

She put her bag down on the table by the door, then went into the kitchen.

"Something smells good."

"I'm making enchiladas for dinner."

"Oh. I'll be sorry to miss those."

Her mother slanted a smile at her. "There'll be leftovers."

"Good. I'm going to go take a shower."

She'd much rather slip into her shorts and a tank top and veg on the sofa with Oliver and her mom tonight, but she'd made this date with Kal, so she was going to have to follow through.

After her shower, she did her hair and makeup. Kal had told her to keep it low-key and casual tonight, so she put on flowered capris and a short-sleeved T-shirt, then slid into her tennis shoes, hoping what she wore wasn't too casual. She put on earrings and a bracelet and called it good.

When she came out, the smell of the enchiladas made her stomach growl. "I'm so hungry."

Her mom cocked her head to the side. "Did you eat today?"

"I had a salad and some apple slices."

"Okay. Where are you going for dinner?"

She shrugged. "No idea. Kal said it was casual."

"You need casual, not fancy and dressed up. Especially after a long day at work. I'm sure you'll have a good time."

"Hopefully."

Her mom sighed. "You could maybe go into this date with a little more enthusiasm."

"I guess. I don't know, Mom. Do I really have the time to be dating anyone? My plate's kind of full."

"You're going out with him tonight, aren't you?"

"Yes."

"Then let yourself have a little fun instead of facing it like an ordeal. Don't you think you deserve that?"

She had a point. She'd been dreading this all week, thinking of all the things she could be doing instead of something frivolous like a night out. But her mother was right. She did deserve a little fun. And what harm could it do? She already knew she wasn't going to get involved with Kal. They'd been down that road once, and she wasn't going there again with him. So they'd have dinner, a nice conversation, and that would be it.

"You're right. I do deserve it. And thank you for watching Oliver for me."

"I'm not doing it for you. I'm doing it for me. Besides, I'm already here, aren't I?"

"But you don't have to do it."

Her mother walked over and grasped her by the upper arms. "Stop trying to act as if this is a burden for me. I love having you and Oliver here. I've been lonely in this big house by myself. Oliver and I are going to have dinner, he's going to help me do some puzzles, we'll play some of those idiotic video games that make my eyes cross, then we'll watch movies."

She laughed. "Okay. Thanks, Mom. I won't be late."

"Oh, please, do be late. Go sit in his car and make out for a while."

Her eyes widened. "Mom."

Her mother laughed. "Have fun, Hannah."

She shook her head and grabbed her keys, then walked out the door.

Make out in his car? No, they were going to have dinner. That's all she was going to do with Kal Donovan.

And then she was going to come home to her son, where she belonged.

CHAPTER 6

HANNAH PULLED INTO THE DRIVEWAY OF KAL'S HOUSE and turned off the engine.

Kal had told her to meet him at his place. She assumed that was so they could take one car to whatever restaurant they were going to.

Nice house. Two stories, big yard, in a perfect neighborhood. The house was older, but looked as if it had been freshly painted, and had cute shutters on the front windows.

The kind of house she'd always wanted. She had once hoped that someday she and Landon could save up for a house just like this. Maybe have a couple more kids.

Ha. That dream died in the dust.

And what exactly was she doing here? Dreaming again? Of what? She'd long ago given up on dreams of some Prince Charming coming along. She knew now the only way to make her dreams come true was to make them happen herself. Yet here she was, having been talked into having dinner with Kal.

Granted, he was charming, for sure. But she wasn't in need of rescue.

She was stalling and she knew it. And why? This wasn't a romance. Sure, Kal was hot as hell, and maybe she had spent the week looking forward to seeing him. At least during those times when she wasn't dreading seeing him.

Conflicted much, Hannah?

She really needed to make a decision and stick with it, one way or another. This was the problem with dating in general. The whole emotional aspect of it. Who had time for that? She certainly didn't.

Then again, when was the last time she'd had an adult conversation with an intelligent, smoking-hot man who was attracted to her? And, even better, who wasn't a stranger? They had a history together. Something to build on.

If she was interested in building something.

Was she? Good question. But either way, she was having dinner tonight. And some relaxation time with good company. Didn't she deserve that?

Hell yes she did.

"Way to make an easy night complicated as hell, Hannah."

She walked over to the door and rang the bell.

She heard footsteps, and Kal answered the door, looking delicious in dark board shorts and a white T-shirt.

Should her heart be racing like this? What the hell. He's a firefighter. He knows CPR. In the meantime, it would be good to remind herself to breathe.

"Hey," he said. "Come on in."

She stepped inside and followed him through a living area and into a brightly lit kitchen that was much more modern than the outside of the house. The kitchen was spacious, with amazing appliances and beautiful countertops. She couldn't get over all this space.

"This is lovely," she said. "So you and your brothers did this?"

"Yeah."

"I'm impressed."

"Thanks."

She inhaled. "And what's that incredible smell?"

"Ziti pasta with meatballs in sauce on the side because you said you don't eat a lot of meat."

He remembered. That was sweet. "Oh. Who's making dinner?"

He smiled. "I am. For you."

Her heart did a tumble. "Really? So we're having dinner here?"

"I thought it would be better than sitting in a noisy restaurant." He went over to the fridge. "Beer or wine? I've got both. I've got a rosé and a sauvignon blanc in the fridge, or if you want red I've got a pinot noir in the cabinet."

He made dinner. For her.

She absolutely would not swoon.

"I'd love the pinot noir."

"Sure." He grabbed a beer out of the refrigerator for himself, then pulled the bottle out of the cabinet.

After pouring the red, he handed her the glass.

"Thanks. This is an awful lot of work for you."

He took a seat at the island next to her. "What is?"

"Cooking."

"I had the day off. You didn't. And I like to cook."

He liked to cook? That was new. "Since when? Because you didn't cook in high school."

"I had other things on my mind in high school. Sports. Hanging out with my friends. You."

She felt that flutter all through her nerve endings. "So when did the cooking thing come to life?"

"College and after, when my mom wasn't around to cook for me. And once you become a firefighter, you're on shift for twenty-four hours. It's not like they have a chef at the fire station. They teach you right away that one of the duties you share in is cooking, and you damn well better not suck at it. My parents were both great about teaching all of us boys to cook decent meals."

"Good for them. It's nice to have guys who know how to fix something other than a burger on the grill."

His lips curved. "I can do that, too. And a steak. And anything else that goes on the grill."

"Of course you can. But not tonight."

"No, I figured you might want something a little homier."

"Hey, I gave up my mom's homemade enchiladas to be here with you."

He leaned back. "And you didn't cancel our date to stay home and eat? Because I've had your mom's enchiladas. I still remember how good they are."

"Trust me. I considered it. Mom wouldn't let me cancel."

He took a swallow of beer, then smiled at her. "Remind me to thank your mom. I'm glad you came."

She picked up her glass and took a sip. It was a good pinot, smooth and mellow. She took another swallow, then set the glass down and looked around. "So where's your brother and his fiancée?"

"He was going to pick her up after work tonight, then they were going out to dinner and to check out a wedding venue and a band."

"So they want a live band for the wedding?"

"They're thinking about it, but they're still undecided. They picked a date, though."

"And when's the big day?"

"July next year."

"That doesn't give them much time to put a wedding together."

"Oh, trust me. Becks is organized and so is Jackson. They'll get it done. She's already been dress shopping, they've got the caterer nailed down, and next week they've got an appointment with the cake person."

"Mmm, I love cake."

"Do you? I didn't think about dessert. I can whip up a cake."

She swirled her finger around the rim of her glass, trying to figure out just who Kal was now. He cooked, and he was telling her he baked, too? "Just like that?"

"Well, it wouldn't be a three-tiered piece of art or anything. But sure."

"I might just let you do that. Just to watch the master at work."

He slanted a look at her. "Funny. I'm not Martha Stewart. I just throw shit in a bowl, mix it up, toss it in a pan and see what comes out."

"Now I have to see this."

"Okay, then. Let's make a cake. We've got about thirty minutes before the food comes out of the oven. Plenty of time."

He scrolled through his phone, settled on a recipe, then started compiling ingredients.

"What can I do to help?" Hannah asked.

"Grab the hand mixer from the cabinet down there." He motioned with his hand to the location, so she crouched down and found the hand mixer and plugged it in. By then he already had the ingredients in the bowl and started mixing them together.

"What else?"

He pulled his attention from the phone. "You can set the table. Dishes are in the cabinet left of the sink. Utensils right here."

He motioned again, and she was happy that he wasn't treating her like a guest. She grabbed plates and utensils and carried those over to the table.

They worked together on the cake. By the time he finished mixing, she had the parchment paper lining the cake pan. He poured the mix in just as the oven timer beeped. He pulled the pasta and meatballs out before adjusting the oven temp and slid-ing the cake batter in.

"Okay," he said after he put the bowl in the sink and ran some water. "Let's eat."

They carried the food over to the table, and Kal went to the refrigerator and brought out a salad he'd also made, along with some dressing.

She scooped some of the pasta onto her plate, along with one meatball, because it looked so good she had to taste it.

"Having a meatball, huh?"

"Hey, I said I limit the meat in my diet, not that I don't eat any. And these meatballs look amazing."

He added Parmesan cheese to both their plates, then Hannah slid her fork into the pasta. It was creamy and flavorful. She tried the meatball next, and her taste buds did a happy dance.

"This is delicious," she said.

"Glad you like it."

The salad was really good, too. The whole meal had been a surprise. Kal was a great cook.

"You must coax a lot of women over here with the promise of a home-cooked meal."

He arched a brow. "I don't bring a lot of women over here. I only cook for the special ones."

"Okay. So only a few."

"Or one." He gave her a pointed look.

And now she felt very special.

When the timer went off for the cake, Kal went over and pulled it out of the oven and onto a cooling rack. Then he came back to the table.

"Once that cools, we'll frost it."

"Sounds fun."

"You probably expected me to take you out to dinner. I hope you weren't disappointed."

"I can't think of anything I'd rather be doing tonight." And she meant it. This night had been perfect so far. And Kal? She was constantly surprised by him. He had a maturity to him that knocked her backward.

Given the man that she'd divorced had been offended at the thought of becoming an adult, being with Kal was utterly refreshing.

She took a sip of her wine and looked over at Kal. He was gorgeous. Sexy as hell, actually. Held an important job in his community, putting his life on the line to keep people safe.

He'd been incredibly sweet to her since the moment they'd reconnected. Every word out of his mouth caused her senses to go haywire.

Plus he cooked, too.

Damn. Who would have guessed that could be so hot? When he was busy eating, she watched his hands. They were . . . large. Which of course meant nothing, and they'd had sex before, and . . .

Well. Maybe large hands did mean something after all.

This sudden awakening of her libido was not convenient.

But as he looked up from his plate and his gaze met hers, she realized there wasn't much she could do about her body's reaction to him. They shared a past, and now her present was very much mixed up with said past.

And wow, did it suddenly get hot in here.

"Mind if I fix myself a glass of ice water?" she asked.

"I'll get it." He stood, and she couldn't help but admire his extremely fine ass as he walked away.

Yes, she was in very deep trouble. Because she'd only had one glass of wine, was definitely sober and was most assuredly fantasizing about getting her hands—and her body—all over Kal.

Deep, deep trouble. Because she had responsibilities and no time for a hot fling with an old boyfriend.

• • •

KAL FIGURED TONIGHT WAS GOING BETTER THAN HE ANticipated. Hannah seemed relaxed, she liked the food he fixed and she was giving him some damn hot looks.

Which might mean nothing. Then again, it might mean something. Either way, things were looking good.

After dinner they did the dishes together. Now it was time to frost the cake he'd made. Since he'd made a simple yellow cake, he figured it needed chocolate buttercream frosting.

He'd gotten out all the ingredients and beat them until the concoction was sweet and creamy.

"I'll frost it," Hannah said.

He knew she wanted to help, so he handed the spatula over to her. "Sure."

She applied the frosting with expertise, and when she was finished, Kal reached into the cabinet and pulled out multicolored sprinkles. Hannah's eyes sparkled with delight.

"It's not even my birthday," she teased.

"No, but since it's only one layer, it needs something extra."

She leaned against him. "You're something extra."

He laughed. "Not sure if that's a compliment or an insult."

She was so close he could breathe in her sweet scent.

"Definitely a compliment."

She lingered there, making him throb with the need to plant his mouth on hers, to taste her lips, to slide his tongue between them until they were both lost. It had been so long since he'd kissed her, so many years he ached with the need to touch her. But he also knew she was wary and needed some time. So he took a step back and focused instead on putting the sprinkles on the cake.

But he'd really wanted to kiss her. And when he heard her sigh of disappointment, he realized he might have missed the opportunity.

Damn.

"It looks amazing," she said.

"You ready for a piece?"

She laid her hand over her stomach. "I'm still full from dinner. I think I need to digest a little first."

"How about a walk?"

"Excellent idea."

It was a nice night. Not humid or too hot, with a little breeze. A perfect evening for a stroll. They took a long walk around the neighborhood, talking about their jobs. He asked her about her day, and she filled him in on what it was like to own the salon.

"It's a lot of work. I not only do hair and have to grow and maintain my own clientele, but I have to hire stylists and manicurists, do advertising, keep the books and make sure the shop meets code and stays clean."

Listening to her talk, Kal knew she wasn't complaining. She enjoyed what she did.

"You love being your own boss."

She smiled. "I do. When I first started out, I spent years working for other people. I hated it and swore that as soon as I could I'd buy my own salon. So I saved and saved until an opportunity came along to start up a place of my own in Georgia."

They rounded the corner by the park, several blocks from the house. It was well lit, and there were always people doing nightly walks there. Kal waved to some of the people strolling by. "How long did you have the place in Georgia?"

"About a year before my divorce. I had just gotten to the point where it was full, running efficiently, and then I had to sell it."

"I'm sorry. That had to hurt."

"It did. But fortunately, it was in a great location and the new owner snapped it up right away for a good price. Plus selling the house in Georgia and splitting the equity with Landon gave me enough money to open the shop here."

"That's a good thing. Other than the divorce, of course. I'm sorry about that."

"I'm not. Getting out of that marriage was the best thing that ever happened to me."

He could tell she bore some bitterness about her ex, but he wasn't sure she was ready to open up to him about it. "You want to talk about it?"

She looked over at him. "My ex? He's a nice enough guy, but he's a child. And I already had one kid. I didn't need another who was supposed to be acting like an adult."

When he gave her a questioning look, she shrugged. "It's a really long story. I'm sure you're not interested."

He stopped to make sure she could see that she had his attention. "I'm interested."

She started walking again, so he got back in step with her. She didn't talk right away, not for about a block. He figured maybe she wasn't going to open up to him. But then she began.

"We got married too young. I was ready to get out of Ft. Lauderdale, and Landon was my ticket out. He had big ideas about opening his own place. He's a mechanic. He had cousins in Peachtree City in Georgia, and they were going to go into business together and open an auto repair shop. Big plans, big ideas. It all sounded perfect."

"But?"

"They started one business, and it did okay for about a year. I thought that was going to be it. That he'd have the success he'd talked about. But he and his cousins couldn't agree on one single thing, and they fought all the time. On the mechanical side, they were all great. As businessmen, they sucked, so the business failed. Landon decided to go out on his own, start up his own shop. But again, he had a great head for mechanics and he completely ignored the business side, so that venture failed, too. And so it went. Landon always had big plans, big ideas. Maybe buy a franchise, that would work out better. Or start something completely new. We argued all the time about finances. And nothing ever came of all his big ideas. So he'd pick up odd jobs—when he actually worked. In the meantime, I had my business going and I was constantly working. And he often wasn't. But there was always 'I've got this great new idea' while I'm working twelve hours a day and trying to take care of a baby. By the time Oliver was four, I knew I was finished. It just took me another couple of years to extricate myself from the marriage."

He could picture how hard Hannah worked and struggled on her own. It couldn't have been easy.

"And how did your ex take the divorce?"

She shrugged. "He knew it was coming. He can barely take care of himself now because he can't hold down a job long enough to get a decent paycheck. He loves Oliver, and I know that, but the idea of a nine-to-five job, to work for someone else? It nearly sends him into a panic. He's just not built that way. He still wants to own his own business. He just can't figure out how to make that a reality."

She sighed. "So, anyway, I left, took Oliver with me, and Landon signed the papers, giving me full custody. I told him he can see Oliver whenever he wants to, and I think that gave him some comfort."

His heart ached for Hannah. And for her son. That had to be a painful end to what had to be a big dream for her. "I'm so sorry, Hannah."

"It's okay. Oliver and I are doing just fine. He's got me, and he knows I love him. And he's got my mom now, and he adores her."

They rounded the corner leading back to the house. "Does he ask about his dad?"

"Sometimes. He knows his dad loves him. He also knows Landon has issues with follow-up that have nothing to do with him. At least as much as a seven-year-old can understand. And maybe someday Landon will get his shit together enough to be a good father, but I don't hold out much hope."

That really sucked. Having come from a background of having lousy, deadbeat parents before he was adopted, Kal knew what it was like not to be loved, not to be put first, to be abandoned by someone who should love you. He never wanted any kid to feel that way.

"Every kid should be the light of their parent's life."

She nodded. "I think so."

They got back to the house and went inside.

"I'll be right back," she said.

Hannah went to use the bathroom, and Kal washed his hands, got out some plates and cut into the cake. When she came back out, he took the cake over to the table.

Hannah fixed herself a glass of water and brought that to the table.

"I still can't believe you made cake."

"I'm a multitalented kind of guy."

She picked up her fork and looked at him. "Yes, you definitely are."

She took a bite, swallowed and then smiled. "This is so good."

"You seem surprised."

"I'm not. Okay, maybe I am. I still can't reconcile this new version of you with the guy you used to be. Carefree, a little bit crazy, but definitely not the cook-a-meal kind of guy."

"Like you said, we grew up."

"This is true." She took a bite, swallowed. "You can definitely bake."

"I'm glad you like it."

She scooped another forkful. "Who doesn't like cake?"

"That's always my question."

They finished off their cake, then took their plates to the sink to rinse and load into the dishwasher.

Kal placed two more pieces onto a paper plate and covered it with foil. He looked up at Hannah. "For Oliver and your mom."

"That's so sweet. Thank you."

"Sure." There was enough cake left for Jackson and Becks, so he put a cover on that. "How about a movie?"

"I'd like that."

He grabbed his beer, and she refilled her glass of wine. He led her into the living room, and they took seats on the sofa. He picked up the remote and turned the TV on.

"If I remember right, you like romantic comedies, suspense, action movies and thrillers."

"I'm impressed at your recall."

"I'm just full of surprises." He scrolled through the list of available movies, and they discussed a few they could watch, finally settling on a thriller.

"I haven't seen this one," she said. "But I've heard good things."

"I haven't seen it, either."

She kicked off her tennis shoes and socks and pulled her feet up on the sofa. He tried not to notice her cute pink-painted toenails, or how dainty her feet were.

He used to rub her feet in high school. She was a cheerleader, plus she ran track, and used to complain about her feet hurting after a long meet, so while they'd sit in her parents' living room watching television, he'd rub her sore feet. And then she'd giggle because her feet were ticklish. He'd bet her feet were even more tired now that she spent long days standing on them.

But he kept his hands to himself and focused on the movie instead. Fortunately, it held his attention because it got off to a fast start. It was gripping, and both he and Hannah were silent during the first half.

"Could you pause this while I switch to a glass of water?" she asked.

He did, and they both got up. She washed out her wineglass and refilled her water, and he grabbed another beer.

After he came out of the bathroom, she was leaning against the kitchen island.

"I needed a breather," she said. "That movie is intense."

"If you're scared, you can lean against me."

She pushed off the island, and they made their way back toward the living room. "Oh, I can, huh? What makes you think I'm scared?"

"You were curling your toes. You always do that when you're tense."

She frowned. "I do?"

"Yeah."

"Maybe I was just cold."

They settled back in, and he reached for the blanket resting on top of the sofa. "You know this was sitting right here."

"I didn't notice it."

"Uh-huh. You're scared."

"Am not." She wrapped the blanket around her legs.

When he restarted the movie, Kal noticed she also scooted a little closer to him, which he didn't mind at all.

By the time the movie approached the climax, Hannah had moved next to him. Her body pressed against his, and her head lay against his shoulder. He put his arm around her and pulled her closer as the main characters fought off the killer and survived.

Hannah exhaled and lifted her head as the credits rolled. "My heart's beating so fast. I didn't think they were going to make it."

"I knew they were gonna be fine."

She gave him a look. "Please. You gripped my fingers so tight I thought you'd break my hand."

"What?"

She lifted her hand, and he realized they were holding hands. And he had a tight hold on hers.

"Oh. Well, I was just keeping you from getting scared."

"Uh-huh. Sure."

"Well, you oozed over here and were practically on my lap."

She lifted her chin. "I was keeping you warm."

"Uh-huh. Sure," he mimicked.

She laughed. "Okay, fine. The movie was tense. I was tense. And so were you. I dare you to deny it."

He started to object, but her stern look made him think twice. "Is that your mom look?"

She burst out laughing. "It might be. Why? Is it effective?"

"Very. Does it work on Oliver?"

"Of course it does. Moms are magical, you know."

"Don't I know it. My mom has a very similar look. Makes me run for the hills every time she levels it on me. Do they teach it to you in Mom School or something?"

"No, I think it's passed down genetically."

"Just so you know, it's extremely effective."

"Good." She glanced down at her phone. "It's getting late. I should go. Oliver gets up early."

"Okay. I'm on shift tomorrow, which means I have to get up early, too."

"You should have said something. We didn't have to watch the movie."

He smiled at her as they walked into the kitchen to put their glasses in the sink. "It's not that late, Hannah."

She leaned against the counter. "Still, I don't want you to miss out on sleep."

"Trust me. I'd rather spend time with you than sleep."

"Well, I had a nice time. Thanks for cooking for me."

"Thanks for coming over. We'll have to do it again."

"Yeah, about that . . ."

Uh-oh.

"Okay, you're gonna tell me I'm not your type."

She let out a short laugh. "I think you know that's not true. But I have a very full, very busy life, and I'm not looking to get into anything serious right now."

"I don't recall asking you to marry me over bites of pasta. So neither am I. How about we just play this loose and easy and maybe have a little fun?"

She paused like she was going to object, then nodded. "I could maybe do that."

"Sounds super enthusiastic."

"I am. I'm just a little leery after, you know."

"I understand. But I promise you that I hold down a job, I don't have nefarious intentions and I'm a really nice guy. Which you should already know."

He took a chance and stepped into her personal space, testing the waters. She didn't skirt out of the way, instead tilted her head back while laying her palm on his chest.

"You broke my heart in high school," she said, her voice lowering to almost a whisper, as if she was afraid to say the words out loud.

"I left for college. And we both made the decision to break up."

"True. But that was the part that broke my heart."

Now it was his heart that squeezed as he remembered that day when he packed up his car, Hannah standing there with tears streaming down her face. Neither one of them wanted to leave the other, but it was something he'd had to do, and he knew Hannah couldn't come with him. It had been his idea to break up. Not because he wanted to date other girls at college, but because he'd wanted her to be free.

Who knows what would have happened if they hadn't split up.

He cupped her hand between both of his. "That was a long time ago."

"Yes."

"I'm sorry about the breakup."

She pressed into his chest with her hand, making his heart kick up a fast beat. "It's okay. Waiting around for you would have been worse. We did the right thing."

"Did we?" He rubbed his thumb across her hand, absorbing the soft feel of her skin. "I always wondered about that. I missed you after I left."

"Did you?"

Now his breathing hitched and he moved in even closer.

"Yes. A lot. I felt lost without you. If it makes you feel better, I didn't date anyone for the first couple of years in college."

Her lips curved. "I find that hard to believe. You're kind of a catch, Donovan."

"So are you, McKenzie. Clark. Whatever you want to call yourself now."

Her lips curved. She pulled her hand away, raised up on her toes and curled her hand around the nape of his neck, drawing his face toward hers.

"Hannah works. Now shut up and kiss me."

He didn't need more invitation than that.

Their lips met. The contact was an explosion of heat, like flames licking all around him, but in the best way. Her body was warm and soft, and she moved into him, sliding her hand along his chest, making his heart pump faster.

Her lips moved under his, slow and deliberate, as if they had all the time in the world to explore this lazy kiss. But he wanted to dive in and get lost in her, so he pressed in, slid his tongue between her lips, and she moaned.

Oh yeah. Now they were getting somewhere.

Until she pushed on his chest. He broke the kiss and took a step back.

"I'm sorry," she said, licking her lips. "I . . . can't. Not yet."

He nodded, giving her more space. "It's okay. We've got time."

"I need to go."

He took a couple of deep breaths to clear his head, then walked outside with her to her car.

She turned to face him with a smile. "I had a good time."

"Me, too. We should do this again."

Her lips curved. "Yes, we should."

She started to lean in again, then stopped. Instead, she opened her car door. "See you, Kal."

"Later, Hannah."

After she drove away, he went inside and locked the door, then fixed himself a glass of water and went upstairs to his room. He got ready for bed and climbed in but couldn't sleep.

How could he when he could still taste Hannah on his lips, when her scent still lingered in a room she hadn't even been in?

Okay, so he still felt it for Hannah. But he was going to have to pump the brakes a bit and take things slow with her.

Because he wanted her back in his life again—only this wasn't high school Hannah. This was adult Hannah who had a kid.

And she was worth taking on the slow ride.

CHAPTER 7

"AND THEN AFTER THE MOVIE WE ALL MET UP AT OUR house to have cake to celebrate James's birthday. Only his sister said we should have gone to her house because she has that big newly renovated kitchen. She said that way all the extended family could be there. Which really meant so she could show off her new shiny things to everyone and brag about her rich lawyer husband. So she was mad about it and refused to come. But his mom and his aunt showed up, and there was plenty of room, so I don't know what Rachel's problem was, other than she's always been a raving bitch who wants everything to be about her."

Hannah finished cutting her client's hair while simultaneously listening to her go off on her sister-in-law. But part of her job also consisted of being a good listener, and sometimes a counselor, depending on the situation. This client needed someone to listen while she vented her frustrations, which Hannah was adept at doing. She nodded, said a lot of "Oh no" and "That's too bad" and "I'll bet that was awful," which seemed to satisfy her client.

She had a short break before her next appointment. Despite the deluge of rain today, the shop was getting a steady stream of clients. It rained a lot in Florida, but that never stopped people from doing their daily tasks. Even a hard rain like today wasn't a deterrent.

She cleaned her station, got something to drink from the kitchen, then took a seat and went through the supply catalog and made some notes about products she needed to order. Occasionally, she'd lift her head to listen in on whatever conversation Delilah or Marguerite had going on with their clients. Josephine had her own station in the corner of the salon with a relaxing mani/pedi chair. She currently had a client sitting there with her eyes closed while Josephine did a pedicure on her, so everything seemed to be going well there. Hannah was happy with the influx of new clients since Josephine had started.

Hannah went back to her catalog until the door opened and a tall, dark and handsome man walked in. He wore his yellow firefighter coat, he was dripping wet from the rain and he looked drop-dead gorgeous.

All work stopped, every pair of eyes immediately turning to Kal, who smiled at Hannah. She got out of her chair as he walked over to her.

"What are you doing here?"

"I was in the neighborhood and thought I'd stop by to check out your place."

"You're on duty?"

He nodded. "On a supply run. There's a shop just a block from here, so I thought I'd take a minute to drop in and say hello." He looked around her. "Are you with a client?"

"Not at the moment." She felt every set of eyes in the place trained on her—well, not on her, on Kal. She should probably introduce him. "Hey, everyone. This is Kal Donovan. He's a firefighter and a friend of mine. Kal, you remember Delilah from high school?"

"Oh yeah. Hey, Delilah."

"And this is Marguerite, and over there is Josephine."

"Hey, Kal," Marguerite said, sporting a wide grin. "Nice to meet you."

"Hi, Kal," Delilah said. "Hannah said you two were dating again."

"She did, huh?"

"And she's said good things about you," Marguerite added.

"Really."

"Oh yes," she said. "Very good things."

He looked over at Hannah. "You've been talking about me, huh?"

"Oh, she talks about you all the time," Delilah said with a grin.

"I do not. Not a word." She shot a look over at Delilah, who laughed.

"Honestly," Hannah said to Kal. "Nothing."

Now Kal laughed. "I don't mind, as long as it's all good."

"I haven't said a word to anyone."

"Oh, so now I'm your dirty secret."

She rolled her eyes. "Kal."

"Come on. I'm teasing. Show me your place. I can't stay long."

The man was exasperating. "Fine. This is it." She held her hands out wide.

He slanted a look at her. "You can do better than that." He walked over to her station. "So this is where you work?"

She sighed. "Yes. This is my station."

"Nice." He leaned down to inspect the corner of the mirror where she had a picture of her son. "This is Oliver?"

"Yes."

He lifted, giving her a warm smile. "He's cute. He looks a lot like you."

"Thank you for saying that."

"It's true."

She could get lost in Kal's eyes, the smoothness of his skin and his mouth—just remembering what it had been like to kiss him the other night . . .

She cleared those thoughts from her head and walked him toward the lunchroom. "Anyway, this way is the break room where we can put our feet up and eat."

He peeked his head in the door, leaning his body against hers so he could see. Her body reacted by quivering all over.

"Sizable enough and you have a microwave and fridge. That's nice."

"Yes." She straightened and moved away. "Here are the washing stations, and our washer/dryer and storage."

"This place is bigger than I thought."

She shrugged. "It's not huge, but it's enough space."

"It's nice, Hannah."

"Thank you." Standing this close to him in the small washing area was sending her pulse racing. Especially since her mind had to go to that place where she remembered kissing him the other night. Clearly a huge mistake.

"Anyway, I came by to ask what you're doing tomorrow."

She frowned. "Why?"

"It's Friday. I'm off shift. I thought maybe you might want to go out."

"I promised Oliver I'd take him to the new movie."

"The one with the fire truck? Come on, I'm dying to see that one."

She cocked her head to the side. "It's an animated movie, Kal."

"And?"

She walked out of the laundry area, and Kal followed.

"You want to see a kid movie. With a seven-year-old."

"Well, yeah. Doesn't everyone love animated movies?"

"I do."

Hannah swiveled toward Delilah, who shrugged. "Well, I do."

"So do I," Delilah's client said. "My husband and I don't even have kids and we love animated movies."

"See?" Kal said. "Let's go see the movie."

She shook her head. "Fine."

"Great. We'll go get pizza first. I assume you have no objection to pizza."

"Oliver loves pizza."

"Who doesn't?" Marguerite said, grinning.

"Great," Kal said. "I gotta go. I'll text you tomorrow."

"Bye, Kal," Delilah said.

Kal grinned and waved, and Hannah waved as well.

Once he left, Delilah said, "He is so damn hot."

"I didn't tell you I was seeing him."

"I know that, but it was kinda obvious the minute he walked in the door. And why didn't you tell me?"

"Because there's nothing going on. We're just friends from high school, and we reconnected at the reunion. Nothing's going on between us."

"She lies," Marguerite said. "Tension was thick in here."

"So thick," Marguerite's client said. "Like, we-need-to-turn-the-AC-down-in-here thick."

Delilah laughed. "They're right. He's hot for you. And you're hot for him. Face it, girl, there's some boiling chemistry going on between the two of you."

Delilah wasn't lying about that. The whole salon had gotten steamy when he'd walked in. The man took up space with his presence. And that space ignited whenever he walked into the salon.

Whew. She was perspiring now.

The problem was, how was she going to keep her very astute seven-year-old son from noticing her interest in Kal?

Because just being next to Kal had a polarizing effect on her. Which meant she was going to have to work very hard to mentally and physically put Kal in the friend zone tomorrow night to avoid confusing Oliver. The last thing her son needed was to see her reaction whenever she was around Kal. And right now that reaction was chemical.

Baby steps. She liked Kal, and if she wanted things to progress with him, she had to take it slow.

With Kal. And with her son.

CHAPTER 8

KAL BROUGHT THE SUPPLIES BACK TO THE STATION, dodging the rain that was coming down harder now. He didn't even mind. Not after his successful visit to see Hannah.

She'd looked so pretty with her hair piled on top of her head, that businesslike focus she'd given him as she showed him around her shop. She was so obviously proud of what she'd created there, as she should be. He'd been impressed.

She had a nice shop, and she worked with good people. He could see she was happy.

And, he had a date with her and with Oliver tomorrow night. It had all worked out, and he couldn't wait to meet her son.

But now it was back to work, so he had to focus.

As one of the junior firefighters on the roster, it often fell to him to do the drudge work like supply runs and inventory. He put the supplies away, updated the inventory and took the report in to his lieutenant. Then he headed to the kitchen to grab some lunch—or what was left of lunch, anyway. They'd had tacos, and it looked as if a plague of locusts had run over the kitchen. Irish was just about to put the leftovers away when Kal walked in.

"You're lucky anything is left," Irish said. "But I managed to set a few aside for you."

"Thanks, Irish."

"Also, you're on dishes."

He shook his head. "Of course I am."

He shoveled the tacos and rice into his mouth, then cleaned the kitchen, listening to the wind and rain pelt against the windows.

It had been pouring outside since he showed up for duty this morning, and it hadn't let up yet. Station 38 had already been on three calls for car wrecks since shift started, one with some fairly bad injuries. It was going to be a hot mess today.

He'd checked in with Jackson and Rafe, and they said it was just as bad at Station 6. They'd no more get back from one call before they had to go out on another.

It wasn't like rain was unheard of in Ft. Lauderdale, but since it was hurricane season, the rain could really perform, and roads became dangerous.

He went to the open doors of the bay and hung out there with a few of the other members of the team, watching how hard the rain was sheeting.

"Forecast calls for this nasty weather all night," Andy said.

"I'm glad I'm here today," Wes Macintosh said, his dog, Winnie, sitting by his side.

"We are, too," Lieutenant Anderson said.

They were lucky to have search and rescue firefighter Wes Macintosh with them today, along with his specially trained dog, Winnie. Wes wasn't assigned to a specific fire station but tended to float wherever he was needed.

Kal hoped they didn't need Wes or Winnie today. But the way it was looking outside, and with the sun going down, they just might.

They all went inside and worked on rope drills. True to form, Starling and Beckwith were hypercritical of his every move, even though he knew he was doing everything right. Kal wasn't in the mood for it today, so he did his best and chose to ignore them.

They had just put the last of the ropes away when the alarm sounded for the TRT. The team ran for the bay to climb into gear and get into the truck.

"Station 6 is on location at the scene of a two-car accident," Lieutenant Anderson informed them as they made their way to the scene. "Car one rear-ended the second, causing the second to slide down an embankment. Because of all the rain and subsequent mud, Station 6 hasn't been able to get down and rescue the occupants of car two. That's our job."

Kal got his mind into work mode. They talked out the potential scenario, who would do what and the type of equipment they'd need at the scene, including ropes and pulleys, rappelling equipment as well as rescue buckets. Fortunately, Station 6 was on the scene, so they'd have extra rescue gear available as well.

They arrived on scene, and as Kal and the team got out of the truck, they were pelted by the rain. Visualization was gonna be hard if not damn near impossible.

Lieutenant Anderson got the sitrep from Jackson, since he was lieutenant for Station 6, while the TRT gathered their gear from the truck.

"Okay, everyone," Anderson said. "Station 6 tried to get to the vehicle that slid down the embankment, but it's too slick with mud, and the last thing we need is to lose a firefighter team along with whoever is down there. So we're going to rappel down with a team at the top to provide balance and safety."

The lieutenant started barking out assignments. Kal, Phil Beckwith and Micah Brown would be rappelling down, and Meg, Dean and Andy would provide support.

Kal felt good about being called on for this job. Despite what Phil and Dean thought about him, obviously his lieutenant was fine with his skill set, because this wasn't going to be easy.

"Wes, I want you and Winnie to stand in wait to see if we need any search and rescue assistance," the lieutenant said. "I'm hoping everyone is still buckled tight in the vehicle."

"You got it," Wes said.

Kal hoped everyone was still inside the vehicle as well. The last thing they wanted was someone ejected. At high speeds and in a rolling vehicle, that could be trouble—and potential for serious injury.

Everyone harnessed up, and the ropes were dropped.

Micah looked over at Kal. "You ready for this?"

He nodded. "I've got it."

Micah gave a quick nod, and they started rappelling down.

Kal focused on his own rope, his feet sinking into the thick mud. His only objective was to make his way down to that vehicle without slipping and becoming another casualty. The last thing the team needed was for one of their own to fall. He looked down to see Micah below him, and Phil was above him, the three of them taking the same route through this blistering rain and in this sucking mud.

"I've got lights," Micah said into his com, letting them know that he'd spotted the vehicle.

That was good. It wasn't as far down as Kal thought it might have been. About fifty feet. Which meant they'd be able to get survivors up with buckets.

First they'd have to assess the victims, determine what they were dealing with.

Micah reached the car first, but waited for Kal and Phil to touch down.

As soon as they did, Micah radioed to the team above that they'd reached the vehicle.

Damn, it was difficult to see, hard to maneuver as they detached, wound their ropes around a nearby tree and drove a spike into the carabiners to hold them in place. The wind was howling, making getting around in the thick muck even more difficult. They grabbed their supplies and made their way to the vehicle, a dark four-door sedan that was sitting right side up—thankfully. It was nestled against a group of trees. Likely, the trees were what had halted its continued slide down the embankment. But the top was smashed in, so clearly a rollover.

They cleared the windows of mud as best they could, but it was still tough to see inside. And the doors were smashed and locked. At least they could get to one side of the vehicle. Since no one inside was trying to get out or making any noise, their only recourse was to break the windows.

Micah was the senior of their group, so Phil and Kal looked to him.

"Break 'em," he said.

Kal was on the passenger side back seat window, Phil on the front seat. He got out his punch and broke the window. He didn't hear any screams or noises. Phil shook his head. They cleared through the glass and shined lights inside.

No one was inside the back seat, so he went to assist Phil, who was checking vitals on the guy strapped into the passenger side.

"Unconscious. Pulse weak. But alive. Assessing for injuries."

"I'll climb in the back window to check on the driver," Kal said.

"No," Phil said. "Let me do that."

"You've got a patient already. I'll get in this way to check on the driver."

Phil paused, then nodded. "Fine. Do it."

He forced the back seat door open and scooted over between the two front seats.

The driver was female. Late twenties was Kal's guess. Her long blond hair was matted and covered in blood. Her eyes were closed, and she wasn't moving. He pressed his fingers to her neck.

Nothing.

Not about to give up, he kept searching, pressing harder.

Come on. Don't give up.

Finally, he felt a faint beat.

"I've got a pulse," he said. "Very weak."

"We've got to get these people out of here," Phil said. "This guy has a leg and arm fracture and possibly spinal. Can't be certain until he's fully assessed."

Micah stuck his head in the window. "I've radioed up to let them know we need advance life support and medical and buckets. Help is on the way."

"They'd better hurry," Kal said as he constantly monitored the vital signs of the driver. They weren't improving, but they weren't getting worse, either, so that was good.

The passenger, on the other hand, had started to regain consciousness and was fighting Phil. Micah had to help restrain him.

"Laura," the guy said. "My . . . my wife."

"We're taking care of her," Phil said. "But you can't move."

"What about Danny?"

Phil's gaze shot to Micah's, then back to the patient. "Who is Danny?"

"Our son. He's in the back seat."

"How old is Danny?" Micah asked.

"Ten."

Oh, shit, Kal thought. There was a kid out there somewhere in this mess of mud and rain. And he was all alone. Maybe hurt or scared.

"Okay, sir," Phil said. "You hang on. It's important that you not move."

"I'll get Wes down here with Winnie," Micah said to Kal and Phil.

The kid had to have been ejected through one of the windows that were now crushed against the tree. But they didn't see anyone on the way down. The problem was, he could be anywhere.

The good news was that the rain was starting to lighten up, which would make search and rescue easier. As would getting these people out of the vehicle and up that damn muddy slope.

Wes made his way down with Winnie, along with several of the other firefighters who brought extrication equipment.

Micah filled Wes in on the missing kid, and Wes and Winnie went right to work on search and rescue. Hopefully, it would be a rescue. Kal's stomach filled with dread. They needed to get that kid back. But Kal had to focus on getting the people out of the vehicle.

Kal prepared the wife for extrication, cutting her seat belt and making sure she was secure at the neck and back.

"Your hands are shaking, kid," Phil said, casting a glare at him. "You need me to call for help for you?"

"No. I've got this."

"And you've got a life hanging in the balance in your hands. If you can't handle it, we'll replace you with someone who can."

The last thing he needed right now was Phil telling him he couldn't do the job. "I said I've got it."

"Concentrate on your own patient, Beckwith," Micah said. "We're on a time crunch here."

"You got it," Phil said.

With a bigger team down to help, they extricated both victims from the vehicle and secured them, using buckets to pull them up the hill to waiting ambulances. It was backbreaking, slippery work, but they got it done, keeping their patients stable on the way up. By the time they got the woman to the ambulance, her vitals had perked up. Kal was relieved about that. He really hoped she was going to make it.

Wes and Winnie located Danny about twenty feet from the vehicle, conscious but with a broken leg and a possible concussion. He started fully coming around when the team got to him, thankfully. Considering how badly it could have gone for the kid,

they were all relieved when the rescue team brought him up. Kal
hoped he was going to be okay. It was a terrible accident, so it was
amazing the whole family had come through this. At least they
were all alive. Since they wouldn't be following to the hospital,
he'd have no way of knowing if they survived. He just had to
hope.

Now all that was left was cleanup. By the time they made their
way back to the station, Kal was filthy and wiped out, the initial
adrenaline rush having left his body. He felt twenty pounds
heavier since he was carrying all that extra mud and water weight
on his body.

He went to the shower to scrub the mud off, then put on a
fresh uniform. He sat in the locker room and tried to keep his
hands from shaking. It had been a tough call that could have gone
sideways in an instant. It didn't, but he had to admit that one
scared him.

Calls like that were why he'd signed on to the TRT. He was
going to have to suck it up and manage the stress of it all. So he
went back into the main room to rejoin his team.

Everyone seemed to be wiped out, but the truck had to be
cleaned up and supplies inventoried and replaced. Fortunately,
they didn't get any calls the rest of the night, so they ate and
chilled out. Which gave him plenty of time to regain his bearings.

He needed some downtime to reflect on that call, on his reaction to it, on how he'd managed it. Because it had been difficult,
but this was what he'd asked for.

So he was going to have to learn how to deal with it.

CHAPTER 9

HANNAH HAD A CANCELLATION ON HER LAST APPOINT-ment of the day, which didn't disappoint her all that much. It gave her time to pick Oliver up from school so he didn't have to ride the bus. Her mom still worked full-time at the county clerk's office, so they'd made arrangements for Oliver to stay at the neighbor's house with his friend. She'd already called Becca to let her know she was picking Oliver up, and texted her mom, too.

"It's so cool you're here," Oliver said when he saw her outside the school.

"I think so, too."

After he got into his seat, he said, "You're usually the last one home. Now you're the first."

"Which is why I wanted to surprise you today."

"So what are we gonna do now?"

"Well, tonight we're going to a movie, remember?"

"Oh, right. Can we have pizza first?"

"Of course. A friend of mine is going with us."

"Do I know her?"

"It's a him. And no, you don't."

Oliver went silent for a moment, and Hannah wondered if he was upset about her bringing a guy.

"Can I bring a friend, too?"

She smiled as she connected glances with him in the rearview mirror. She should have known he was playing an angle. "Sure."

"Can you call Jeff's mom and ask if he can come?"

"I'll do that as soon as we get home."

Becca agreed to let Jeff go with them for dinner and a movie. In fact, she sounded deliriously happy. Becca was just coming out of her first trimester of pregnancy with her second child, and she told Hannah she was looking forward to having a few hours of rest and relaxation with her husband, Tony. She said they'd probably both pass out on the sofa after dinner. Hannah had laughed at that mental visual.

Hannah couldn't blame her for wanting to enjoy some quiet time.

When they parked in the driveway, Oliver sprang out of the car. "I'm gonna go next door and get Jeff."

"Okay. Come right back."

"We will."

She shook her head and went to the mailbox to grab the mail, waving at Becca as she answered the door to let Oliver in. She went in the house and laid the mail and her purse on the kitchen counter.

Her phone buzzed. It was a text from Kal.

Movie times are 6, 7:30 and 9. What works for you? I'll order tickets.

She looked at her phone, calculating the time it would take for pizza and getting to the movie theater, then sent a text back to Kal.

I think 7:30 works the best so we have time for pizza. And we'll need four tickets. Oliver is bringing a friend.

Kal texted right back with: *Got it. What time should I pick you up?*

She replied: *I'm home early today, so 5:30 is good. We can take our time with pizza.*

He sent a text back: *See you then.*

Sounds good, she replied, then realized he'd be coming over to her mom's house instead of meeting her somewhere. Then again, he was going to meet Oliver, so it didn't really matter if he came here.

When Oliver and Jeff came running through the door, she sent them to Oliver's room to play and told them to stay inside, then went to take a shower. Once that was out of the way, she got dressed and went into the kitchen to flip through the mail.

Junk mail and bills. And more bills. "Living the Cinderella life here, aren't you, Hannah?"

She tossed the mail back on the counter, fixed herself a glass of iced tea and sat at the table to pay a few of those bills before she forgot about them, since no prince was coming to save her. It appeared as if she was going to have to save herself, which she was damned used to since she'd been doing it for years.

Being married to Landon had taught her one valuable lesson, and that was to never rely on anyone but herself. She'd been young and stupid, and she'd fallen for the fantasy of a good-looking guy who'd promised this fantastical future in which he was going to take her away from all of this and set her up for life.

Ha. He'd set her up, all right. He'd set her up with a pack of lies and nothing but disappointment. She'd never fall for that again.

She was much better off on her own.

"Mom. Mom. Momma. Mommmm."

She blinked and lifted her head to find Oliver standing next to the table. "Yes, sweetie?"

"Jeff and I want something to drink. Can we have a soda?"

"You can have water right now and sodas when we have pizza."

"Okay." He climbed up to the cabinet and grabbed two glasses, then stuck them in the spigot outside the fridge and filled them with water. He started to walk off.

"Nope. Drink them in the kitchen."

"Aww, Mom. We won't spill."

She'd heard that one before. "In the kitchen, Oliver."

"Fine. Come on, Jeff. Let's sit at the table and play the game on my tablet."

They sat at the table with her while she finished paying bills. Her mom came home, so she put her paperwork away in the drawer and went into the living room with her mother.

"How was your day, Mom?"

"Good. Yours?"

"Fine. I'm taking Oliver and Jeff to the movies tonight."

"That sounds nice. I'm going out to dinner with Carole and Amanda, then we're heading over to the casino in Hollywood."

"To make millions, no doubt."

Her mom laughed. "No doubt."

"Oh, and Kal is going with us."

She saw the brow raise her mother made. "Oh, really? That's interesting."

"It's not that interesting. He wants to see the movie."

Her mother gave her a smile. "Honey, he wants to see you, not the movie."

She glanced into the kitchen, but the boys were engrossed in conversation about the game and not at all interested in what she and her mother were discussing. "It's not like that."

"If you think that boy isn't interested in getting you naked, then you haven't gotten any in a while."

Now it was Hannah's brows that shot up. "Mom!"

Her mom looked over her shoulder, and so did Hannah. The boys had disappeared back into Oliver's room.

"What? Look, Hannah. I may be a widow, but I still think about sex."

"Apparently, you're the one who needs to get some."

Her mother shrugged. "Who says I don't?"

"Mother. Really."

"Yes, really. We're all sexual creatures, Hannah. And especially you. You're young and vibrant, and you should be getting out there, living it up. There's no reason why you can't have some fun. You got divorced, Hannah. You don't need to put all the good china in the cabinet to gather dust, if you know what I mean."

She could not believe she was having this conversation with her mother. "Yes, I know exactly what you mean, and I'll take that under advisement."

"You do that. Make a date with the boy for Saturday night, too, and I'll watch Oliver. So maybe you two can fool around a little."

She shook her head and stood. "This conversation is over."

She could still hear her mom laughing as she made her way into her bedroom to finish getting ready.

After putting on her makeup, she stared into the closet. Pizza and movie night was super casual. She chose black capris and a cotton short-sleeved shirt, then grabbed a lightweight cardigan since movie theaters were sometimes cold. She slid on her canvas tennis shoes, brushed her hair and came out into the kitchen, looking to see where everyone was.

The boys were still in Oliver's room. Her mom was gone as well, which meant she was probably in her room getting ready, so Hannah went into the living room and opened her phone, selecting her book app, deciding to take a few precious moments to get caught up on the romance novel she had been reading. She was only a few pages in when there was a knock on the front door, so she got up to let Kal in.

"Hey," he said. "You look pretty."

She thought she looked pretty basic, but it was always nice to be complimented. "Thank you. You look nice, too. Come on in."

He walked in, and the two boys came running out.

"Who are you?" Oliver asked, looking Kal up and down.

"I'm Kal Donovan. Are you Oliver?"

Oliver nodded.

Kal held out his hand to shake Oliver's. "I went to high school with your mom. We've known each other a long time."

"Oh, I saw your picture with my mom. You were her boyfriend."

Kal looked over to Hannah, who shrugged. "Yup. I was."

"So you're old like her."

"Thanks, Oliver," Hannah said with a wry smile.

Kal laughed.

"This is my friend Jeff," Oliver said. "He lives next door and we're best friends."

Jeff smiled to show off his missing front teeth.

"Hey, Jeff," Kal said. "So we're going to see the new fireman movie tonight. Did you know I'm a firefighter?"

Oliver looked over at Jeff, then back at Kal. "Nuh-uh. Really?"

"Yup. And I can't wait to see the movie."

"Me, too," Jeff said. "Do you go into burning buildings like they show on TV?"

"Sometimes, but we try to put the fire out as best we can first."

"And do you save people's lives?" Oliver asked.

"Sometimes."

"Cool."

True to the attention span of seven-year-olds, the boys ran off back to Oliver's room just as her mom walked in.

Her bright smile lit up her face. "Kal. It's so good to see you."

"Good to see you, too, Mrs. McKenzie."

"Please. It's Paige." She hugged Kal, then held on to his arms while she inspected him. "You've grown up."

"And you've grown even more beautiful than you were the last time I saw you."

Hannah caught that telltale blush on her mother's cheeks. "You've always known just the right thing to say to make a woman feel special. Thank you."

"Are you coming with us tonight?" he asked.

Her mother shook her head. "No. It's girls' night out. Dinner and then casino."

He turned to Hannah. "Hey, that sounds fun. Maybe I'll go with Paige instead."

Hannah laughed. "Knock yourself out, buddy."

"No, you're going with Hannah." She pushed at Kal. "Now the four of you should get going."

"She's pushy, isn't she?" Kal asked.

Hannah rolled her eyes. "You have no idea. Boys, it's time to go."

Oliver and Jeff ran out, Hannah grabbed her cardigan and her bag and they headed out. Since Kal had his truck, she suggested they take her car, much to the boys' disappointment since they wanted to ride in the truck.

"It has a regular back seat," Kal said to Hannah. "With seat belts. I promise it's safe."

"Come on, Mom," Oliver said. "It's a cool truck."

"It looks like a souped-up version of a road monster."

He laughed. "What? It's a black truck with appropriately sized tires and all the prominent safety features. I promise it won't make weird noises or anything."

She supposed she was used to her small car, so Kal's truck seemed huge to her.

"Please, Mom?" Oliver asked.

"Fine. Go on and get in."

Kal grinned, opened the back door of the truck and helped the boys climb inside. He made sure their seat belts were buckled, then opened the door for Hannah and held his hand out to help her climb in.

She had to admit, the truck was very nice on the inside. All the gadgetry and nice soft seats, and since it was humid out, the air-conditioning was a great relief. There were even vents blowing in the back for the boys, who were busy playing together on Oliver's tablet and completely ignoring her and Kal.

He climbed in and buckled up. "Okay?"

She smiled. "Perfect. Also? Nice truck."

"Thanks. Hungry?"

"Starving. Let's go eat some pizza."

He grinned and put the truck in gear, then backed down the driveway.

She'd initially had reservations about doing this, but now she was looking forward to it. Plus, she was hungry, and she loved pizza. The pizza place was kid friendly with arcade games to keep Oliver and Jeff busy, as well as a nice seating area where the adults could sit but still keep an eye on the kids. All in all, kind of perfect.

They ordered their drinks and pizza, then found a table with a great view of the arcade, so Hannah let Oliver and Jeff wander off.

"I've never been here before," Kal said.

"No reason for you to, since it's mostly an adults-with-kids kind of restaurant."

"It looks fun. Want to play some games?"

She laughed. "At the moment, I'm happy being off my feet and drinking my soda. If you want to play, by all means go and join the boys."

"At the moment, I'm happy sitting next to you."

His statement warmed her. "Thanks. I like having you here next to me."

"How was your day?"

"Crazy busy. But my last appointment canceled, so I got to pick Oliver up from school."

"That was nice. I mean, not the canceled appointment, but it was good you got to pick him up and spend more time with him. I'll bet he was excited to see you."

"He was, actually. Though probably more excited to see Jeff."

Kal shrugged. "Hey, he's seven. Hanging with his friends is everything."

She looked over to the play area to see Oliver and Jeff nudging each other while they played an arcade game. Her little boy was growing some long legs. It used to be he was barely tall enough to reach the controls. That wasn't the case anymore. She sighed. "They grow up fast."

"He's a cute kid, Hannah. He looks a lot like you."

She dragged her attention from Oliver and looked at Kal. "You think so?"

"Yeah. He has your eyes and your smile."

That made her happy. She'd compared their baby pictures a few times and tried to gauge who he looked like. Her mom said he looked like her, but she wasn't sure. "That's nice to hear. Thanks."

She took a sip of her soda, then asked, "What did you do on your day off today?"

"Went to the gym and worked out, then washed the truck and did some grocery shopping."

"How very domestic of you."

He laughed. "It was my week to buy groceries. We take turns."

"I see. So you all make a global list and then one person buys?"

"Usually. Though sometimes we'll run out of something in the middle of the week, or someone will want to make something specific for dinner and they'll pick that up at the store. But yeah, it's one list and we all use it, then we take turns buying. It works out."

"Like a commune."

"Funny. Actually, more like a family. We all share duties."

"Was it always like that? When you were growing up?"

"Yeah. We each had a chore list. Mom made sure it was split evenly. Someone had to empty the trash, one of us had to unload the dishwasher, stuff like that. And then we'd all argue over who had more work to do."

She didn't have any siblings, so she didn't know what that would have been like. It had always been her parents and her, and she'd been assigned chores when she was a kid. But she'd had no one to share the chores with, to argue with.

She glanced over at Oliver. He had chores to do as well, but no one to fight with, to play with other than his friends. She wished she could have given him a sibling, but it hadn't taken her long to figure out that Landon wasn't the best father figure and she didn't want to bring another child into the picture.

"It must have been great to grow up with siblings."

His lips curved. "Depends on the day. Most times we got along, especially when we lived on the street. Then we depended on one another for survival, especially me since I was the youngest. After we got adopted and we adapted to family life? It didn't take long for the fights to start."

"Real fights?"

"Nah. Just how boys squabble. It meant we had gotten comfortable. Mom said it meant we were happy. And that we should knock it off before we ended up stuck in our room staring at the four walls."

She laughed. "I can imagine that probably happened a time or two."

"Damn straight it did. We were all hardheaded boys. And she was right—we were happy for the first time in our lives. Once we adjusted, we started knocking one another around like real siblings. And then Mom or Dad would step in and we knew we were in deep shit. We'd get sent to our room and have nothing to do but stare at one another. It wouldn't take much time before we were all laughing and hanging out together again."

She could feel the love that Kal had for Jackson and Rafe. She'd seen that herself when they had been dating. Kal had been close with his brothers even then. She could only imagine that bond had deepened over the years.

Their pizzas arrived, so Hannah gathered up the kids, who scrambled to the table like voracious velociraptors.

"I'm so hungry," Oliver said.

"I'm hungrier than you are," Jeff replied.

"Nuh-uh."

Hannah looked over at Kal, who said, "I'm bigger and hungrier than both of you. And I'm gonna eat all the pizzas."

Oliver gaped at Kal. "You could eat two pizzas?"

"Easy."

"I wanna see you do that," Jeff said.

"Not me," Oliver said. "I'm too hungry."

"Okay, fine." Kal slid slices of pizza onto the plates. "Since you're too hungry, I'll share. This time."

Oliver giggled, and it made Hannah's heart squeeze. She had no idea why that moment hit her, and she didn't want to analyze it.

After all, it was just pizza.

Kal handed her a plate. The pizza smelled delicious, and her stomach grumbled at her to get eating, so she dived in, watching happily as Oliver and Jeff stuffed their faces.

"What's your favorite topping?" Kal asked the boys.

"Pepperoni," Jeff said.

"Mine, too," Oliver said. "And hamburger. And cheese. And mushrooms."

"What?" Kal gave him a surprised look. "You like mushrooms? What else?"

Oliver lifted his gaze to the ceiling, something he always did when he was thinking hard.

"Um . . . broccoli."

"No way. I like broccoli, too. But not on my pizza. How about onions?"

Oliver shrugged. "Sure."

"Ew," Jeff said, making a face. "Gross."

"No, they're good," Oliver said.

"So you'd eat an everything pizza," Kal said.

Oliver chewed and swallowed and nodded. "I guess. But no fishy things."

"Yeah," Kal said. "No fishy things. I'm with you on that one, buddy. But everything else."

Oliver stared down at his slice. "Okay. Next time we'll have an everything else pizza."

Hannah was surprised at how easily Oliver said "next time," as if Kal had already been accepted.

Kids. They made friends so easily, and obviously Kal was a friend now. Then again, if he'd been a jerk and had ignored him, Oliver wouldn't have been so eager to invite Kal to a "next time" for pizza.

They finished eating, and their server cleared the table.

"Now," Kal said, "let's go play some games."

Hannah went with them, laughing as she watched Kal play Skee-Ball with the boys, followed by pinball and a driving game. Hannah estimated he let them win at least half the games, which she appreciated.

Soon, Oliver had grabbed Kal's hand and dragged him from game to game, and at no time did Kal say he was too tired or didn't want to play. But Kal did pull Hannah into a few of the games, making sure she had some time to play with her son as well. She had to admit, she had a good time, even though she lost on several occasions.

They made it to the movie with plenty of time to get popcorn and soda. Kal sat on her left, and Oliver and Jeff on her right. The movie was cute, and the boys behaved themselves—all three of them. Kal didn't even try to hold her hand, obviously respecting that they were there with her child.

On the way home, Kal and the boys discussed their favorite games at the pizza place, along with their favorite parts of the movie. Oliver had always been a talker, but he and Jeff both were more animated than usual, and very engaged with Kal.

Hannah couldn't believe how easily Oliver had accepted Kal. Then again, Kal didn't talk down to Oliver or treat him like a baby. He was easygoing with him, and he spent time with him. To Oliver, that was everything. It made it even more obvious how much Oliver had missed having a male influence in his life.

When they got home, she walked Jeff next door to his house. Becca thanked her for taking him to dinner and said she and her husband had a quiet, restful evening.

When she got back home, she didn't see Kal or Oliver. She found them both in Oliver's room.

"And these are my trains."

"Wow. Those are awesome, Oliver. I like how you have them up on a shelf."

"Thanks. Mom and Grandma put the shelves up for me when we moved here."

"They did a good job. And the trains look great up there."

Hannah leaned against the doorway listening to Oliver tell Kal all about his trains. He'd always loved them from the time he was little, so every birthday and Christmas Hannah had been buying him new pieces for his set.

"Okay, Oliver," she finally said. "Time to get ready for bed."

"Aww, Mom. I want to stay up for a while."

She shook her head. "You have an early game in the morning, remember?"

"Soccer?" Kal asked.

Oliver grinned. "Yup. I'm a halfback, and sometimes I get to play goalie."

"That's pretty cool. Maybe I'll get to come to your game sometime."

"Great. Mom doesn't get to come because she works on Saturdays. But Grandma is always there."

That twinge of guilt hit her right in her stomach. She pushed it away because there was nothing she could do about it. She had to work. "That's right, and your grandma loves watching you play. Now go brush your teeth and get your jammies on."

"Okay."

She and Kal left the room. As they made their way into the kitchen, she asked, "Do you want something to drink?"

"I'm good right now, thanks."

"I'm ready, Mom," Oliver yelled from the bedroom.

"He reads a chapter of his book to me before he goes to sleep," Hannah said. "We're on the Magic Tree House books right now. Do you mind?"

"Not at all. Go ahead."

She left the room and went into the bedroom, sitting down on the side of the bed to snuggle up next to her son.

"Did you brush your teeth?"

Oliver gave her a toothy smile. "Yes."

"Good. Okay, let's read."

He pulled the book out. "Mom?"

"Yes?"

"I like Kal."

Her heart fluttered. "Me, too."

"Can he come over again sometime?"

"Sure."

"Okay. Good."

He started reading, and Hannah hoped it was the whole pizza and playtime thing and Kal being someone new that sparked Oliver's enthusiasm.

After all, it had just been tonight. And Kal was a nice guy. Everyone liked him.

No big deal, right?

Except it kind of had been, she realized after they finished the chapter. She kissed Oliver good night and turned off the light.

Kal was in the living room playing a game on his phone. When she came in, he shut it off, got up and slipped his phone in his pocket.

"I'm sorry," he said. "I could have left so you could have had some quiet time with Oliver."

"It's okay. It really was time for him to go to sleep. He was yawning while he was reading."

"I can go now if you'd like me to."

"No. Let's sit and talk for a while if you're up for it."

"Sure." He waited while she found a spot. When she did, he sat next to her on the sofa, making her body warm up in all the places it shouldn't.

"I had a good time tonight," she said.

"Is there a 'but' in there?"

She frowned. "No. But there's a 'thank you' in there. Oliver had a good time, too. Thanks for spending so much time with him."

"Hey, he's a great kid. Hanging out with him wasn't a chore."

"Most adults wouldn't think so."

"Then most adults are dicks. Your kid is smart and fun. Who wouldn't want to spend time with him?"

He said all the right things, did all the right things, which was so unusual considering getting her ex-husband to spend any time with his own son had been an effort. And yet, it had seemed so easy for Kal.

She didn't understand it, but she wasn't going to question it. Kal had seemed at ease with Oliver tonight, and she was grateful.

"You're a good guy, Kal."

He looked over at her. "Hey, thanks. What brought that on?"

She shrugged. "No reason. Other than you're nice."

"You know what they say about nice guys."

"That they finish last?"

"Which could be a good thing in some cases."

She laughed. "Not at all what I'm talking about here."

"But you might want to bookmark it for future reference."

She leaned against him, pressing her body against his side. "Or, for now."

He looked down. "This isn't the same sofa we made out on when we were in high school, is it?"

"No. Mom got a new one a few years back."

"That's too bad." He pulled her toward him. "It was a pretty comfy sofa."

This close, she felt his heart pounding. Hers was, too. Their faces were so close all it would take was her leaning in and their lips would touch.

She did, and he kissed her, his soft lips melting her. He took it slow and easy, just the way she liked it, sliding his arm around her waist to tug her closer. She sighed against his mouth and he uttered a groan and it was all she could do not to climb on his lap, but she was conscious of where she was. They weren't alone. But she could indulge in a little kissing. And this was very good, reminding her of just how long it had been since she'd been thoroughly kissed.

"Mom?"

Kal broke the kiss so fast it made her head spin. He also got up and moved clear across the room.

Hannah couldn't help but smile at his quick moves. She stood. "I'll be right back."

He nodded. "Sure."

She went into Oliver's room. "What's up?"

"I heard a noise."

"Yeah?" She went to sit down on the side of his bed. "What kind of noise?"

"I dunno. A noise. Like bumping against the wall outside."

"It's windy outside. Probably that piece of guttering that's loose. But I'll go check it out, and you go back to sleep, okay?"

"Okay." He yawned, and she pulled the covers up, bent and kissed his forehead.

"I love you, Oliver."

He was already falling back asleep. "Love you."

She came back into the living room.

"Is he okay?" Kal asked.

"He said he heard a noise outside. There's some guttering that's loose above his window, and sometimes when the wind kicks up it rattles. I'm sure that's what it was."

"Want me to go look?"

She shook her head. "No, it's fine."

"I'm gonna go check anyway. I'll be right back."

"Okay."

He went out the front door and was gone for a while. When he came back in, he shook his head. "Nothing and nobody out there, just in case he wakes up again. But you're right about that gutter. It's loose."

"I'll have it taken care of so it doesn't bother him anymore."

"Okay." He looked toward Oliver's room. "I think I'm gonna go."

She didn't want him to, even though she knew it was the right thing. "Sure."

He walked toward her and pulled her into his arms, giving her a brief brush of his lips across hers. "See you soon."

"Thanks for tonight. I had a good time. So did Oliver."

"Me, too. Good night, Hannah."

"Night, Kal."

She walked him to the door and waited while he left.

"Lock the door behind me," he said over his shoulder.

She smiled. "Okay."

She closed the door and locked it, then sighed and went to her room, knowing she was going to be way too pent-up to sleep.

She had a hot man on her mind.

CHAPTER 10

KAL GOT UP EARLY, WENT TO THE GYM WITH JACKSON, then they met Rafe at his house. Carmen had the day off, so she fed them a breakfast of huevos rancheros with tomatillo sauce. Kal could have downed that all day long.

"How's the new house coming along?" he asked as they sat at the kitchen table in front of the bay window.

"It's perfect," Carmen said. "Since the house was new, there wasn't much to do, but we've started to put things on the wall, added shelves and area rugs here and there. It's starting to feel like home."

Rafe shot a smile across the table at Carmen. "It felt like home the minute you and I walked in here."

"True. And soon we'll be married. That's hard to believe."

"Yeah," Jackson said. "Hard to believe anyone would be willing to marry this jackass."

"Hey. You're the one who took forever to ask Becks to marry you."

Carmen nodded. "Sorry to say he's right. What took you so long?"

Jackson looked at all of them, then shrugged. "It was Becks. She kept saying she wasn't ready."

Kal sputtered out a laugh. "Yeah, right. She'd have married you a year ago and you know it."

"No, seriously. I asked her several times if she wanted to get married, and she kept saying things were fine as they were. I think she was scared."

Carmen leveled a serious look at Jackson. "Scared of what?"

"I don't know. Things changing between us, maybe."

Kal nodded. "Okay, I get that. Our lives were always in flux when we were kids. Foster homes and being homeless. Maybe she was afraid of upsetting the status quo, of you changing your mind about the relationship."

"Poor baby girl," Carmen said. "I'm glad you were patient with her, Jackson."

Jackson took another scoop of food onto his fork, then looked up at them. "Hey, I wasn't going anywhere. She just had to come to that realization on her own time."

Kal loved that his siblings were both happy. And the women in his brothers' lives? He couldn't imagine anyone more perfect for them. Becks and Carmen were kind, sweet, beautiful and smart. And, more importantly, took no shit from his brothers. Both Becks and Carmen were like sisters to him.

After breakfast, they all cleared the table and took the dishes to the sink. They started to help wash, but Carmen shooed them away.

"It's enough that you guys are helping Jackson build the backyard deck today. I'll take care of feeding you and cleaning up."

"We have to help him," Kal said. "Otherwise, how would we know he did it right?"

Jackson nodded. "This is true. Everyone knows Rafe couldn't build his way out of a wet paper bag."

"Fuck you both," Rafe said. "And get your tools."

Kal laughed.

They all grabbed their tools and met out back. Concrete had been laid where the deck was going to go. It was a decent-sized deck. Not ridiculously huge, but enough for the grill, a table and several chairs.

"This looks good," Kal said. "You can have some kickass parties out here."

"That's the idea. And still leaving plenty of space in the yard for a pool, a swing set and stuff for the kids."

Jackson arched a brow. "Planning ahead, huh?"

Rafe grinned. "We both want kids. Like, right away."

"I'm going to go ahead and speak for Jackson and myself and say we are so ready for nephews and nieces. So get started."

Rafe laughed. "First the wedding. Then the babies."

Kal could already imagine kids running around back here. Birthday parties and summers in the pool. He couldn't wait to be an uncle. He'd had a blast with Oliver last night. Hell, he couldn't wait to have his own kids.

The thought hit him hard as he worked with his brothers to lay out the wood piles and get started on the deck. He'd never felt solid enough in his life to even begin to think about settling down. All he'd wanted to do was work and have fun.

But now? Now those thoughts about establishing a foundation and starting a family had started to creep in. Maybe it was because Jackson and Rafe had both found love and were building a future, and those things he'd blown off before were beginning to make sense to him.

First he had to find a woman to share his life with. Which brought his thought process back to Hannah, to last night, when they'd kissed.

He'd wanted more. So had she.

He wanted to take her out someplace nice, and then get her alone to see what could happen between them. For him, that spark was still there. From Hannah's reaction, it sure felt like it had been there for her, too.

He wanted to see if they could fire that spark up into a flame.

And speaking of burning up, it was humid as hell out today. By the time they broke for a late lunch, they had a good half of the deck completed. The one good thing about Kal and his brothers was that they worked well as a team. There was no bullshitting when there was serious work to be done. They got in and they did it.

Kal went into the bathroom and washed his hands, splashed cool water on his face, then headed to the kitchen.

Carmen handed him a tall glass of iced tea.

"Thanks." He gulped down two large swallows.

"I'm melting out there," Jackson said.

"I'm sorry it's so humid today," Carmen said, offering him a sympathetic look.

"The weather isn't your fault, babe," Rafe said, coming over to sweep his arm around her and give her a kiss.

She smiled. "You're sweaty."

"You like me sweaty."

Jackson curled his lip. "Gross. What's for lunch?"

"I made turkey sandwiches and fruit salad, and I have cheesecake for dessert."

"Yum," Kal said, eyeing the food as his stomach grumbled at him. "What's everyone else having?"

She laughed, and they all sat and ate.

Kal launched right into his sandwich, which was loaded with lettuce, tomato and avocado, along with a spicy mustard.

"So Kal, you're dating your high school sweetheart?" Carmen asked.

Kal choked on his sandwich. "How did you know that?"

"Becks told me. You went out last night with Hannah and her son?"

The other thing about families was that they tended to know everything about your personal life.

"Yeah. We had pizza."

"How's that going?" Carmen asked.

"Slowly."

"Understandable since she has a child. But it's sweet that you two have reconnected."

He noticed his brothers were dead silent. But it gave him an idea.

"Yeah, we're trying. It's hard to carve out some alone time, though. Hannah and Oliver are currently living with her mom."

"I see."

Carmen took a bite of her fruit salad and chewed thoughtfully but didn't say anything else, so Kal went back to his food, too.

"I have an idea," Carmen said.

"An idea about what?" Rafe asked.

"About Kal and Hannah and giving them some alone time."

"Oh. You know, babe, maybe we should just leave them to—"

"Jackson and Becks could come over here for dinner and game night. Then Kal could have Hannah over to the house while no one's there."

Jackson grinned. "I'm always up for game night. Becks would love that."

"But we have the wedding coming up, and you said—"

Carmen waved her hand at Rafe. "The wedding stuff is all in order." She turned to Kal. "You tell me what day works for you and Hannah, and I will make it happen."

Kal turned to Rafe. "Your woman is a force."

Rafe slanted a wry smile at his brother. "Tell me about it."

But it was a great idea. And he had his future sister-in-law to thank.

Now he just had to make a plan. And hopefully Hannah would be interested in spending some alone time with him.

CHAPTER 11

WHEN KAL HAD TOLD HER HE WAS FORMULATING A PLAN to organize some alone time for them, Hannah had been thrilled. That had been the easy part.

Getting their schedules to mesh hadn't been as easy as she had anticipated. She was off on Sundays and Mondays. Kal's schedule varied since he was on shift one day, then off for two. And those days didn't always coincide with hers. And then Oliver had come down with an icky stomach bug that had been plaguing the school, so she'd had to shuffle clients around to stay home with him for a couple of days.

By the time she was free, a week had gone by and it was the weekend of Rafe and Carmen's wedding. And since Kal was in the wedding, it wasn't like they'd get any time to themselves, though Kal had asked her to be his date. She'd been touched to be asked, and of course she'd said yes. She'd known Rafe and Jackson when she dated Kal in high school, and she was looking forward to seeing both of them again at the wedding.

She had worked Monday of that week, so she could take off early that Saturday to get ready for the wedding. She knew Kal was busy with the wedding party, so she told him she'd meet him there, but he insisted he'd pick her up.

She'd gone shopping to buy a new dress, since she had nothing fancy to wear to an evening wedding. She'd found a cute fitted dress, black with embroidered vines and blooms to add a pop of color. It clung to her curves, but the bottom flared out so she could dance in it, and she had a pair of gold heels that would be perfect. Since it was a sleeveless dress she grabbed a cardigan to bring along for the church, then added her gold pendant and gold earrings. She curled her hair and put on her red lipstick, something she saved for special occasions.

When she came out of her room, her mom's eyes widened.

"Gorgeous. Simply gorgeous."

"Thanks, Mom."

Oliver looked up from the kitchen table where he was working on a puzzle with her mother. He smiled. "You look pretty, Momma."

"Thank you, sir."

"Where are you going tonight?" Oliver asked.

"To a wedding with Kal."

He cocked his head to the side and frowned. "You're getting married to Kal?"

"No, honey. Kal's brother's getting married, and I'm going to help celebrate."

"Oh." He shrugged. "Okay."

She'd forgotten her lipstick for touch-ups, so she went back into her bedroom to tuck it into her bag, then came back out.

"Momma?"

"Yes?"

"If you marry Kal, I'll get to come to that wedding, right?"

Oh, wow. Now that was a question. "Yes, baby. If I get married again, you'll definitely be there."

"Okay." He went back to doing the puzzle.

Hannah looked over at her mom, who smiled and shrugged.

Sometimes her son would ask her things that she thought would require a long explanation, when in fact it ended up being nothing at all. At least nothing to him, anyway.

The doorbell rang, so she went to answer it.

Whoa. Kal in a tux. Now that was something to behold. They'd gone to prom together, and he'd looked amazing. But they'd been kids then. Now? Now he was a full-grown man who looked like a secret agent she wanted to undress. He made her heart beat faster.

"You look incredible," he said.

"Thank you. So do you." She itched to run her hands over all that muscle. But since her family was right there, she resisted.

Barely.

She held the door while he stepped inside.

"Hi, Paige."

"Hi yourself, Kal."

"Hey, Kal." Oliver put on a big grin. "You're all dressed up, just like Momma."

"Yup. Doing the fancy thing tonight. How about you?"

"I'm not fancy. I'm workin' puzzles with Grandma."

"Puzzles, huh?" He took a seat next to Oliver and spent a few minutes putting some pieces in. Since he didn't seem to be in a hurry to shuffle them out of there, Hannah sat and also helped Oliver with the puzzles, while appreciating that Kal took some time with her son. Finally, Kal stood.

"Hey, Oliver. I gotta go, but next time I see you we'll have to do something together, okay?"

"Yeah. See you, Kal."

"See you, buddy."

He got up and hugged her mom goodbye.

"Don't be home too early, you two," her mother said. "I've got this covered."

Hannah rolled her eyes. "Mom."

Kal slanted a smile at her mother. "Thanks, Paige."

When she walked outside, she was surprised to see a sleek black Lexus instead of his truck.

"What's this?"

He opened the door for her. "I can't have you climbing into my truck in that outfit. I rented this for tonight."

She slid inside, her butt cupped by the smooth leather.

When he got in, she smiled at him. "Wow. Impressive."

"Well, it's not as cool as my truck, but it'll do." He put the car in gear, and they drove off.

"How have the wedding activities gone this week?"

He let out a soft laugh. "It's been good. We had the rehearsal dinner last night. Rafe is nervous as hell."

"Aww. I'm sure he is. I'm sure Carmen is, too."

"Actually, Becks said she's cool as could be."

"Rafe will probably calm down after the ceremony."

"He's been walking a tightrope for a couple of weeks now. I think he's nervous that something will go wrong at the wedding, and he wants everything perfect for Carmen."

Hannah smiled. "Weddings rarely go off without some small issue or another. No one seems to care because it's all about the bride and groom. As long as they're happy and in love, nothing else matters."

"I guess that makes sense."

She noticed him flexing his fingers on the steering wheel as they drove down the highway.

"And what about you?" she asked. "Are you nervous?"

"Me?" He gave her a quick glance before turning his attention back on the highway. "No. Why should I be nervous?"

"Best man, right?"

"Sort of. Jackson and I are sharing best man duties. But I'm mostly giving them up to Jackson since he's the oldest brother."

"Uh-huh. But still, you have things you're responsible for."

"I guess, yeah."

"Are you in charge of the rings?"

He blew out a breath. "No, thank God. That's Jackson's job."

She laughed. "So you didn't want the responsibility for the hardware?"

"Not at all. I mean, not that I couldn't handle it. I could. But, you know, Jackson's got that covered. Or at least Becks does."

She heard the nervousness in his voice. So despite him saying he didn't, he most definitely had a case of the jitters. Which was sweet. "Of course. So what's your job?"

"Making sure that Carmen's grandfather's wife is seated comfortably in the front of the church before the service. Carmen's parents aren't around, so her grandpa is going to walk her down the aisle. I offered to pick them up, but Jimmy—her grandpa—said he and his wife, Felice, would get themselves there, that way they could leave when they got tired."

"Independence is important when you're older."

"He's very independent. We also offered to get them a car service. He turned that down, too. Said they could still drive just fine."

Hannah smiled at that. Her grandparents had been the same way. Fiercely independent for as long as they were able to be.

The church sat on a corner, a small brick building that looked as if it had been around for quite a while. It was quaint and beautiful. Kal told her that Carmen's grandmother had belonged to this church, and it held sentimental memories for her.

Inside was lovely, with wooden pews and beautiful windows that let in tons of light. There were flowers decorating the end of each row of seats, and the altar was decked out with roses and lilies.

"I have to go do best man duties," Kal said. "Can I walk you to your seat?"

She slipped her hand in his arm. "I'd like that."

The first few rows had been reserved for family members. Kal sat her in the third row on the groom's side. Then he bent and kissed her hand.

"I'll see you soon."

Her stomach fluttered as she smiled up at him, then fluttered again as she watched him walk down the aisle.

There was a harpist playing lilting music as guests filed in. She recognized a few people from high school, since all three brothers were so close in age. She also enjoyed watching everyone else come in, because she loved clothes, and seeing how everyone was dressed was fun. The weather today was beautiful—bright and sunny and warm, and women dressed accordingly in colorful dresses. Hannah enjoyed perusing the short dresses, the longer ones and everything in between. She particularly liked when Jackson walked Mrs. Donovan down the aisle and saw the amazing dark copper dress she wore. She looked beautiful in it.

All the groomsmen took their place in the front of the church, and Kal had been right about Rafe. He looked like he was about to pass out. But then everyone stood, and the harpist started playing Canon in D as Carmen and her grandfather appeared at the back of the church.

Carmen looked stunning in a silk cream-colored princess dress that swayed back and forth like a softly ringing bell as she walked down the aisle. She had the biggest smile on her face, her gaze riveted to Rafe's as they made their way to the altar. And Rafe had tears in his eyes, which made Hannah tear up as well.

Now that was love, when you could see it on their faces, could feel it as Rafe and Carmen looked at each other. And when they said their vows, Hannah's heart swelled with emotion as they spoke their words of love to each other. She sent up a fervent wish of forever happiness for these two.

When the priest pronounced them husband and wife, they

kissed, and everyone applauded. The whole ceremony had been lovely. Everyone walked down the aisle, then the guests started filing out of the church.

She stood outside and chatted with a few people she knew, until Kal came out of the church and made his way to her.

"The ceremony was so nice," she said.

He smiled. "Yeah, it was. I can't believe my brother is married."

"He looked so happy."

"And he didn't pass out."

She laughed.

"I have to go back inside and take some pictures. But I've arranged for one of my work friends and her husband to give you a ride to the reception, if you're comfortable with that."

She nodded. "Of course. That's fine."

He signaled to a beautiful redhead who in no way would Hannah have ever guessed was a firefighter. She was tall and slender, and her husband was just as good-looking.

"Hannah Clark, this is Callie Vassar and her husband, Aaron."

She shook hands with both of them. "Nice to meet you."

"You, too," Callie said. "Wasn't that a great wedding ceremony?"

"It was lovely."

"I almost cried," Aaron said.

"You had tears in your eyes," Callie said.

Aaron lifted his chin. "Did not."

Callie shot a knowing smile over to Hannah.

"I definitely got teary-eyed," Hannah said. "Especially when Rafe and Carmen said their vows."

"Right?" Callie said. "So sweet."

"I gotta go," Kal said. "I'll see you at the reception."

Hannah nodded. "Okay."

She followed Callie and Aaron to their car. On the way to the reception she learned that both Callie and Aaron were firefighters, and they had a little boy named Max who was a year old. Callie showed her photos of their son, who was just as cute as could be with the most adorable dimples. Hannah told them she also had a son, so they talked about their kids on the drive over.

Hannah was excited about the reception at the Sonesta on the beach. The venue was beautiful, right on the water, and she breathed in the nice cool air as they walked inside the hotel lobby and made their way upstairs in the elevators.

"Fancy," Aaron said as the doors opened and they were directed to the penthouse ballroom.

Hannah gasped as they walked inside to see the floor-to-ceiling windows with stunning views of the ocean.

"Wow. This is amazing."

People were already starting to arrive, and drinks and hors d'oeuvres were being served.

"Let's get a drink and some food," Callie said.

"I'll get the drinks," Aaron said. "What would you like?"

Callie looked to her. "Glass of white wine for me. Hannah?"

"Same," Hannah said.

"Got it," he said, then looked over at Callie. "Grab me some food, would you, babe?"

After Aaron walked away, Callie slipped her arm in Hannah's. "Let's go find the food."

Hannah grinned. "Yes, let's. Apparently weddings make me hungry."

"Me, too."

The table where the snacks were located was swarming with other hungry people, so they had to wait their turn, which was fine, because Hannah had an opportunity to scope out this amazing ballroom. The tables were beautiful, with turquoise and bronze décor to match the wedding colors. It was absolutely gorgeous, and all the fresh flowers adorning the table smelled incredible.

So did the food, and when they got their plates, Hannah piled hers high with some tasty snacks, before she and Cassie spotted Aaron over at a table by the window and joined him.

"I hope some of that is for me," Aaron said, eyeing the plates.

Cassie laughed. "Don't worry. It is."

"Good. Because otherwise I wasn't going to share the booze." He slid the glasses of wine over to them, and they were joined at the table by several firefighters from Rafe's station. She met Ethan Pressman and his wife, Penny, along with Adrienne Smith and Miguel Acosta. All of them were super friendly and included her in conversation.

Ethan and Penny had a kid as well, and Adrienne and Miguel were EMTs who had just gotten engaged, so there was a lot to talk about.

Hannah chatted with them, noshed on the food and sipped the wine, which was smooth and delicious, just like the appetizers. Tables started to fill with people, and the ballroom quickly became populated. Soft music was playing, the lights were low as they watched the sun disappear and the water take on a silver hue.

Then the deejay came on to announce the arrival of the wedding party. She looked toward the door to see the bridesmaids and groomsmen walk in arm in arm, her pulse spiking as she saw Kal come in with a beautiful redhead who looked to be about midway through a pregnancy. Kal had his hand firmly wrapped around hers as they shimmied into the ballroom while wild music played and the lights shone on them.

And then Rafe and Carmen came in, everyone applauded and the wedding party took their seats at the main table. The best men and the matron of honor gave toasts to the bride and groom, everyone applauded and then there was a break.

"Rafe looks damn happy," Miguel said.

"Doesn't he?" Adrienne nodded.

Hannah felt a touch on her shoulder and turned to find Kal smiling down at her. "How's it going over here?"

"Just fine."

"Hey, we're taking good care of your woman," Aaron said.

Hannah's entire body warmed at Aaron's comment. She most certainly was not Kal's woman, but she appreciated that they thought she was.

"Thanks. Got a second, Hannah?"

She nodded and took Kal's hand as she stood. He walked her past the tables and outside the ballroom.

"I'm sorry to leave you for so long. I had no idea all that picture taking and the rest of this stuff would take so much time."

She laid her hand on his forearm. "Don't worry about it. Your friends are great, and we're having fun."

"You sure? I have to sit at the main table for dinner, and then once we do the official wedding party first dance thing, I'll be free and I can come sit with you."

She loved that he was thinking of her comfort. "I'm fine. Really. You do what you need to do for your brother."

"Okay. But I want you to know I really want to spend time with you tonight."

"Thanks. I appreciate it, but really—don't worry about me. I'm having a great time."

He escorted her back inside, and Hannah saw that they were serving dinner, so Kal walked her back to her table. He leaned in and kissed her, briefly, then headed to the main table. She couldn't help but let out a soft sigh.

"Hmm," Adrienne said, offering up a smile. "He really likes you."

"We're just friends."

"I don't kiss any of my friends like that," Penny said.

"Can't tell you how relieved I am to hear that, honey," Ethan said.

Penny laughed, and Hannah's cheeks warmed. Fortunately, at that moment, the servers started delivering their food, so she and Kal ceased being the topic of conversation. Then all the talk was about the delicious seafood and steak and amazing side dishes.

Hannah absolutely loved the sea bass, which was melt-in-your-mouth tender. And she couldn't get enough of whatever that sweet potato fluff was, but she wished she had a recipe for it. She also had brussels sprouts, and it was the best wedding food she'd ever eaten. Certainly better than the homemade food they'd had at her super small wedding to Landon.

Of course they'd had no money, but to her it had seemed fine. At the time she'd been way more interested in their impending move to Georgia and less engaged in the fuss and expense of a wedding. Her mom had been the one who'd insisted they do something, so she'd agreed to the bare minimum, just to get it over with.

She should have taken her lack of enthusiasm over the whole ceremony as a warning. But she'd been oblivious back then, only wanting to escape. Seeing Rafe and Carmen's wedding today made her realize what she'd missed out on—and what she hadn't had with Landon in the first place.

She wouldn't make that mistake again.

Not that she was planning on another wedding, or falling in love again. She had way too many things going on in her life to even entertain the idea. Her focus was on raising Oliver and growing her business. And that was all she had time for.

But tonight? She intended to enjoy this wedding and have some fun.

CHAPTER 12

THERE'D BEEN STANDING AND PHOTOS AND TOASTING
and photos and eating and photos and smiling and photos and
dancing and photos. And videos. All the videos. So much talking
and videos. Hopefully, now he was done. Because if he never got
his picture taken ever again for the rest of his life, Kal would be
a happy man.

Though he had to admit, he couldn't have asked for a better
partner in all this than Tess Blackstone. She was Carmen's co-
worker and good friend, and she was funny and sarcastic. And
also six months pregnant, so he'd been solicitous of her feelings
and her condition the entire time they'd had to pose together. Not
that she'd needed it. She was a nurse and on her feet all day. She'd
told him this had been easy. Except for wearing heels.

Once they finished the wedding party dance, she looked at
him. "I am so putting my sandals on."

"Jealous."

She laughed. "What? You didn't bring yours?"

"Didn't think of it."

"Loser."

"You said it." He kissed her cheek, then turned her over to her husband, George, who had showed up on the dance floor to take over.

"Thanks for taking care of her," George said.

"It was truly my honor. You have a treasure in this woman."

George's eyes sparkled with love as he drew Tess into his arms. "Don't I know it."

Tess shot Kal a look over her shoulder. "Because I tell him every day how awesome I am."

Kal laughed as he left the dance floor. He stopped at the bar and grabbed a beer, then wandered through the crowd, stopping at a few tables to say hello to people he knew. But the person he really wanted to see was currently laughing with her head thrown back at something Miguel Acosta had just said.

He was glad she was comfortable with the people at the table. He felt bad about inviting her to the wedding just to abandon her for half of it. There wasn't much he could do about it since he'd had brotherly duties he had to perform, but at least now he was free.

He made his way to the table to hear the end of a dirty joke that Adrienne was telling everyone.

"The more you play with it, the harder it gets."

Everyone groaned, then laughed. He was sorry he missed it.

"About time you made it," Ethan said. "I was about to fix Hannah up with another guy."

Kal pulled up the empty chair next to Hannah and sat. "Not funny."

"Three guys have already asked her to dance," Callie said. "We had to run interference for you."

"Also not funny."

"And not true," Hannah said, laying her hand on his arm. "I'm just sitting over here like a wallflower."

He cocked his head to the side. "Now that I don't believe."

"Okay, maybe one man asked me to dance. I politely declined."

He was relieved to hear that. If he'd seen her dancing with some guy—especially if it was someone he knew—he wasn't sure how he would have reacted.

Okay, he knew exactly how he would have reacted. He'd have been jealous and pissed-off. He stood and held out his hand for her. "Then may I have this dance?"

She stood and put her hand in his. "I'd love to."

He led her out onto the dance floor, happy to hear a slow song playing so he could hold her against him. He drew her into his arms. Her body was warm, and she smelled so damn delicious he wanted to lick her neck. He laid his cheek against hers and whispered in her ear.

"You smell nice."

She pulled her head back, swept her knuckles over his lower jaw. "So do you. And you look pretty, too."

He laughed. "Pretty, huh? I prefer ruggedly handsome."

"I don't know about that. You're wearing a tux. You're a little too *GQ* right now to be considered rugged. Maybe in your jeans and T-shirt when you're all sweaty."

"I'll keep that in mind."

Just then a hand touched her arm. She looked around to see the beautiful bride grabbing her hand.

"Time to meet the family, Hannah," Carmen said.

Kal bit back a groan at the interruption. "We're dancing here."

"You can have her to yourself later," Carmen said, giving Kal a look. "Becks and I are dying for a chat."

Hannah was amused by Kal's worried look, but actually, she'd been waiting for a chance to congratulate Carmen on her marriage to Rafe. Now was her opportunity. She followed Carmen off the dance floor and out of the ballroom. Carmen used a key card to enter a private room with tufted seats. There was champagne chilling in a bottle there.

"This is for the bride and groom to have time away from the stress of the wedding reception," she said. "If we need it."

"It's very nice."

There was a knock on the door, and a beautiful blonde came in. She was wearing a short yellow dress, her hair plaited in a braid that rested on her shoulder. Hannah was drawn immediately to all of her amazing tattoos.

"Hannah, this is Becks, Jackson's fiancée."

"Hi, Becks, it's wonderful to meet you."

"Nice to meet you. Wow, what a party, right?"

Hannah nodded. "It's lovely here. You picked an amazing reception venue."

"All Rafe's idea," Carmen said. "I would have been happy with the church hall, but he said I deserved something spectacular."

Becks popped the cork on the champagne, then poured it into three glasses and handed them out. "It's definitely spectacular." She held her glass up. "Here's to you and Rafe, Carmen. May your life be as fizzy and fun as this champagne."

Carmen laughed. "Thanks."

They all sipped the champagne, which tasted delicious. "The food was amazing, too."

"That was my favorite part," Carmen said. "Okay, the wedding part was nice, too, but I was starving. Don't tell Rafe I said the food was my favorite part."

"What happens in the private suite stays in the private suite," Becks said, leaning back on the chaise. "And speaking of that, we wanted to get to know you, Hannah, since you're dating Kal now."

"Oh. We're just friends."

Becks looked over at Carmen, and they both laughed.

"What?" Hannah asked.

"We've both heard that one before," Becks said.

"Yes," Carmen said. "Because we both said it before. To each other."

Hannah looked at both of them. "No, really, we are just friends. I mean, we dated in high school, but we broke up and then we saw each other at our ten-year reunion. Now we're just catching up. As friends."

Becks kicked her heels off. "Uh-huh. And does any of this 'just friends' stuff involve smoking-hot chemistry between the two of you?"

"Or kissing?" Carmen asked. "Have you kissed him yet?"

"I . . ." Hannah was at a loss for words. "Yes. We've kissed."

"I don't know about you, Becks, but I don't kiss my guy friends. And I sure don't dance close with them and run my hand over their muscles like Hannah was doing with Kal out there on the dance floor."

They noticed all that? She thought they'd just been on the dance floor for about a minute, and she couldn't remember touching him like that, or him looking at her that way. Then again, she'd been happy to be with him, and maybe she had smoothed her hand up his arm, and maybe he had given her that hot look that never failed to turn her temp up a few degrees.

They definitely had chemistry. They always had. There was no denying it.

"Okay, so maybe more than just friends. But it's complicated."

Becks nodded. "It always is."

"And we have history together."

"So did Jackson and I. When we first ran into each other again, he didn't even remember me."

Hannah stared at Becks in shock. She had strawberry blonde hair and was covered in tattoos. She was gorgeous. Who wouldn't remember her? "What?"

"To be fair, I was a kid the last time he'd seen me. I'd changed a lot."

"Okay, so that makes sense."

"And he'd been called to a fire scene—my tattoo shop. So he was kind of busy that day."

"Oh, Rafe told me this story," Carmen said. "But Rafe said he recognized you right away. So Jackson doesn't get a pass."

"True. But Rafe and I always hung out together when we were kids. To Jackson, I was just one in a long line of kids he had to watch over on the streets. So it made sense he wouldn't remember me."

"So you were homeless with the Donovan boys?" Hannah asked.

Becks nodded.

"That must have been so hard. I'm sorry you had to go through that."

"Thanks. It wasn't easy, but I had Jackson and Rafe and Kal. They were like my brothers. Okay, Rafe and Kal were like my brothers. I crushed on Jackson hard when I was a preteen. And when we ran into each other again as adults?" She gave an enigmatic smile.

"Then it became love," Carmen said with a wide smile.

"It did. Well, first we argued with each other a lot. Then it became love."

Hannah laughed.

"See?" Carmen said. "It was complicated."

She did see. And then again, she didn't. Not the same way as her situation, anyway. "Not at all the same thing."

"Well, no one's relationship is the same," Carmen said. "Mine and Rafe's was completely different from Becks and Jackson's. But ours was complicated as well. The thing is, we made it work because we had feelings for each other. So we worked our way through the complications."

Okay, that part she did see. Sort of. "I'm divorced. And my ex was a lot to handle. And while Kal is nothing like my ex-husband,

I'm just not ready to jump back into a relationship yet. Plus I have a seven-year-old son to consider, too."

"I can understand that," Carmen said. "I went through the same thing. Marriage, divorce, you feel like you made all the wrong choices and you don't want to do it again. It's hard to put your heart into the hands of another man when someone hurt you."

"You do get it."

Carmen smiled and stood. "Yes, I do. But I also wasted a lot of time second-guessing myself and all the choices I made. Don't do what I did. And speaking of time, I have a husband waiting for me."

They all left the room, and Hannah was happy to have finally met the women who captured Jackson's and Rafe's hearts.

Those guys were very lucky, because Becks and Carmen were incredible. Open and honest and fun to hang out with. She hoped she'd have more time with them in the future.

They met up with the men, and Kal slipped his hand in hers. "I thought maybe they kidnapped you for an inquisition."

Her lips curved. "More like getting acquainted. Becks and Carmen are lovely."

She followed Kal's glance to the table where Rafe and Carmen sat with their hands entwined, their gazes only on each other, then to the dance floor where Jackson and Becks rocked slowly together.

"Yeah, they are. They're family."

She knew that Kal loved his brothers, so she was happy to see how much he appreciated the women who were now part of their lives. He walked her over to the main table and pulled up an extra chair for her to sit.

"Something to drink?" he asked.

"Wine would be great, thanks."

He dipped down to drop a short kiss on her cheek, then whispered, "Be right back."

She smiled up at him, then watched him disappear into the crowd. While he was gone, she observed Carmen and Rafe, the way they held each other's hands and looked at each other. There was so much love on their faces. Even if someone stopped to chat with them, they'd still steal glances at each other while they were talking to the other person.

Her attention drifted over to Jackson and Becks, who walked off the dance floor. They did the same thing, focusing only on each other as if no one else existed for them. Jackson had his arm around Becks, holding her close, his love for her obvious.

If she ever fell in love again, that's what she wanted. She realized now she'd never had that with Landon. Even at her wedding reception he'd been in a corner with his best buddies getting drunk and laughing while she'd mostly entertained their guests.

Of course they'd been so young. But was that really an excuse? She'd long ago had to face that they'd never really shared the kind of love she'd witnessed today. Landon had been her escape, and he'd just wanted a partner—maybe even a mother figure, and he'd targeted her because she'd been mature enough to deal with all his bullshit.

Which hadn't been romance. Or a marriage. Or anything even close to love.

She inhaled, then blew out a breath, determined to eliminate those memories. Tonight wasn't the night for it. Not when so much love and happiness surrounded her.

Kal came back with her glass of wine.

"I ran into Rafe at the bar. He told me they're going to cut the cake next. You like wedding cake?"

She tipped her head back to meet his gaze. "I'm fine with cake. But I know how much you like it."

"It'll be the high point of the night for me."

She fought back a laugh. Kal always did have a thing for sweet stuff.

He took a seat, then draped his arm over the back of her chair. "Are you having a good time?"

"Yes. It's a lovely wedding."

Just then, Kal's parents came over, so Hannah stood while Mrs. Donovan pulled her into a hug, then held on to her hands.

"Hannah McKenzie? It's so good to see you again."

"You, too, Mrs. Donovan."

Mrs. Donovan looked over at Kal. "You didn't tell me you were dating Hannah again."

Kal scratched the side of his nose. "You've been busy with wedding things, and we haven't had a chance to talk. There's a lot to catch up on."

His mom sent him a look. "Apparently, there is." She turned her attention back to Hannah. "I heard you were in Georgia."

"I moved back not too long ago."

"Well, we're glad you're here. And I'm very happy to see you."

Kal's mom had always been great to her. Warm and welcoming and made Hannah feel like family. "Thank you. And congratulations on Rafe's marriage."

"Thank you."

Mr. Donovan gave her a hug, too. "Been a long time. How are you?"

"I'm good, thanks, Mr. Donovan."

"We're really glad you came tonight," Mr. Donovan said.

Kal's mother took her hand. "And you're an adult now. You can call us Laurel and Josh."

"Okay . . . Laurel." Hannah smiled shyly at the unfamiliarity.

"Kal, go get me a wine spritzer," Laurel said, taking his seat, "while I catch up with Hannah."

"Yes, ma'am."

Kal and his dad walked away, and Hannah and Laurel sat.

"So your mom told me you got a divorce. I'm sorry."

"Thanks. But it was the best decision for me and for my son."

Laurel smiled and patted her hand. "Sometimes it is. And you have a little boy. Tell me about him."

"Oliver is seven. He's smart and full of energy and just the sweetest little boy ever."

"I'd love to meet him sometime. You'll have to bring him by the house. Oh, we bought a new house last year. I don't know if Kal mentioned that. Does Oliver like to swim? I have a pool now."

Hannah smiled. "Kal told me about your new place. How exciting for you. I would love to see it. And Oliver loves to swim."

"Then you have to come over. Have Kal make arrangements when you're both off."

"Thank you for inviting us. That's so sweet of you."

"We'll have more time to catch up on our lives then."

"I can't wait."

Kal came back with his mom's drink. "Carmen said to tell you that they're cutting the cake now, Mom."

"Okay." She bent over and kissed Hannah's cheek, then squeezed her hand. "So good to see you again."

"You, too."

After she walked away, Kal slid back in the chair. "Sorry about that."

"Don't be. I like your mom."

"Yeah, the drawback to bringing you to a family wedding is . . . the family."

She laughed. "Stop. I've always loved your family. Your parents are wonderful, and your brothers are great."

"Yeah, they really are."

She appreciated that he didn't complain about his family, that he truly loved them all.

Rafe and Carmen cut the cake and they watched as the photographer took photos of them feeding each other a bite. Hannah tensed, waiting to see if Rafe would smash the cake into Carmen's face. Thankfully, he gently slipped a bite into her mouth and Carmen did the same. She should have known the way the two of them were so sweet with each other that there'd be no cake she-nanigans.

Then Hannah watched Kal rock back and forth impatiently while the staff cut the cake. He was like a kid, waiting expectantly until they were finished.

Fortunately, the wedding party received their pieces of cake first. Kal brought a plate to her at the table and set it down.

She was about to slice into the beautiful cake when Kal stopped her.

"Wait," he said, then slid his fork into his cake and offered her a bite.

"I'm surprised you can wait that long to eat. And that you're willing to share yours."

His lips curved. "All worth it to feed you."

She took the bite from his fork. It was melt-in-your-mouth delicious, with a subtle flavor of almond and the most delectable buttercream frosting she'd ever tasted.

"It's so good."

"Yeah, it is," he said, but he was looking at her and not the cake, making her entire body flame up.

She ate a few more bites, then offered up the rest to Kal, who greedily cleaned her plate.

Jackson and Becks went out on the dance floor, followed by Rafe and Carmen, so Hannah and Kal joined, too. They danced and laughed, and there was a photo booth where they all stopped to take silly pictures with props. She couldn't recall when she'd had more fun.

The slow dancing was her favorite part, because she got to be in Kal's arms, and even though the ballroom was filled with people, the way he looked at her made her feel as if they were completely alone.

She waited for the warning bells to sound off in her head, the ones that would tell her she was moving too fast, that she should slam on the brakes.

Nothing. Maybe she was just having too much fun. Maybe it was the wine and Kal's family.

Either way, she was going for it, because she was enjoying herself too much tonight to let any warning bells get in her way.

When the night got late and lots of people had left, they swayed together on the dance floor to a slow, sexy song. Kal's hands moved up and down her back, and the feel of his fingers sliding along her skin caused delicious pinpricks of need to skitter through her nerve endings.

"I got a room at the hotel tonight," he said.

"That's okay. I can call for a car to take me home."

"Or . . . you could stay with me."

Could she? Her mind filled with the possibilities. The logical part of her said no.

But the part of her in Kal's arms right now? The part of her that felt his hands roaming down her back, tingling all over as his fingers teased the nape of her neck? That part of her wanted to scream yes.

But could she lose herself in the moment?

CHAPTER 13

AS HANNAH LOOKED AT KAL, SHE THOUGHT OF ALL HER responsibilities. Her son. Sunday was grocery shopping and laundry day.

Then again, her mother did tell her to have fun. To stay out late. Overnight might be too late, though.

But was it? She knew her mom. She wouldn't care, as long as Hannah sent her a text to let her know she'd be out with Kal all night. Knowing her mother, she'd probably send out a cheer emoji.

It had been a long time since she'd spent the night with a guy. And it wasn't like Kal was a stranger. As he held her in his arms and moved her around the dance floor, she realized this felt right.

"I could stay with you," she finally said. "I just need to clear it with my mom so she's okay with it."

His lips curved. "Back when we were teens there was no asking permission."

She laughed. "Back when we were teens we'd have gotten killed for sleeping together."

"True."

"I'm going to send her a text now, before she goes to bed."

He nodded and let go of her hands. She went to the table and grabbed her purse, pulled out her phone and sent her mom a text message letting her know she was going to hang out with Kal at the hotel tonight.

It didn't take her mom long to reply.

Yes! Have fun! Don't come home too early tomorrow. Love you.

And her mom *had* used a celebration emoji. Hannah rolled her eyes. So predictable, that woman. But she was also always in Hannah's corner, and she loved her mother for that.

She went back into the ballroom to see that everyone was packing up to leave. Carmen and Rafe had already headed up to the honeymoon suite, and then tomorrow they'd take off for St. Lucia in the Caribbean for a weeklong honeymoon, which sounded decadent and delightful.

They helped Josh and Laurel load the wedding gifts in the cars and said their good nights. Jackson and Becks stayed to visit with Kal's parents. Kal pulled Hannah along toward the entrance to the hotel.

"In a hurry?" she asked as they made their way to the elevator in the lobby.

"Do you know how long I've wanted to get you alone?"

The doors opened, then closed. Kal pushed the button.

"About as long as I've wanted to be alone with you?"

He pinned her against the wall of the elevator, his mouth coming down on top of hers, hard and hot and filled with the same urgent need that fueled her. She wound her fingers into his hair, breathing in his scent as his tongue ramped up her desires to a fever pitch.

When the doors opened, he broke the kiss, took her hand and they walked at a brisk pace toward his room.

Hannah's heart raced as he opened the door and flipped on the entryway light. He didn't turn any other lights on, so Hannah barely registered the room's layout. She didn't care, and Kal seemed to know the way to go, so he led her by the hand into the room, took her bag from her and laid it on the dresser, then sat her on the bed.

"You thirsty?" he asked.

"No."

"Need anything?"

"Just you."

"Good." He knelt and took off her shoes, taking his time to rub her feet, her calves, sliding his hands along her skin, eliciting shivers all over her body.

"Cold?" he asked.

"Exactly the opposite."

He spread her legs and moved between them, laying his hands on her hips.

"Did I mention how much I like this dress you're wearing?"

She could barely breathe right now since his hands were gripping her hips, clenching and unclenching in a way that made her want to wrap her legs around him and draw him inside of her. It had been so long, and this slow tease of his was making her tense.

"Thank you. You look pretty hot, and I don't want to mess up your tux. You should take it off." She reached out and undid the bow tie, pulling it away from his collar, and tucked it into the pocket of his jacket.

He shrugged out of the jacket and stood, laying it over the chair. Then he toed off his shoes, took off his socks and undid the buttons of his shirt. Fortunately, her eyes had adjusted to the darkness and she had a lovely, if dimly lit, view of him removing his shirt.

Damn. He'd grown some muscle over the past ten years. And his shoulders were so broad. She couldn't resist getting up to smooth her hands all over the amazing skin he'd just revealed.

She walked over and ran her palm across one shoulder, then

down his arm and back up again. She stopped when she saw the tattoo on his right biceps. It was dark so she couldn't make it out all that well.

"You got a tat."

"Yeah. A couple of years ago. Jackson, Rafe and I all got the same one."

"I'll have to check it out when it's light." She continued to touch him, smoothing her hand over the top of his shoulder, then paused.

"Is this okay?" she asked.

He looked down at her. "Your hands on me? Very okay."

She moved her hand across the top of his chest, feeling his muscles jump as she shifted lower, down across his chest to his wow-are-these-even-real sculpted abs.

"So, you work out, huh?"

"A little."

"More than a little, I think." She walked around behind him to admire his broad back, wondering how much work it took to get all this muscle. He'd been in good shape in high school; he'd always worked out. But his body now? This was a man's body.

He turned to face her and drew her against him, putting his lips on hers and taking her breath away with a deep, lingering, hot kiss that made her toes curl into the carpet. And when he reached for the zipper of her dress and drew it down, she sighed against his mouth.

She pulled back so she could draw the dress off her shoulders, letting it pool into a puddle at her feet.

"Wow," he said, staring at her. "You're gorgeous, Hannah."

She blushed under his perusal of her body. "Do you remember how fast and furious sex was when we were in high school?"

He grinned. "Yeah. I can count on one hand the number of times we actually had the opportunity to get fully naked. Mostly it was fumbling around with our clothes half on so we wouldn't get caught."

"Right." She moved closer to him, winding her hand around his neck. "But it was still really great sex."

"Now it'll be even better."

She arched one brow. "Oh, we're boasting?"

He laughed. "No, I meant we'd have more time to enjoy each other."

"So you're not any better?"

He cocked his head to the side. "Hannah."

Now she laughed. "Sorry."

"Devil." He bent and kissed the side of her neck, reaching around her back to unhook her bra with one hand.

"Still good at that, I see."

"The kissing, or undoing your bra?"

She smiled. "Both."

He slipped his hand under her bra and cupped her breast. Her breath caught at the warmth of his hand, the tease of his fingers across her nipple.

"So soft," he murmured against her neck as he swept his hand across her breasts and her nipples hardened, sweet pleasure shooting directly to her sex.

He'd always had the touch, knew exactly what to do, how to touch and kiss her to take her right to the edge of madness. They were just getting started, and she was already quivering all over.

He pulled the bra from her arms, then undid his pants and let them drop, along with his boxer briefs, revealing his glorious cock. She couldn't help but lick her lips.

"Stop that," he said.

She arched a brow. "Stop what? Remembering what you tasted like in my mouth? The way it used to drive you crazy when I—"

She didn't get to finish her sentence, because she'd been lifted and thrown onto the bed. She couldn't help but erupt in squeals of laughter.

Her laughter died when Kal's hand cupped her sex. "I seem to remember you going a little mad when I put my mouth on you."

She gave him a thoughtful look. "Really? My memory is a little dim in that regard. You might have to refresh it."

He gave her a devilish smile, then slid his hand under her panties, making her gasp as he rocked his fingers back and forth over her already primed flesh. "Does that help?"

Her breathing quickened. "Somewhat. But don't stop."

He didn't, instead teasing a finger inside of her, then two, pumping a delirious response from her that made her lift her hips against his hand. She was so ready to go off, all he had to do was rub the heel of his hand against her clit and she'd be there.

But he was deliberately avoiding her hot button, taking her so close she grabbed his hand to put his fingers right where she needed them.

"Oh no, babe," he said. "I know what you need."

He slid down her body, taking her panties off as he did, then spread her legs and put his mouth on her overheated flesh. She tilted her head back and rode the wave of orgasm that hit her almost instantaneously as he rolled his tongue over her and took her right to the promised land and beyond. And then he eased her down with soft licks and brought her right back again with his fingers and mouth until she cried out hard with a second orgasm, this one more intense than the first. And even sweeter.

Could this be heaven? If it was, she was more than happy to stay here forever.

It took her a while to come down from the utter high. Kal kissed her hip and her belly as he made his way up her body. She rolled over to face him, sliding her fingers over his jaw.

"And that," she said. "I remember so very well."

He grinned. "Good."

She walked her fingers down his chest and abs until she circled his erection, taking in the way his breathing changed when she began to stroke him.

Touching him excited her, spiked her adrenaline, made her want to climb on top of him and slide his cock inside of her and ride them both to an explosive climax. But first she wanted to tease him, making him want and need in the same way he'd done to her.

Except he rolled her onto her back and kissed her, driving her legs apart with his knee and sliding his erection against her sex, and now she was the one who wanted, who needed. She reached up to dig her nails into his back, moaned against his lips and arched into him.

He pulled his mouth from hers. "Gotta grab protection. Now."

"Yes."

He left her and opened the closet door, dug into his bag and came back with a condom, then climbed back onto the bed.

"I'm so glad you were prepared," she said, enrapt as he tore open the wrapper and applied the condom.

"I was hoping we might have some time together."

She lifted her arms and pulled him down on top of her. "Lots of time. All night long."

His mouth met hers, and then it was lips and tongues and his body against hers. And when he slid inside of her, she stilled, absorbing the way he fit her so perfectly, the way her body quivered and tightened around him in reaction. She couldn't help but react with a moan of pleasure, which elicited his groan in response.

She rolled her foot across his calf, slid her hand down his arm, needing to touch him everywhere she could, to feel that skin-to-skin contact. Kal's mouth was everywhere—on her lips, her neck, his tongue licking along her skin like flames, making her feel as if she were burning from the inside out. The only thing that was going to douse this inferno was the orgasm that quickly built inside of her.

Kal scooped his hand under her butt, lifting her against him. He ground against her as he moved, and that was all she needed to explode into a blazing climax that sent sparks of pleasure shooting through her. She dug her nails into his arms and rode out her release, then wrapped her legs around him to draw him in when she felt his body go taut. He shuddered against her, burying his face in her neck as he rocked through his own orgasm.

They stayed connected like that for a while, Kal continuing to stroke his hand along her side. She had to admit it felt good to be caressed.

He finally lifted his head. "Sorry."

She arched a brow. "For?"

"I wanted it to last longer."

Her lips curved. "I was barely breathing by the end. Any longer and you might have endangered my life."

"Good to know." He disengaged and went into the bathroom to dispose of the condom, then came back and flopped onto the bed. He pulled her against him. She settled her head on his shoulder, mapping her fingers over his chest.

"That was a decent start," he said, sliding his fingers into her hair. "Next time we'll go longer."

"I might need vitamins."

She heard the rumble of his quiet laugh, but she had to admit it felt good to be here, in bed with him. She was relaxed, naked and utterly comfortable.

Then again, it wasn't their first time together.

She tilted her head back. "Do you remember our first time?"

He grimaced. "I try not to think about that. It wasn't my best performance."

"Hey, it was the first for both of us."

"I know. I tried to be gentle with you."

"Which you were."

"But I was also very excited to get you naked."

She smiled. "I was pretty excited about it, too. And super nervous, and also I wanted to just get it over with."

"Hey."

She laughed. "Not get it over with, in that I wanted to get away from you. But the whole virginity thing. I wanted to get past that part."

"Oh yeah. Me, too. I came too fast."

"Which I appreciated, actually. It wasn't like I wanted you inside of me for hours or anything. Not the first time."

"That makes sense."

"And you were so sweet, asking me the whole way through if I was okay. You were the perfect guy to have my first time with."

"So it was horrible, then."

She rolled over and laid on top of him. "It most definitely wasn't horrible. And after that it got better."

He smoothed his hands down her back and rested them on her butt. "Better, huh?"

She rocked against his quickly hardening cock. "Much, much better."

She raised up and slid against him, and as he grabbed another condom, she realized she was going to get no sleep at all tonight.

Oh, the sacrifices she had to make for really great sex.

CHAPTER 14

KAL WAS NEVER HAPPIER TO FINISH A SHIFT. IT HAD BEEN a grueling twenty-four hours. They'd been called to a scene of a crush accident, with multiple stations responding. There'd been hazardous chemicals involved, two semis that had wedged a truck between them. It had been the TRT's job to get the wedged truck's occupants out of harm's way while the hazmat team managed one of the semi's chemical load.

It had been nightmarish and precarious, but fortunately, they'd managed to get the two occupants of the truck out without further injury. Some broken ribs and a busted ankle, but otherwise, all had come out of it alive, much to the team's relief. But it had taken a lot of hours of painstaking, careful work. It had been both nerve-racking and exhilarating.

Now Kal was just damned exhausted. Normally, he went straight to the gym for a hard workout after he got off shift. He'd had plenty of workout finishing up that rescue, so all he wanted was to eat a decent breakfast and then face-plant in his bed.

As he climbed into his truck, he was surprised to see a text message from Hannah.

Are you off shift yet?

He'd dropped her off at her house yesterday morning since he had to be on shift. There'd been a hot kiss in the car, but otherwise, he'd told her he'd call her. He knew she was off today since it was Monday, but he figured she'd be busy.

He texted a response. *Just getting in my truck now. What's up?*

She replied right away. *My car won't start. Would you mind helping? Only if you're free.*

He sent a reply: *On my way.*

She sent a thanks and a heart emoji. He put his truck in gear and headed over to her house. He was at her house in fifteen minutes and pulled up next to her car. Hannah came outside, looking beautiful as always. Her hair was pulled up into a high ponytail, and she was wearing dark capris and a short-sleeved T-shirt.

"I'm so sorry to bother you right after you got off duty."

"Not a problem. What's going on?"

"I don't know. I turned the ignition over, and I got nothing. It sounds like it wants to start, but it won't."

"Okay. Let me check it out."

She handed him the keys, and he slid inside the car. He put the key in and turned. He heard the crank, but the engine didn't fire. He popped the hood to take a look to see if any wires had come loose. After inspecting the battery and anything else it might be, he looked up at her.

"I think there's something wrong with your starter. I can work on it for you."

"Oh, you don't have to."

"I don't mind. But I need to eat first. Want to come out to breakfast with me?"

She looked at him for a few seconds. "I have a better idea. Come inside."

"Okay."

He locked her car and his truck, then followed her into the house, which he noticed was quiet.

"Your mom and Oliver not home?"

She nodded. "Mom took Oliver to school this morning before she went to work." She led him into the kitchen. "Want some coffee?"

"That'd be great, thanks."

She brewed him a cup in her Keurig, then handed it to him. They'd barely gotten the truck resupplied by the end of shift this morning, so he hadn't had a chance to even grab a cup before the next shift had come on. The smell alone helped to perk him up.

"This is great, thanks."

She leaned against the kitchen counter. "What would you like for breakfast?"

"You don't have to cook for me."

"And you don't have to fix my car."

"Okay, then. Whatever you want to make, I'll eat."

"Good enough." She pushed off the counter and went to the fridge, pulling out eggs, sausage, milk and butter. Then she grabbed flour, and he watched while she started mix for biscuits.

Since he wasn't one to just sit and watch someone else cook, he put the sausage into the pan and made that while Hannah baked fresh biscuits. After the sausage was done, she crumbled up some of it to make gravy. His stomach grumbled.

"Smells good," he said as he finished up the eggs and she poured juice.

"It does. Let's eat."

They served up the food onto their plates and carried them to the table. Kal dug in because he was so hungry he couldn't wait another second. He ended up eating three biscuits and most of the eggs.

"Sorry," he said after he finished cleaning his plate.

"No, it's okay. You obviously needed the food. Busy shift?"

"Crazy busy. And we had a rough call that lasted until almost the end of shift. I was so ready for some food by the time it was over."

"And then I texted you."

"Hey, it's not a big deal." He wiped his mouth with the napkin and stood to help clear the table.

But Hannah stopped him. "Absolutely not. I'll do this."

"Okay. I'll go work on your car and see if I can get it started."

"Thanks."

Once he figured out what the issue was, he ended up having to go to the auto parts shop to buy a starter. Installation took a couple of hours, but after that Hannah's car fired up just fine. He took the car for a short drive, parked and turned it off and on again several times, and everything seemed to be working okay. Satisfied that he'd solved the problem, he went inside to wash his hands.

Hannah was doing paperwork at the kitchen table.

"Paying bills?" he asked as he finished drying his hands.

She looked up at him with a grimace. "Unfortunately, yes."

"An evil necessity for all of us."

"True. How's the car working?"

"Like new. Or at least your starter is new."

"What do I owe you for the parts?"

"Nothing."

She shook her head. "That's not how this works, Kal. What do I owe you?"

He rolled his eyes, but he understood why, so even though it cost less than twenty bucks, he dug the receipt out of his pocket. She looked at it and pulled out her wallet and paid him cash.

"Thanks."

"No, thank you."

"When was your last oil change?"

"About two weeks ago."

His lips curved. "Good for you."

"Hey, she's gotta last me, so I do my best to take care of her."

"While I was under the hood I checked everything out, and it all looks like it's in working order, so I think you'll be good to go for a while."

"That's a relief. Thank you. I can't tell you how much I appreciate you doing this for me."

"No problem. I'm gonna head out."

She got up and walked around to stand next to him. "I thought maybe you'd stay. We have the place to ourselves for the day."

The offer was tempting. Way too tempting. "I'd like to, but I didn't sleep last night since we were on scene all night. I'm dead tired."

"Oh, of course," she said. "You want to sleep and I made you work. I'm sorry."

He wrapped his arm around her. "What I want is you. What I need is sleep. Two different things."

She laughed and laid her palm on his chest. "There'll be other opportunities for us. Go get some rest."

He appreciated that she understood and wasn't making a big deal out of him leaving. He brushed his lips across hers for a kiss that was all too brief, but he knew if he went in deeper, he'd never leave. And then he'd end up even more tired. "I'll talk to you later."

"Okay. Thanks again."

She walked him outside to his truck and waited while he climbed in. For a brief few seconds there he had second thoughts about leaving. But then he put his truck in gear and backed out of the driveway.

Damn common sense. Where had that ever gotten him?

Just into a great career with the future he wanted. Getting his head on straight and having goals for his future meant everything to him. And right now he was exhausted and knew he needed sleep more than anything. Even more than he needed Hannah.

He yawned and turned onto the highway, headed for home. For his bed. Where he'd sleep alone.

This time.

CHAPTER 15

HANNAH'S LAST APPOINTMENT OF THE DAY ENDED AT four, which meant she could get out of the salon early. Oliver had soccer practice, but he was carpooling with Jeff, and Becca offered to take the boys for tacos afterward and hold a playdate at her house. She told Hannah the boys would do homework after school, and Hannah agreed. Her mom was leaving right from work to go to dinner with her book club. A free night was a rare occurrence.

She stopped at the grocery store and then headed home. After she put everything away, she got out her phone and texted Kal.

What are you doing today?

It took him about twenty minutes to reply to her text.

Mowing the lawn. You still at work?

She smiled and replied: *Just got off. How about dinner? I'm cooking.*

He answered with: *Sounds great.*

After they agreed on a time, she began prepping the lasagna she had planned to make. Once it was in the oven, she went into her bedroom to change clothes. After a long day at the hair salon, she felt like she was covered in hair and hair color, even though she knew she wasn't. Still, she'd feel better after a shower, so she got in to wash off, then put on a sleeveless sundress and slipped into her sandals. Since it was warm and sticky outside, she didn't even bother reapplying her makeup. If Kal wanted a woman who was all dolled up, he'd have to choose a different one. She was just too damn hot to bother. She brushed through her hair and wound it up in a bun on top of her head, pulling it off her neck.

That was better.

She went into the kitchen and fixed herself a glass of ice water, then sorted through today's mail. Fortunately, it was all junk mail, so she tossed it.

Any day where bills didn't show up was a good mail day.

She heard a car door open and took a peek outside to see her son climbing into Becca and Tony's car. She smiled as she caught sight of Oliver and Jeff gesturing madly to each other in the back seat as Tony pulled down the driveway.

Just as they left, she saw Kal's truck pulling into the driveway. Her heart immediately started skipping.

She walked away from the window, shaking her head. Her reaction to him was utterly ridiculous. She was like an infatuated teenager whenever he was around.

"Get over yourself, Hannah."

She went to the door and opened it. He was wearing shorts and a sleeveless tank.

"Hot?"

He grinned. "You sure are."

She laughed. "Come on in." She led him into the kitchen. "Something cold to drink? I have iced tea."

"That sounds really good. Mowing the lawn nearly killed me today."

"You poor thing." She fixed him a glass of iced tea and handed it to him.

He took a couple of gulps, then sighed. "That's what I needed. Thanks. Why is it this damn hot in October?"

She leaned against the counter and shrugged. "Because we live in Florida?"

He grumbled and took another sip of tea. "Whatever." He looked around. "Where's Oliver?"

"Soccer practice and out to dinner with Jeff."

"Oh. And your mom?"

"Book club night, so she's gone, too."

"Huh. Okay. How was your day?"

"Productive. How was your day off?"

"I did some things. Mostly sweaty things."

"Oh, really? I like sweaty things."

He laid his glass on the counter and stalked over to her, slid his arm around her waist. "Is that right? What kinds of sweaty things?"

She laid her palm on his chest. "Not mowing-the-lawn kinds of sweaty things. More fun stuff."

He pushed in against her chest. "I like fun stuff."

She hadn't wanted him to leave yesterday morning, wished she could have lounged around with him all day. But he'd needed sleep, and she had things of her own to do as well. Sometimes parenthood and responsibility had to take precedence over what she wanted.

But now? Now he was close to her, and the hungry way he looked at her told her all she needed to know. He wanted what she wanted, what they hadn't had the time or the luxury for yesterday morning. She hadn't had nearly enough alone time with him, and she craved his touch on her skin.

"How long will we be alone here?" he asked.

"Long enough." She lifted his shirt and put her hands on his deliciously warm bare stomach, feeling his muscles clench under her hand. His mouth came down on hers, and she barely had time to take in a breath before his tongue searched for hers. The way he kissed her, the barely leashed passion in the way he grabbed the material at the back of her dress and tightened it in his fist, was the strongest aphrodisiac. She whimpered against his mouth and inched herself closer, needing to climb inside of him because she craved more of what he gave her.

"Hot in here," he said. "Let's go somewhere cooler." He lifted her, and she wrapped her legs around his hips while he carried her down the hall into her bedroom. He deposited her on the bed and climbed onto it, continuing his exploration of her mouth with his until she writhed against him, every part of her body aching with the desire to be touched.

And oh, did he deliver. His hands roamed her body like an explorer searching for a lost treasure, and she was the prize he was looking for. His fingers slid under her dress, teasing her thighs. She parted her legs, and when he cupped her sex, everything inside of her quivered in anticipation.

"This would be much better if we were naked."

He lifted his head to stare down at her. "You in a hurry?"

"Kind of."

"Are Oliver and your mom coming home soon?"

"No. But my lasagna might burn."

"We could wait until after dinner."

"Or, you could get me naked and get your cock inside of me."

He laughed. "So you're saying you want a quickie instead of slow lovemaking."

"Exactly what I'm saying. But I still want to come."

"Oh, you'll come. You'll come first." He bent his head toward hers and kissed her, then slipped his hand inside her panties, making her breath catch as he expertly found all the right spots to wind her up.

He slid her underwear off, shrugged off his shorts and underwear, then stopped.

"Oh, shit. I don't have a condom."

"I do." She motioned to her nightstand. "In the drawer."

He went over to the drawer and pulled a box of condoms out. "Look at you, being all prepared for sex."

"Because of you, dumbass. I just bought them."

His lips curved. "I like that."

After putting the condom on, he climbed back on the bed, hiked up her dress, rolled her over to face him and lifted her leg over his hip.

"Now this is like high school," he said.

She laughed. "Shut up and fuck me."

He slid inside of her, and all conversation ended. His mouth was on hers, his tongue doing wild things to her tongue, and his hands slid over her body, teasing her breasts and grabbing her ass to hold her against him while he drove his cock into her. The way he moved never failed to bring her right to the edge. It didn't take her long to explode into a shuddering climax, with Kal going right after her.

She wasn't certain she'd taken a breath the entire time. But now she did, exhaling and inhaling to bring in the oxygen she so desperately needed. Kal kissed her lightly and held on to her while he stroked her back. Even when they were teens he would always hold her after sex. It had been one of the most romantic things about him.

She sighed, feeling that natural relaxation an orgasm gave her. "That was nice."

"What? Not terrific, or stupendous, or the best sex you ever had? Just nice?"

She pushed on his chest and rolled off the bed. "It was mind-blowing. I doubt I'll recover from the amazingness of it."

He grinned. "Better."

"I'm going to check the lasagna."

"I think I'll just lie here and bask in the glory of my amazingness."

She shook her head as she slipped her underwear back on. "You do that."

She'd just finished washing her hands in the kitchen when Kal joined her. "That was a quick inventory of how amazing you are."

"I'm just that good." He brushed her lips with his. "What can I do to help?"

She scrunched her nose as she thought. "How about a salad?"

"I can do that."

"Stuff's in the fridge."

"Got it."

Kal washed his hands and then got to work making the salad, while Hannah pulled the lasagna out of the oven and placed it on the kitchen table. She set the table, then made dressing for the salad. They took their seats and she scooped out the lasagna.

"I might have forgotten to mention that it's eggplant lasagna."

He looked up at her. "I'm sure it's great. And you can't scare me away with your meatless meals."

She laughed. "I wasn't trying to. I just make the food I like to eat. You're either along for the ride or you're not."

He leaned over and pressed a kiss to her neck, then gave her a lopsided smile. "Definitely along for the ride. Plus, I like food. And this looks good."

"So does your salad." She scooped a pile of the greens onto her plate. Since she'd left him to make the salad, he'd added tomatoes, slivered carrots, mushrooms and bell peppers. It looked fabulous.

She waited while Kal took a bite of the lasagna. People could pay lip service to eating a meatless meal, but that didn't mean they'd actually like it. He didn't say a word, just shoveled in three forkfuls, then looked up at her.

"What?"

"Nothing. I was waiting to see you grimace."

"It's really good, Hannah. The eggplant is tender, and this sauce is killer. Plus, it has cheese. Anything with cheese on it is a good meal."

Her lips curved. "I'll make a note of that."

She dug in and ate, and Kal was right. It was tasty.

"So I was thinking," Kal said between bites. "This weekend there's a fall festival. They're doing hayrides, pumpkin patch, rides and things."

"That sounds fun."

"It's also a fundraiser for the homeless."

"Oh? Tell me more."

"They're collecting donations for discounted entry. Like socks, hygiene products, soaps, shampoos, things like that."

"What a wonderful idea."

"I thought maybe you and Oliver would like to come with me. Jackson and Becks are gonna go, too."

"It sounds fun. When are you going?"

"Sunday. I'm on shift Saturday, and I know that's a workday for you, too."

"Sunday sounds perfect. We'd love to go."

"Great." He sent her the kind of smile that warmed her all the way to her bare feet. Not that she wasn't already completely heated from the inside out after that hot sex session, but this kind of warm was different. It was the way he looked at her, the way he thought to include her in his life that made her feel . . .

Special. It also sent warning bells pinging in the logical part of her brain, the part of her that told her to hit the brakes on this— hard. But she also knew how much giving back to the homeless community meant to him and to his brothers, and now wasn't the time.

They cleared the table, wrapped up the leftovers and put those in the fridge, then settled on the sofa to watch TV. She chose a baseball game, and they argued over balls and strikes, something they used to do when they were younger.

"Good call," Kal said after the ump made a call for ball four and the batter walked to first base.

"You must need glasses, because it was right over the plate, and he should have been called out on strikes."

He shook his head. "I see just fine. Not my fault you've never known where the strike zone is."

She sat up straight and swiveled to face him. "Excuse me? Who pitched for the varsity softball team?"

"Who was the catcher on varsity baseball? Trust me. I know my strike zone."

"So do I."

They glared at each other, and then she launched herself on top of him. They wrestled until she laughed so hard she was out of breath.

"Give up?" he asked.

"Never."

He flipped her over on her back and came down on top of her, smoothing her hair away from her face. "That's what I like about you. You never give up."

Kal's lips met hers, and she wrapped her leg around his as his tongue slipped inside and made her instantly hot and needy. She arched her hips to feel that sexual connection with him, and he ground against her in the most intimate of ways.

"Mom, I'm home."

She shoved Kal so hard he almost fell off the sofa. Instead, he hurried to the corner of the sofa and dragged his fingers through his hair.

Hannah stood and smiled while trying to regain her composure. Fortunately, Oliver had headed down the hall and hopefully hadn't seen the two of them making out on the sofa.

"Hey, kiddo. How was soccer?"

"Good. Oh, hi, Kal."

"Hi, Oliver. I heard you had soccer practice. How was it?"

"It was good." Oliver plopped down on the sofa right next to Kal. "What are you doing here?"

"I ate dinner with your mom tonight."

"Cool. What did you have?"

"Eggplant lasagna."

"Oh. We had tacos. I got to play forward and halfback today at practice. I did my homework already, Mom."

"Okay. I'll check it later. You need to go take a shower."

"Right now?"

"Yes, right now."

Kal stood. "I gotta go anyway. I'll see you this weekend, Oliver."

Oliver looked up at him. "You will?"

"I will. We're gonna go do something fun."

"All right! See you later, Kal."

"See ya, buddy."

Oliver went down the hall toward the bathroom, and Hannah walked Kal to the door. "Sorry about that."

"Don't worry about it. It's life with a kid."

He didn't seem upset about it, and she appreciated that he understood that her life was filled with interruptions. "I'll talk to you soon."

He wrapped his arm around her and tugged her against him, long enough to press a steamy kiss to her lips. Then he let her go. "Yeah. Soon."

She didn't want to let him go, and there was that problem again. "Bye, Kal."

"Bye."

He turned and walked out the door, and she lingered to watch him, far longer than she should have.

CHAPTER 16

AS THEY MADE THEIR WAY TO THE SCENE OF THIS ACCI-
dent, Kal mentally prepared for how they were going to conduct
the rescue. It always helped him to walk through the steps of what
gear they'd need, how they'd work the scene, what role he'd take
and how dangerous it was going to be. Though everything the
TRT did was dangerous, some situations were worse than others.
He hoped this wasn't one of the worse ones.

They arrived on scene at the large farm and immediately
started unpacking their gear. Kal caught sight of the nervous parents standing on the side of the road.

Lieutenant Anderson stepped up to talk to the parents, who
hurriedly motioned them toward the back.

There was an old well that had been broken apart and a black
hole where their ten-year-old son had fallen.

The parents were John and Belinda Lindquist.

"We haven't used this one in years, and we knew it was a danger, so we were planning to fill it in," John said. "We told Caleb
to stay away from it, but he must have come out here to take a
look and fallen in."

"When he first fell in we heard him cry, and now we don't hear anything," Belinda said, tears filling her eyes. "Please, get him out of there."

"Any water down there?" the lieutenant asked.

The man shook his head. "No. Well's been dry for a while."

"We'll take care of it," Lieutenant Anderson said. "Now you need to step back and let us get to work."

John and Belinda also had a thirteen-year-old daughter named Roberta who looked just as worried as her parents.

The thing he liked the most about his lieutenant was how calm he was under pressure. He also made sure to fill in the parents about what they were doing and how they planned to get their son out.

He gave the team their assignments, and they all jumped to perform the tasks. They began to set up the tripod, get the ropes in line, and both Meg and Micah harnessed up. While all this was going on, their lieutenant laid out what was going to happen and what everyone's job would be.

Meg would go down first, with Micah as backup if needed, though with the hole being so tight, hopefully they'd only need one of them. Dean and Phil would provide weight on the tripod. Kal was in charge of the blue rope that would be used to pull Caleb up. Irish and Andy were in charge of the red rope and lowering Meg.

They were a well-oiled machine, but all this took time to set up. They were thirty minutes in by the time they were ready to lower Meg into the hole.

"Oh, please hurry," Mrs. Lindquist said.

"He's gonna be fine," Mr. Lindquist said, putting his arm around both his wife and his daughter.

EMTs were also on hand to provide aid for the child as soon as they pulled him out. Kal hoped the kid was okay enough to not need EMTs. He hated to think of the other outcome, not with the parents and his sister standing right there.

"You ready?" Lieutenant Anderson asked, looking around at all of them.

"Yes, sir," they all said one by one.

His gaze landed last on Meg, who nodded, gave the rope team controlling her a thumbs-up, then slid over the edge and into the abyss.

Kal's muscles tensed as he waited for the signal, hoping he'd get to pull up a survivor. He knew the entire team was focused on their duties, all connected via their mics to listen to Meg's descent into the well.

He watched as Irish and Andy continued to give rope to Meg's descent, which meant she was going pretty far down. He had no idea the depth of the well, but it was obviously a ways.

"Okay, I see something," she said. "Looks like a figure curled up at the bottom. White T-shirt, blue jeans. No movement."

Kal's stomach clenched as he waited for her to reach Caleb.

"Feet on the ground," she said.

And then nothing but silence. They knew she was checking Caleb's vital signs, examining him for injuries, so it'd be a few minutes before they heard back from her. To the team it seemed like an eternity. To Caleb's parents, even longer.

"He's conscious. He was asleep. Amazingly, nothing is broken. He has some deep cuts and scrapes, but nothing major. Looks like he might have a sprained ankle. Maybe a concussion. Says he's hungry and really thirsty. I'm harnessing him to pull up."

They all exhaled in relief. The lieutenant reported Meg's findings to Caleb's parents, who both burst into tears, and the family embraced one another.

Within a few minutes, Meg gave the okay to pull Caleb, so Kal gently retracted his rope, not wanting to jar him or bump him against the side walls of the well. EMTs stood at the entrance to grab hold of him as soon as he appeared and put him on the stretcher. They headed straight for the hospital, the family following in their car. After he was up, Phil and Dean pulled Meg out.

"Whew," she said after she disengaged from the pulleys. "Dark and tight down there."

"Long way down, too," Kal said as he was folding up his rope.

"No kidding. Caleb was lucky to have escaped with only minor injuries."

Phil walked by, then paused. "Your rope was slack on the withdrawal. You could have banged that kid against the wall. Do better next time."

Kal just stared after him as he walked away, then turned to Meg. "My rope was fine. Taut. Fucking perfect."

She shrugged. "Ignore him."

"Kind of hard to when he rides my ass every chance he gets."

They packed up their gear and headed back to the station. Since it was late afternoon and they'd worked through lunch, Irish put together some bacon, lettuce and tomato sandwiches and tomato soup for them to eat. Simple, but it tasted great.

"Heard you fucked up handling the rope today," Dean said to Kal after everyone else had left the table. It was only Kal, Dean and Phil.

"No, I handled my rope duties just fine."

Dean looked over at Phil and smiled, then sent a smirk back at Kal. "Not what I heard."

There was so much he wanted to say, but what was the point? All it would do was cause more animosity with two of his teammates, so he let it go.

Then again, he was tired of having to take it almost every day.

"What's your issue with me?"

"We worked our asses off to land a position on the TRT, kid,"

Dean said. "While you just waltzed in and were given the job by your daddy, the battalion chief with connections."

That's what they thought? "Look. I applied, I tested, I trained and I got in, just like everyone else. My father had zero influence in my getting in here."

Phil let out a laugh. "Yeah, right. Everyone knows how you got here, and it wasn't your skills."

Now he was pissed. He stood up. "Bullshit. Talk to the lieutenant if you don't believe me. Talk to anyone else."

Phil leaned back in the chair. "No need to. Everyone knows the truth, and the truth is you didn't earn your way here, Donovan. You got in through family connections."

"You believe that, then prove it. Otherwise, shut your fucking mouth."

"Is there a problem here?"

Kal snapped to attention when his lieutenant walked in. "No, sir."

Phil and Dean went back to relaxed mode.

"Nothing going on here, Lieutenant," Dean said. "Just having lunch."

Lieutenant Anderson gave them all the once-over as if he didn't believe what they told him.

"Donovan."

"Yes, sir."

"Is there a problem I need to know about?"

"No, Lieutenant. No problem."

He stared at all of them for a few more seconds, enough to make Kal really uncomfortable. And judging from the squeamish looks on Dean's and Phil's faces, they weren't comfortable, either. The lieutenant finally left the room. Kal glared at Phil and Dean, then he left the room, so wound up he needed to punch something. And since he couldn't punch Dean or Phil, he headed to the workout room, deciding to take it out on the weight equipment.

He might not be able to beat the shit out of the guys who irritated him, but he could burn some of the rage off in there.

This time, anyway.

But one of these days, they were going to push him too far, and he was going to knock them both on their asses.

And that was going to feel really damn satisfying.

CHAPTER 17

"OLIVER, IF YOU AREN'T READY IN FIVE MINUTES, I'M GOING to call Kal and tell him we're not going."

"Mommmm. I'm in the shower now."

Hannah rolled her eyes and took in a deep breath. "You are not. Get in there right away."

There were days when being a parent took every ounce of energy she had. Today was one of those days. Oliver had woken up cranky and obstinate, fighting her on every single thing. Even though he was excited about going to the festival, he was doing everything he could to not take a shower, like lying around on the sofa all morning and playing in his room.

But she did finally hear the bathroom door close, and when she walked down the hall, the shower was running.

Progress.

She pivoted and headed toward her room, running into her mother. "Kids, huh? Pain in the ass. Wonder where he gets it from," her mother said with a knowing smile.

"His father, probably."

"You'd like to think that, but I had to light a fire under your butt to get you moving all the time. So the hard-to-get-moving part? That's on you, honey."

She scrunched up her nose. "Well, I'm not like that now."

"That's because you married a boy even lazier than you. You had no choice but to grow out of it."

"I guess you're right. I won't let Oliver grow up that way."

She patted Hannah's shoulder. "That's my girl."

After her mother walked away, she went down the hall and into her room. Now that she'd gotten Oliver started on getting ready, she had to do the same. She'd already showered, but she had to get dressed and put her makeup on. The weather was nice today. The temperature wasn't unbearable for a change, so she put on a pair of capris and a short-sleeved T-shirt and slid into her canvas tennis shoes. After applying makeup, she brushed her hair and put it in a high ponytail. Perfect for a festival. She didn't have to be glamorous, and it wasn't a date, anyway. Anytime you brought your kid on an outing, it wasn't a date.

After Oliver got out of the shower, she went into his room to supervise the rest of his routine, since he tended to get easily distracted. He got dressed and put on his shoes. She made sure he combed his hair and brushed his teeth. After that, he was required to pick up his room, since it looked like a tornado had swept through it after he'd slept. They'd argued about that, too.

It was just going to be that kind of day.

By the time Kal showed up, she was already exhausted and would have happily opted to spend the day curled up on the sofa reading a book.

He swept his knuckles over her cheek. "You look tired."

"Kid's giving me a hard time today."

"Boys. They'll do that. Or at least that's what my mom always told us."

She smiled. "Please tell me you grow out of it."

"Some of us do and become amazing specimens of the male species." He gave her a wickedly sexy smile.

She raised her hand and coughed into it. "Sure. Keep believing that."

"Hi, Kal." Oliver ran over and put his arms around Kal's middle.

Kal seemed surprised but looked over at Hannah and grinned before hugging Oliver back. "Hey, buddy. How's it going?"

"Mom made me take a shower."

"Did you stink?"

"I dunno. Maybe."

"Then you probably needed one. I took a shower, too. Now we can both smell good for your mom today. How's that?"

"Okay, I guess. When are we going? I'm bringing my Iron Man costume. Jeff is going as Black Panther. Are you wearing a costume?"

"That sounds perfect. I'm not wearing a costume, buddy. How could I possibly compete with your awesomeness?"

Oliver laughed. "Mom, can I go get Jeff?"

"Sure, honey, but be careful."

"Okay. I'll be right back, Kal. Don't leave without me."

"I'll be here."

Oliver ran out the front door just as Hannah's mother came down the hall.

"Hi, Kal."

"Hello, Paige. How's it going?"

"Oh, you know. Aging by the minute."

He laughed. "Don't believe it. Look at how beautiful you are. Are you coming with us today?"

She shook her head as she grabbed her purse. "No. I have plans with a certain gentleman for brunch."

"Wait." Hannah frowned. "I didn't hear about this."

Her mother came over and kissed her cheek, then patted her arm. "No, you didn't, did you? You all have a nice time today."

Hannah just stared after her mother as she walked out the door. "Huh. I had no idea she was even seeing someone."

"Maybe it's a first date and she doesn't want to talk about it just yet."

"Maybe." It was none of her business who her mother saw anyway. But it was great that she was getting out and seeing someone.

Kal stepped over and pulled her into his arms. "Before the kids come back."

He brought his lips to hers and kissed her. It was light and easy, but enough to let her know he'd been thinking about her. She fell into the kiss that suddenly turned more passionate, making her wish they had more time alone.

He pulled back and swiped his thumb over her bottom lip. "Damn."

"Yeah," she said, blowing out a breath. "I wish we had more time, too."

"We'll make the time. Somewhere. And today we'll have some fun with the boys."

She smiled, happy that he wasn't frustrated or mad. "We will. I have a bag packed with donations for today. I got some hygiene items and some socks and a box of diapers for the homeless shelter."

"Oh, that's great. I have some stuff, too. I know they'll appreciate it."

The boys burst through the door. Jeff flung his backpack by the door, and they raced into Oliver's room.

Hannah shook her head. "Let me give you the donation bag, and I'll round up the boys."

Once she made sure Oliver had his costume in his backpack, she hustled the boys out the door and into the truck.

Since the festival was in Pompano Beach, the drive took about a half hour. On the ride there, Kal engaged the boys in conversation about sports, comic books and superheroes. Hannah was amazed at Kal's knowledge base about all kid things. Maybe boys retained all that knowledge from their own childhoods. She had to know stuff so she could talk to Oliver about his interests. It certainly wasn't necessary for Kal to know any of it, since he didn't have kids. She was impressed.

They parked in the lot and handed over their donation bags at the gate. Hannah's eyes widened when she saw the multiple bags that Kal had in the truck.

"It's not all from me," he said as he easily hefted her two bags plus three more of his own. "Rafe and Carmen don't come back from their honeymoon until tonight, so they wanted me to add stuff in on their behalf."

"What are all the bags for?" Oliver asked.

"They're donations for homeless shelters around the area."

Jeff gave him a questioning look. "What's a homeless shelter?"

"It's a place for people to stay when they don't have a home of their own," Hannah said.

"Like an apartment?" Oliver asked.

"No," Kal said. "Sometimes people don't have a place to live at all. They live out on the streets either alone or with their families."

"That sounds sad," Oliver said.

Jeff nodded as they handed the bags to the people at the gate and got their wrist bracelets.

"And scary," Jeff said.

They were given a pamphlet, and Hannah looked it over to decide which direction to go first.

"Do kids live on the streets?" Oliver asked.

Kal looked at Hannah as if to ask if it was okay to answer. She nodded.

"They do," Kal said. "That's where I lived when I was a kid."

"No way," Oliver said. "Were you scared?"

"Sometimes. But I stayed close with people I knew so I was never alone. In fact, my brothers that I have now became my brothers when I was homeless. We got rescued from a fire together when I was living on the streets, and we all got adopted by my firefighter dad and my amazing mom."

"Whoa. That is awesome. You have the best life, Kal."

Kal grinned. "Yeah, I sure do."

Hannah thought it was incredible how kids could hear the worst circumstances but pull the highlights out and absorb only the best parts. She supposed that was the child in them. But Hannah had seen the shadows in Kal's eyes and knew he was still haunted by his past. He probably always would be.

And who wouldn't, having lived in those circumstances? She couldn't imagine going to sleep night after night hungry, homeless, not knowing where your next meal would come from, or if you would ever be able to eat again. And being tossed away by your parents as if you never mattered. It made her love her mom even more fiercely, and determined to love her son the best she could.

She sighed.

"Okay, where to first?" Kal asked, oblivious to the deep emotions rolling through her. Obviously, the boys' heavy questions hadn't bothered him. But she still had to ask.

She put her hand on his arm. "Are you all right?"

He cocked his head to the side. "I'm fine. Why?"

"The boys. Their questions."

"It's all good. Thanks for asking, though." He brushed his lips across hers, then immediately drew back, no doubt realizing what he'd done. They both looked at Oliver, who was staring at them.

"I'm thirsty," Oliver said. "Can we get something to drink?"

"Sure," Hannah said. "Drinks first, then we'll go on a hayride."

And later, when she had Oliver alone, she'd ask him how he felt about seeing her and Kal together.

He might just be seven years old, but he had feelings, and they were important to her.

The hayride was fun, and they were seated with eight other people, several of them kids, so Oliver and Jeff had a great time laughing and talking with the other kids. After that they had lunch, though the boys could hardly sit still since they knew the costume contest would be next and they could barely contain themselves, so it was like trying to eat a sandwich around a couple of bouncing balls.

"Oliver, Jeff, sit and eat your food or we won't be able to make it in time," Hannah said.

"But we want to go now," Oliver said.

"It doesn't start until two, and it's only one thirty."

"So how much more time is that?" Jeff asked.

"Thirty minutes. And it's only a five-minute walk to the arena, so there's plenty of time to make it there. Now sit and eat."

They finally settled and found something to talk about while they ate their food.

"You're good at that," Kal said.

"At what?"

"Parenting."

She laughed. "It doesn't always work."

"I don't know. You've got that magic voice that makes people want to do what you ask them to do."

She leaned into him. "Really? Does it work on you?"

"You bet your—" He looked over at the boys. "Anyway, you should try it on me sometime. Anytime."

"So if I wanted the house painted, for instance . . ."

He cocked a brow. "Not exactly the direction I was headed."

She gave him a small smile. "I know. Come on. Let's get these boys into their costumes."

On the way to the costume contest, Kal got a text from Jackson.

"Jackson and Becks are here. I let them know where we were headed so they could meet us there."

"Oh, good."

Kal went into the men's restroom with Oliver and Jeff while they changed into their costumes. When they came out, Iron Man and Black Panther were outfitted in full glory.

"My two favorite superheroes, ready to head into action," Kal said, toting both their backpacks.

The boys struck fighting poses.

"I feel protected already," Hannah said.

"We're ready to kick some butt," Oliver said.

"I'm so glad we have superheroes here to protect us." Jackson leveled a grin at the boys as he approached.

"Me, too," Becks said. "Nice costumes."

Hannah stood. "Oliver, Jeff, this is Kal's brother, Jackson, and Becks, his fiancée."

"What's a fiancée?" Jeff asked.

"That means we're getting married," Becks said.

"Oh. I knew that."

Hannah smiled.

"How come you're brothers but you aren't the same color?" Jeff asked.

"Because we were adopted together," Kal said. "We didn't have the same parents when we were born. But we grew up together. We lived together. That made us brothers."

"That's so cool," Oliver said. "Does that mean Jeff and I can be brothers now?"

Hannah smiled. "Not exactly. You have me and Jeff has his parents. And the two of you don't live together. But you can be best friends."

Oliver scrunched his nose as he thought. "I guess that's okay. Mom, can we go now? I don't want to miss the contest."

"Sure."

They all made their way to the entry point near the stage. There were quite a few kids entering the contest, so Hannah, with Kal's help, registered both Oliver and Jeff. They were led to a gate where they'd go up on stage to show off their costumes.

Everyone took a seat, and the parade of costumes began.

"There are some really cute kids up there," Becks said. "Yours included, Hannah."

"Thanks." Becks was right about that. She enjoyed watching kids of all ages walk across the viewing area. She clapped for all of them.

In the end, no one was singled out as the best. All the kids received a bag of treats and an award badge, which Hannah appreciated. Best of all, both boys were thrilled and already digging into their bags, which meant the adults could wander over to the wine and beer area without the boys complaining about it.

Kal got a beer and Hannah a cup of wine, and then they walked around the vendor booths to see what was being offered. Nothing she really wanted, actually, but it was still fun to browse to see what crafty items people made. She sniffed some soaps, ogled quilts, ran her fingers over some amazing woodcrafts and pondered buying a pink flamingo for her mother's front yard.

"Does she like flamingos?" Becks asked.

"She's crazy about them. But shockingly, she doesn't have one in her front yard. And this one is adorable." It was made out of brass and wasn't pink, which was what made it so unusual and unique. She knew her mother would love it.

"Grandma would like that one," Oliver said. "We should buy it."

"Oh, we should, huh?"

"Yeah."

"You're right. We totally should." She pointed to the flamingo and dug the money out of her purse. The vendor wrapped it up nicely for her and put it in a bag.

"Cute flamingo," Kal said as they continued to walk along.

"I hadn't intended to buy anything. But my mom will love it."

She stopped at another vendor that sold spices. She sniffed a few of them and loved the way they smelled. She could already imagine the different dishes she could make with those spices.

But she'd already bought the flamingo, and since she was on a tight budget, she walked away without buying them, catching up to Jackson and Becks, who were with the boys. They'd found a pet adoption corral, which made her heart squeeze.

"Look at the dogs, Mom," Oliver said, already heading toward a small brown-and-white mixed-breed dog. It was cute and furiously wagged its tail when Oliver went into the corral to play with it.

Jackson and Kal were in there as well, both of them squatting down to pet the dog.

This was not going to end well.

"Which one of them do you think will end up with the dog?" Becks asked.

"My mother would kill me if I came home with a dog," Hannah said.

"She doesn't like dogs?" Becks asked.

"I actually don't know. I never had pets as a kid. My dad never wanted them around, for sure, and after he died, my mom just didn't have the time to take care of them."

"We would make friends with the dogs on the streets," Becks said. "Feed them scraps of food if we had some. I always wanted one."

Jackson looked up at her. "You did? Why didn't you say so?"

Becks shrugged. "It's never come up."

Jackson stood and came through the gate to walk over to Becks. "We should get a dog, babe."

"Oh, it's all right. I don't need one."

"Need isn't what I'm talking about. What do you want?"

Hannah watched with interest as Jackson and Becks talked together about something as simple, and yet so complex, as adding a dog to their lives. It was something she and Landon had often argued about. He thought getting a puppy would be easy, when she'd been struggling with dealing with Landon's job issues while working and raising Oliver, mostly by herself. After months of arguing, she'd told him if he brought a dog home, she was going to take Oliver and leave him and the dog and he'd never see them again. He'd finally let the topic drop, but she'd felt like the worst mother ever. But someone had to be the adult, and that responsibility had often fallen on her shoulders.

"Look how cute he is, Momma."

She looked over and smiled at Oliver, who was playing with the same dog. "He's very cute, Oliver. But we're living with Grandma, and she doesn't want a dog in her house. Maybe someday when we get our own house, okay?"

Her stomach twinged when she caught sight of Oliver's crestfallen face.

"How about we do this another time?" Becks said to Jackson.

Hannah laid her hand on Becks's arm. "It's okay. You make your own decisions and don't worry about Oliver. He'll understand."

Oliver got up and went over to the part of the corral where Becks and Jackson were looking at an adorable German shepherd mix who seemed to be a bundle of energy.

"He's cute," Oliver said, reaching out to pet the dog. "Do you like this one?"

"I do," Becks said.

"You gonna take him home? I think he likes you."

Becks looked at Jackson, who nodded. "I think we'll apply to adopt him. If Kal's okay to share the house with a dog."

"Hey, I'm good," Kal said.

"Did you hear that, Momma? They're gonna adopt him."

She was happy that Oliver wasn't too upset about not being able to get his own dog today. But Jeff had a Labrador at his house that Oliver loved to play with, and maybe a surrogate dog was enough for him for now.

But someday? Someday she'd have her own place again. And then Oliver would have a dog of his own.

After Jackson and Becks filled out the application to adopt the dog, they wandered around and found a designated play area. The boys ran loose, and the rest of them sat at tables to watch them while drinking their wine and beer.

"I remember having that much energy," Kal said as they watched the boys chase after each other, along with a few other kids they'd made friends with.

Jackson grinned. "You still have that much energy."

"I don't know about that." He took a long swallow of his beer. "I'm pretty sure those two could wear me down in a hurry."

"Trust me, they could," Hannah said. "Oliver will go the entire day until he hits his bed at night."

"Bet he sleeps well, though," Becks said.

Hannah nodded. "Once he's asleep, he's out cold."

Jackson turned to Becks. "Like you."

She nudged him with her elbow. "At least I don't fall asleep standing up leaning against a wall."

"Really?" Hannah asked.

"In my defense, it was a long shift the day before and I hadn't gotten any sleep. I was really tired."

"He has been known to be talking one minute, asleep the next," Kal said.

"I've never known anyone who could fall asleep mid-sentence," Hannah said.

Becks held her hands out toward Jackson. "And now you do."

"Whereas my brother here will just disappear in the middle of a party and go to bed." Jackson shot a wry grin at Kal.

"Not true. I threw up first. Then I went to bed. That was one wild party."

"You were the first to leave."

"You kept feeding me shots of Fireball followed by tequila shooters."

Hannah looked over at Becks, who shrugged. "Clearly before my time. And mixing those two sounds awful."

"It was," Kal said. "Group of firefighters went out one night, and we all decided to do shots."

"Only the rest of us were smart enough not to mix our alcohol."

Kal glared at Jackson. "Hey. I was the youngest in the group."

"And the dumbest," Jackson added. "When we came back to our house, we kept drinking. Only the rest of us switched to beer. Not my brother, though."

Kal shrugged. "I was wasted by then. What did I know?"

Hannah grasped his arm. "Fireball and tequila, Kal?"

"Let's just say it was a painful lesson learned, and one I never repeated."

Hannah's stomach rolled just thinking about it.

"I only overindulged once," Becks said. "Up all night sick was enough for me. I've never done it again."

"Same," Hannah said. "There's nothing like waking up in the morning, sick *and* still drunk, to cure you of ever wanting to do it again."

Becks's eyes widened and she nodded. "Right? It's such an awful feeling."

Suddenly, Hannah wasn't in the mood to drink wine any longer. Maybe it was the memory of overindulging, or maybe the way the weather had warmed up today. Either way, she finished her glass, then went to get herself some water, along with some for Oliver and Jeff.

When the boys finished playing, they headed over to the pumpkin patch, wandered around in there, then each boy chose a pumpkin to take home.

"Do you want to come over for dinner?" Becks asked. "I think we're going to toss some skewers of chicken on the grill, along with some veggies."

That did sound good. "I have to take Oliver and Jeff home, and I'm not sure if my mom is back yet. Let me check with her."

"Sure."

She texted her mother, who was home and fixing dinner. Hannah asked if it would be all right if she dropped Oliver with her and went out for dinner. Her mother said it was fine with her.

"What would you like us to pick up?" Hannah asked as they made their way to the parking lot.

"I think we have everything we need at the house already, Hannah, but thanks."

Hannah thought this would just be a one-off at the festival with the kids, but now her day with Kal was going to go longer.

She had to admit, she was excited about that, because now she'd get some more time with him.

Alone. Without kids. And that sounded fun.

CHAPTER 18

THEY SAID THEIR GOODBYES, AND KAL DROVE HANNAH and the boys home. She thought maybe Oliver would be upset about not being able to go with her to Kal's house, but he said goodbye to Jeff outside, then dashed into the house with his pumpkin and started talking all about his day to Hannah's mom.

"When can we decorate the pumpkin, Momma?" Oliver asked.

"We'll do that tomorrow after school. Right now you need to go wash your hands because they're filthy."

"I got dirty today, Grandma," he said with a wide grin.

"You definitely did."

"We'll be leaving, but I'll be back later," Hannah said.

Oliver waved as he headed down the hall. "Bye, Momma. Bye, Kal. Today was so much fun! Thanks!"

"See ya, buddy," Kal said.

Her mother looked at her and Kal. "Seems like he had a good time."

"He did. Are you sure you don't mind watching him?"

"He lives here, Hannah, so get over it and quit worrying about asking me to watch him. He's my grandson. I love every minute I spend with him."

"Okay. Thanks, Mom." She started to turn away, then stopped. "Oh. How was brunch today?"

Her mother gave her a half smile. "Brunch was very good."

Hannah waited for more details, but it was obvious her mom wasn't going to divulge information about the mystery man.

So disappointing. "You're not going to tell me anything?"

"Nothing to tell . . . yet. It was nice. Now go have dinner with your boyfriend."

She cringed at the word *boyfriend*, but Kal laughed and slipped his arm around her waist, so it obviously didn't bother him.

"Thanks, Paige," Kal said. "See you later."

"Bye, Mom."

Once in the truck on the way to Kal's house, he asked, "So she won't divulge the goods on the mystery date, huh?"

Hannah shook her head. "Nope. Not a word."

"Huh." He turned onto the highway and sped up to merge with traffic. "Maybe it's new so she doesn't want to say any more about him in case it doesn't work out."

"That could be. She hasn't dated much since my dad died. She's never had a serious relationship since my dad, as far as I know."

"She loved your dad. I imagine it's been hard for her to meet people."

"For her it has been."

"But she is getting out there now, so it's a good thing, right?"

She looked over at him. "It's a very good thing. I've been encouraging her to have a relationship for years. She just hasn't seemed interested."

"Or maybe the right man hadn't come along yet."

"Maybe." She wanted her mom to be happy. If that meant she was alone, that was fine. But alone was lonely. Hannah knew that since her divorce.

Of course, Hannah didn't need a man in her life. She had her friends, her family, her work and Oliver. She was plenty busy. Fulfilled. More or less.

But now, being with Kal made her realize how much she'd missed dating. Just hanging out and having fun and sharing her life with someone.

And sex. The sex part was definitely a good time. She wanted a lot more of that, especially with Kal.

"Hey, can we stop at the grocery store before we go to your place?" Hannah asked.

"Sure. What do you need?"

"I know Becks said not to bring anything, but I want to make a watermelon salsa."

"Okay, now I'm hungry."

She grinned.

After she picked up what she needed at the store, they headed to the house. When they walked into the kitchen, Becks saw the bag Kal was carrying.

"I told you we had everything covered."

"Hannah's making a watermelon salsa," Kal said.

Becks smiled. "Then by all means, carry on."

Hannah washed her hands and, with Kal's help, sliced up watermelon, mango, cucumber, jalapeno, onion and basil, then added lime juice, a little sugar, some garlic and salt. She scooped a bit onto a spoon and slid the spoon between Kal's lips for a taste test.

"I'm about to go run out the front door with this bowl and eat all of it by myself."

"No, we'll share."

"Why? I don't even like my brother."

"Yes, you do. And you like Becks, too."

"Glad you added me in there," Becks said.

He sighed. "Fine. Sharing sucks, though."

She laughed and tucked the bowl into the fridge to cool.

"Anything I can do to help you?" she asked Becks.

"Nope. Everything is on the skewers and ready for Jackson to grill."

The kabobs looked great, with chicken, pineapple and green peppers all strung along in neat rows. After the guys went outside to grill, Becks poured wine for Hannah and herself.

"It was a good day. And your son is adorable, Hannah."

"Thank you. He's a good kid. I'm very lucky."

Becks took a sip of wine. "I'd say a lot of that has to do with having a good mother."

"It's been a rough ride for both of us. Deciding to divorce and then relocate wasn't easy on either of us. But Oliver is a smart kid. And he wasn't happy living with his dad any more than I was. Landon liked to pull disappearing acts, or didn't show up for important occasions. Reliability isn't his strong suit."

"I'm sorry."

"It's okay. I got used to it. Much harder for a child to accept. It was easier to remove Oliver from Landon's presence than to have his heart broken all the time. And once I sat down with Landon and explained to him that he couldn't keep shirking his duties as a dad, and how much he was hurting Oliver, he agreed. He really does love his son. He's just not father material."

Becks shrugged. "Some men aren't. At least your ex realized that. He gets props for that and for letting go of Oliver without a fight."

"I give him huge points for that. Oliver misses him—theoretically, I think. He doesn't miss being hurt by him. He has more stability in his life now than he had before, and that's more important than having a father who wasn't around half the time."

"Agree. My parents were . . . well, let's just say they weren't the best role models. Trust me when I tell you that having no parents at all is better than bad parents."

"I'm sorry you had to go through that."

"I turned out okay. I ended up with some great foster parents, and they loved me. I had security and stability and got to see what it was like to have a family. And now I have love and a family who means the world to me. And someday I'll have kids, and they'll know what it's like to feel safe and loved every day of their lives."

"That's pretty awesome, Becks. A lot of people don't come through what you experienced without scars."

She shrugged. "You can either take it with you or you can leave it behind. I faced all my demons a long time ago and left them in the past. I refuse to continue to relive it when I have so much awesomeness ahead of me."

"That's a good philosophy. I should probably work on doing the same thing."

Becks studied her, then asked, "Still leery about relationships?"

"You could say that. I mean, I get that not every guy is going to be like my ex. But I have Oliver to think about. The last thing he needs is for some man I decide I'm in love with to suddenly not be there for him. It would break his heart."

"And yet you've let Kal into Oliver's life."

Hannah's gaze drifted toward the back door where Kal and Jackson were talking and laughing. "Yes, I know."

"Regrets about that?"

She returned her attention to Becks. "I don't know. I guess I'm letting things happen organically. I can't control everything that happens."

"And maybe you can't protect Oliver from everything that happens, either." Becks took a sip of wine and laid the glass on the kitchen island. "Look, I don't know what's going to happen with the two of you. I don't know where you are in your relationship. I know the two of you have a past that I know nothing about, and that's not my business. But I can tell you that Kal's a good guy. He cares about children. He wouldn't intentionally hurt Oliver."

Hannah nodded. "I know that. I see that and I feel it whenever he's with Oliver."

Becks reached out and laid her hand over Hannah's. "None of us can predict the future. Sometimes you just have to go with your gut. And maybe a little bit of your heart."

Hannah drew in a deep breath, realizing that what Becks had said made a lot of sense. "You're right."

Then again, logic had never failed her. That's how she had gotten out of her marriage. She'd been rational, had thought it all out and had made a sensible decision. She'd done her best to keep emotion out of the equation and had done what was best for both her and Oliver.

It was whenever she'd let emotion in that things became messy.

But she also liked spending time with Kal, and logic had nothing to do with that.

The door opened, and Kal came in bearing a plate full of delicious-smelling food. And speaking of delicious, she realized that whenever she caught sight of him, her entire body nearly vibrated.

That was a physical response, so she couldn't even call that emotion.

She sighed.

See? Complicated.

But not all bad, either.

After Kal washed his hands, he came over and threaded his arms around her waist, pressing a kiss to the side of her neck. Sensation traveled down her body like a slow-moving river, giving her goose bumps and endorphins and making her smile.

"Wait 'til you taste these."

She tilted her head back to look at him. "You were taste testing outside?"

"Someone had to make sure the chicken was done."

She reached up to smooth her hand over his square jaw, drinking in the way his gaze caught and held hers, as if he was looking inside of her, could see all her secrets, could feel how she felt.

That part was definitely emotion, and she needed to brush it away, so instead, she said, "Good of you to take one for the team."

"That's me, babe. Always one to sacrifice."

"Okay, you two," Becks said. "Enough with the romance. Time to set the table, because I'm hungry."

They grabbed the food and plates and placed everything up on the table, then they sat and dived into the food. From the utter silence and groans of pleasure, it appeared that everyone must have been hungry.

"This is so good," Hannah finally managed in between bites of food and sips of water.

"This watermelon salsa is to die for," Becks said.

The guys didn't speak. They were too busy shoveling food into their mouths. Which, Hannah supposed, was complimentary to the food.

"How's things at the TRT?" Jackson asked Kal.

Kal shrugged. "About the same."

"Those guys still giving you shit?"

"Yeah. I tried talking to them again." He took a swallow of his beer.

"And?" Jackson asked.

"They seem to think that Dad had a part in giving me a leg up in getting my spot on the TRT."

Jackson frowned. "That's bullshit. The department never lets nepotism favor one candidate over another. It would be a violation of standards. You got in on merit and nothing else, same as when you got the job at Station 6. Dad was excluded in making the decision on your hire. Your assignment was the captain's decision. Even Rafe and I weren't included in that."

"I know. We were all just lucky to be assigned to the same station."

Hannah hadn't heard any of this. "Someone on your team is giving you a hard time?"

Kal nodded. "Two guys have been riding me since I first started there. They criticize everything I do and think I don't deserve to be on the TRT."

"But his lieutenant thinks he's doing a good job," Jackson said, dipping a chip into the salsa and shoving it into his mouth. After he swallowed, he said, "So as long as his superior is okay with his performance . . ."

Hannah looked at him. "Then those guys have it out for you for other reasons. Jealousy, maybe?"

Kal shrugged. "I guess. I don't really know. I've given up trying to figure it out."

"Do you get along with the other members of your squad?" she asked.

"Yeah. We all get along great."

"Then screw those guys," she said, rubbing her hand along his forearm. "You're good at your job, your boss knows you do it well and you have coworkers who think you do it well. No one else matters."

He smiled at her, but she could tell it bothered him. "Thanks."

She wished she could do or say something to take his pain away, but she knew better than anyone that conflicts with coworkers could only be solved with either time or replacement of said coworkers. And since that appeared unlikely to happen, all she could do was offer moral support.

She knew how hard Kal worked, knew how much he loved his job. It pissed her off that some people were making it harder for him to do the job he cared so much about.

After dinner they cleaned the dishes and the kitchen. Jackson and Becks were going to a late movie, so they said their goodbyes.

Hannah hugged Becks. "Thanks for the invite to dinner. I had fun."

Becks squeezed her. "I'm so glad you came over. Let's do this again."

After they left, Hannah took Kal's hand. "I'm sorry you're having conflict at work."

"Hey, don't be. It's not all the time. And I can handle it."

"You shouldn't have to. Those guys are dicks and need to get punched in the face."

He laughed and pulled her against his warm body. "Yeah? And do you think you could take them?"

"They'd never see it coming. I'd lay them flat."

"Okay," he said, stepping back. "Show me what you've got."

She arched a brow. "You don't wanna mess with me. I really do know how to knock you on your ass."

He gave her a benign, patronizing smile. That did it. She had planned to lie back, but now she was going to show him just what she could do.

"Come at me," she said, turning her back to him.

"You sure about that?"

"I'm waiting."

She tensed, waiting for him to strike. When he put his arms around her she stomped on his foot, the least amount of damage she could do.

"Ow, dammit!"

She pivoted and directed a palm strike, stopping just shy of his nose. He hadn't expected it, and he reared back. She also caught the shocked look on his face.

"Really?" he asked.

She shrugged. "The next step would have been to break your nose. Still don't think I have it in me to defend myself?"

"My damn foot hurts."

"That's the idea."

"Okay, you took self-defense classes."

She nodded. "Several. I wanted to be able to take care of myself."

"I'd say you can do that just fine. Also, my foot still hurts."

She looked down at his feet. He was wearing tennis shoes, and she hadn't stomped with all her might. "You'll live."

"You're mean."

She laughed. "I can be. But you doubted my ability to defend myself."

He started to say something, then stopped and looked at her. "You're right. I was wrong. You're a badass, Hannah Clark. I should have remembered that from the time you threw rocks at me when you thought I was cheating on you with Penny Fairbanks junior year."

She blinked, then laughed. "I'd totally forgotten about that. I did throw rocks at you behind the school. I was so pissed at you."

He pointed to his chest. "At me? It was Penny who was flirting with me, trying to break us up. And when that didn't work, Penny told you that I asked her out, when in fact I never did that, would never do that. And what did you do? Did you come to me and ask me if it was true? No, you didn't. You threw rocks at me instead."

It hadn't been her finest moment. "I apologized, didn't I?"

"Yeah, after about the twentieth rock, when I finally convinced you I never asked her out. Those rocks hurt, by the way."

"But did you die?"

He rolled his eyes. "No, I didn't. And you have trust issues, Hannah."

He was so right about that. "I can't help it. Besides, Penny Fairbanks was beautiful. Smart. And popular. Who wouldn't want to go out with her?"

"Me. I didn't want to go out with her. I had you. Plus, *you* are beautiful, and smart, and everything I wanted. I wasn't in love with Penny Fairbanks."

Her heart did a little jump. "Point taken." She stepped toward him and wound her fingers around his neck, nestling her body against his. "Maybe it's time you forgive me for the rock throwing."

"You hurt my foot."

"Poor baby. Maybe I could help you forget about your foot." She lifted up on her toes, drawing his lips to hers.

It was a fiery-hot kiss, no preliminaries, nothing soft about the way his mouth claimed hers so deeply, the way his tongue dived in to tease and flick and make her breath come in gasps. She fisted a handful of his shirt to pull him nearer to her, as if by holding on to a part of him she could draw in his scent, could feel the skin-to-skin contact she craved.

He grabbed on to her butt and picked her up. She wrapped her legs around him and held on while he carried her up the steps. They stopped at the landing. He pushed her against the wall, his cock grinding against her pussy. She wanted to hold him there—right there—until she came in a blistering orgasm that made her scream.

"We might not make it to my room," he said, his voice tight.

"I don't care. Just make me come, Kal."

His mouth met hers again in a feverish kiss that made her blood run hot. His hands seemed to be everywhere—on her stomach, on her breast, grabbing her butt so he could pull her close and grind against her, making her head bang softly against the wall because it felt so damn good.

And then he slipped his hand inside her pants to cup her sex and she thought she might explode from the heat of his fingers teasing her clit and dipping lower to slide inside of her pussy. He rubbed and fingered her until she rolled against his hand in search of the orgasm that was hovering just on the brink of explosion.

He flicked his tongue against hers, nibbled at her lips, whispering to her in that dark, sexy voice of his.

"After you come I'm gonna get you naked and eat your pussy until you scream for me."

She was breathing so hard she was getting light-headed, the sensations swirling around her so strong she half thought she was going to die. But this would be the best death, because her climax burst and she cried out, rocking against his hand in uncontrollable spasms that left her weak and spent in his arms.

He picked her up and carried her the rest of the way to his room, laid her on the bed and stripped off her clothes while she lay there like an overcooked noodle, unable to move.

"You've killed me," she said.

He gave her a half smile. "Not yet. We haven't even started."

After she was naked, he took off his clothes, and she couldn't help but admire his body as she did every time she was alone with him. He went into the bathroom for a second and came back with a condom packet, tossed it on the table next to his bed, then climbed in next to her and pushed her onto her back.

"What did I say I was gonna do to you?" he asked.

"Oh, right." She stretched, feeling the pull in her muscles that had tightened during her epic orgasm. "Maybe I could get my heart rate back to a nonlethal level first?"

He swept his hand over her breasts, teasing the nipples to a sharp, tight point before bending to suck one tip into his mouth, causing her to gasp as pleasure shot straight to her core.

He lifted his head and smiled at her.

"Cardio's good for you."

Her heart rate started pulsing. "This kind of cardio might kill me."

He continued to smooth his hand over her body, snaking his fingers over her belly and lower until he once again cupped her sex. This time his movements were slow and easy, lulling her into a dreamlike state where there was only pleasure, only the feel of his fingers gliding over her slickened sex.

He eased down her body and spread her legs, replacing his fingers with his mouth, and that easy, dreamlike state heightened into gasping intensity. His tongue was hot and wet, rolling over her like he was well familiar with the map of her body and knew exactly where he wanted to go. All she had to do was hold on for the erotic ride.

But holding on wasn't going to be easy, because he had her right there, hanging off a cliff and ready to plunge into the fires of ecstasy. All she had to do was fall.

She fell, losing control of her senses, feeling only the thrilling pleasure of soaring through her climax. Kal held on to her while she shuddered and rolled through the most magnificent sensations until she felt as if she were floating.

Then he was right there, pulling her to face him, his cock sliding into her while she was still pulsing from her orgasm.

"You haven't screamed my name yet," he said, withdrawing and easing back into her, making her take a breath. It was as if every sensation was heightened. When she didn't think she could feel anything after those two mind-blistering orgasms, he had her rising again, climbing again, ready to take that plunge one more time.

"I never scream."

"We'll see."

He rocked against her, ground against her, and her body heated with every stroke. He swept her sweat-soaked hair away from her neck and licked her skin, possessing her in a way she'd never been possessed before, taking her mouth in a deep, soulful kiss that felt less like sex and more as if he were trying to tell her without words that she belonged to him, and that he belonged to her, that they were forging some kind of bond together with every movement they made.

Or maybe this was all some fantasy concocted by her sex-soaked brain, and it all just felt like she was on another level with him in this moment because he'd wrung everything out of her.

But then he pushed her onto her back and made eye contact with her as he moved within her. And the way he looked at her, his eyes so clear, the emotion so present, she was sure it wasn't a fantasy, and she was certain what she felt was way more than sex.

He grasped her hand as he began to drive harder, and she lost all sense of reality. All she could think about was reaching the climax. And when it hit, she didn't close her eyes or bury her face in his shoulder. She kept focus on his face, letting him see what he'd done to her, letting him see how she felt in the moment. And when he came, he looked at her and she could swear he'd bared everything to her right then.

It was a heart-hitting power she'd never experienced before, something she felt deep in her soul.

It had been magical.

Kal collapsed on top of her and rolled over, pulling her next to him. He caressed her hair, stroked her back and kissed her face for the longest time. It was as if he had felt the same kind of power that she had felt in their lovemaking.

Or, maybe, just maybe, she had made it all up in her head and it had meant nothing at all, that it had just been sex. All she knew was she wanted to stay like this—with him—for as long as they could. And since Kal didn't seem to be in any hurry to disengage, she was content.

But finally, he got up and went into the bathroom to dispose of the condom. When he came back, he stood at the side of the bed.

"I don't know about you, but I'm sweaty."

She smiled. "Me, too."

"Shower?" He held out his hand.

She took his hand, and he helped her out of the bed. "Sounds like a great idea."

She followed him into the bathroom and waited while the shower warmed up. Kal looked over at her and gave her his usual sexy half smile.

Everything was back to normal, as if what she'd thought was some momentous thing hadn't happened.

She supposed it *had* been just sex. Maybe what she'd thought was an extraordinary moment hadn't been anything at all.

Which was probably a good thing, because this wasn't the right time in her life to fall in love anyway.

After she'd had that long talk with herself tonight about using logic and not emotion, after one excellent night of sex, she'd allowed emotion to enter the picture.

Just how dumb are you, Hannah?

Pretty dumb, obviously. Time to right the ship again and let logic take over.

She was in this for fun. Not love. Fun. And only fun. She was going to keep reminding herself of that until it sank in.

"You coming in or are you going to hang out in the bathroom all night being sweaty?" Kal asked.

She took a deep breath and answered. "I'm coming in."

But she was going in with her logic armor firmly covering her heart.

She stepped into the shower with him.

CHAPTER 19

KAL CAME OUT OF THE BATHROOM AND STARED DOWN AT the hot, sexy woman asleep in his bed.

It took some convincing, but he'd gotten Hannah to agree to spend the night with him last night.

She'd been tired, and frankly so had he. Since they were both off work today, it made sense for her to spend the night. She'd talked to her mom, who said she could take Oliver to school this morning, and Hannah would pick him up after.

Which meant they could spend at least part of the day together.

He tossed on a pair of shorts and a T-shirt, then went downstairs to grab a cup of coffee. Jackson and Becks were already dressed and down there.

"Where are you two headed today?" he asked.

"We're going out to breakfast, then running some errands," Jackson said. "And we'll hit the grocery store since it's our week."

"Okay."

"I have a list a mile long," Becks said. "And there's a couple of wedding things I want to look at."

Kal noted the way Jackson smiled over at Becks.

"Sure, babe," Jackson said.

Becks looked happy. Kal liked seeing her happy. And in love with his brother.

She slung her backpack over her shoulder. "We'll probably see you tonight, Kal. Say goodbye to Hannah for us."

He grabbed his coffee and leaned against the counter. "Will do. Have a good day."

He knew that Becks and Jackson were aware that Hannah spent the night. Nothing happened around this house that everyone else didn't know about. Which got him to thinking about Jackson and Becks getting married.

It had been different for Rafe and Carmen. They'd gotten a house of their own. They could have their married-people privacy without having a third wheel underfoot. Maybe it was time he moved out so Jackson and Becks could have their space. Hannah had alluded to it, and now that he'd had some time to think about it, it was starting to make sense.

"Hey, you left me."

He looked up to see Hannah leaning against the railing. She was wearing one of his firefighter T-shirts that hung all the way past her thighs. Her hair was messy from sleep, and she was the hottest woman he'd ever laid eyes on. The way she smiled down at him stirred both physical and emotional things inside of him that were way too deep to think about on a Monday morning.

"I needed coffee and didn't want to wake you."

"I'm awake now. And I definitely need coffee. Should I get dressed first?"

He shook his head. "Jackson and Becks left for the day."

She came downstairs and got on her tiptoes to press a kiss to his lips. "Mmm. You taste like coffee. Where's mine?"

"Coming up." He brewed her a fresh cup and handed it to her. "Cream is in the fridge, sugar on the island."

"Thanks." She went to the refrigerator and poured a small amount of cream in hers, put the cream back and stood facing the fridge while she took her first couple of sips.

"I thought we might—"

She held out her hand, palm facing toward him to silence him, then took another couple of sips before she headed over and climbed onto one of the chairs at the island. "You always this cheery and talkative in the morning?" she half grumbled.

"It's not like you don't know me." Kal grinned at her.

"I knew you at school. That's not first thing in the morning."

"Ohhkay, and you're not a morning person. Obviously."

"I'm a delightful person—after I've had a cup of coffee."

"Duly noted." He went quiet and climbed onto the chair next to hers, trying not to notice how his shirt had ridden up on her, showing off her amazing legs. Instead, he grabbed his phone and checked the news and weather for the day, giving Hannah the space she needed. He noticed she drained her cup and went to the Keurig to make another.

After taking a few more sips, she asked, "Where did Jackson and Becks go off to?"

"Breakfast. Then to run errands and do stuff for the day. They weren't too specific. I think some wedding planning things were part of the day."

"That could be fun. For Becks."

"I dunno. I think Jackson is really into all the wedding planning."

"Really? I'm surprised. He doesn't strike me as the type to want to get involved."

"He loves all things Becks, and he wants to marry her. So if she's excited about wedding planning, he will be, too."

"Aww. That's sweet. How about you?"

"The wedding? I'll be there for both of them."

"No, not theirs. Your own someday. Will you be as excited about it?"

He shrugged. "Depends on the woman I marry, I imagine."

She frowned. "What do you mean?"

"I mean if I'm heart and soul, head over heels in love, and she's the be-all and end-all of my existence? Then yeah. I'll be into it."

She laughed. "What other woman *would* you marry, Kal? Some chick you met when you swiped right on Tinder?"

"Hey. It could happen. People who met on Tinder have gotten married."

"Really? You know this for a fact?"

"Well, no. But I'm sure it's happened. It has to have happened."

"Not a single person I know of has ever met a decent match on a dating app. Most men are only looking for a hookup."

"Not true. I've met women on dating apps. And went out with them."

"And subsequently had sex with them, right?"

He didn't answer.

"I thought so. And since you're not currently in the process of marrying any of them, I rest my case."

He rolled his eyes. "You can't damn an entire dating app based on my history. I was out for fun. And, for your information, so were the women I dated."

"And you know this to be true, how?"

"I put in my profile I wanted fun, not forever."

She gave him a scathing look. "Aren't you just the most charming asshole? So you set the women up at the beginning not to fall in love with you. Or else, right?"

"Hey, I was being honest. I wasn't in a place to be in a relationship at the time I was on those dating apps. I figured being up-front and clear with anyone I met was the right thing to do. Tell me that's a bad thing."

Now Hannah was the one who went silent.

He reached out to grasp her hand, but she pulled it away.

"Hannah."

"I don't know."

"Talk to me, Hannah. Tell me what you're thinking right now."

She took in a breath and let it out, then swiveled her chair around to face him. "What about now? How are you feeling about dating now?"

"You mean with you?"

She nodded, and he read the uncertainty on her face. Did she really think he was comparing her—them—to what he'd been doing four or five years ago?

Then again, she hadn't been in his life then. She'd known nothing about what his life was like in his early to mid-twenties. Or anything after they'd broken up when they were eighteen until now. Ten years was a long gap.

"After I . . . got over you, I partied my ass off in college. I met a lot of girls. But I also studied my ass off, too. My parents wanted each of us to get a degree, even though it's not required to apply to be a firefighter. So while I had a lot of opportunities back then, I didn't take as many as you might think. I mostly hung out with my friends.

"After college, I applied to the Fire Academy. Once I got in, I put everything I had into making it through that first probationary year. Not only to prove myself worthy as a firefighter, but to make sure I didn't do anything stupid to disgrace the Donovan name. So while I dated, I didn't want to get serious about anyone—not when I couldn't put a hundred percent of my focus on a woman. It wouldn't have been fair to them when all of my efforts were going into becoming a firefighter."

Hannah was listening with interest. Not judgement. So he continued.

"It wasn't until the past couple of years that I'd say I've done any long-term dating. My first and only serious relationship was with you, Hannah. And if that makes me an asshole for being honest with the women I went out with, then I guess I'm an asshole." He shrugged.

She reached out and swept her palm against his cheek. "You're not an asshole. And I'm sorry I said that. I guess I just had some different experiences with guys on those dating apps."

"I'm not surprised. A lot of guys on those sites *are* assholes. I just don't happen to be one of them."

"I'm sorry. Again. Sometimes I react instead of thinking things through. It's my worst fault. Forgive me?"

He took her hand, flipped it over and kissed her palm. "Forgiven."

"You know, I always had it in my mind that you were sleeping your way through the entire state after I left."

He laughed. "No. That's not how it went down. For a long time I kind of just . . . wallowed."

She tilted her head to the side. "Wallowed?"

"I missed you, Hannah. I took our breakup pretty hard."

"You broke up with me, remember?"

"Yeah. And I felt shitty about it. But staying together wouldn't have worked, and we both knew it. Doesn't mean leaving you was easy."

She gave him a sympathetic look. "It wasn't easy for me, either. And then I rebounded with Landon. He was supposed to be my escape, my ticket to freedom, and well, we know how that ended up."

"I'm sorry."

"Not your fault. My choices were my own, and I've had to live with the consequences of them. I've also left them in the past."

"Not me, though."

She frowned. "What do you mean?"

"I mean I was part of your past. But you haven't left me there. The exceptional part of your past."

She laughed. "Yeah, okay, sure. Most of my past has been left behind. Except for you."

"Good enough. Hey, how about we go out for breakfast?"

"That sounds good. I need to make a stop at home to change first, if you don't mind."

"I don't mind."

He went upstairs to put other clothes on, then they drove to her place. He was surprised it only took her ten minutes. She came out of her room wearing jeans, a white button-down shirt and white tennis shoes, her hair pulled up into a messy bun at the nape of her neck. She'd scrubbed her face, and she looked fresh and unmade-up, with only gloss on her lips.

"You remind me of high school," he said.

She flipped her head to the side. "What?"

"No makeup, tennis shoes, your hair pulled back. You look exactly the same as you did when we were in high school. Fresh and beautiful."

She stepped forward and smoothed her hands over his chest. "That might be the nicest compliment any man has ever given me." She raised up and kissed him.

Her kiss was a soft caress across his lips. He let her lead, and when she wanted more, he opened, her tongue slipping inside. When she grabbed hold of his tongue and sucked, his cock went instantly hard. The kiss was hot and passionate and demanding. He grabbed her butt and drew her against him so he could rub his aching erection against the softness of her body.

She moaned, then pushed at him and stepped away, taking his hand and leading him into the living room.

"Sit on the sofa," she said.

He wasn't about to argue with her, especially if that meant they could get more comfortable and make out some more.

"Undo your pants."

He blinked. Okay, more than making out. He was down for that. He undid his pants.

"Drop them to your ankles."

Now it was getting even better. He shrugged out of his pants and boxer briefs and slid them down. He expected Hannah to get naked, but instead, she got on her knees in front of him, spreading his legs apart so she could crawl between them.

His balls quivered at the sight of her sliding her fingers over his thighs, lifting his shirt and smoothing her hands over his skin.

"Babe," he whispered, but that was all he could manage because she took his cock in her hand and began to stroke his length. He kind of forgot to breathe because all he could do was watch the way her hand slid up and down on his shaft, her thumb rolling over the crest, teasing so softly he thought he might die from it.

And then she leaned over, tilted her head to look up at him and smiled in the most wickedly sexy way, right before she took him in her mouth. His cock disappeared inch by inch into her warm, wet mouth, her tongue swirling over his flesh as she took him to heaven with torturous licks and sucks. He tensed up and grabbed hold of the couch cushions to keep from blowing his load right then and there.

He breathed heavily, lifted up to feed more of his cock into her mouth and leaned forward to grab hold of her hair—one, to keep it off her face, and two, because he had to be able to see the beauty of her mouth moving, to see what he was feeling.

It was good. So damn good. And he was about to lose it, because she had taken him all the way in, and he was going to come.

"Hannah, I'm gonna come."

She kept working him, though, reaching under to massage his

balls with one hand and using the other to stroke the base of his cock. And there was nothing he could do to stop the explosion now, because he was there, his body jerking in hot spasms as he came with a groan and a hard shudder.

He fell back against the sofa and lay there, utterly useless and completely satisfied. Hannah kissed his thigh, climbing up his body to press a kiss to his neck and then his mouth.

She licked her lips and smiled at him. "Be right back."

He nodded, only vaguely aware of reality at the moment. His pants were still around his ankles, and he wasn't even sure what time it was, or what day it was. His brain had gone into a fog.

Eventually, he managed his bearings and got up, got dressed and went into the guest bathroom to clean up a little. When he came out, Hannah was in the kitchen going through her purse. He went over to her and turned her to face him.

He planted a long, deep kiss on her lips, then said, "Thank you for that."

"Oh, it was my pleasure."

"Definitely mine, too. Are you sure I can't return the favor before we go?"

She patted his arm. "I'd love that, but maybe later, because my stomach is telling me I'm hungry."

He couldn't argue with that, so they got in his truck and headed a few miles down the road to a restaurant. Hannah ordered a mushroom and spinach frittata, and Kal decided he wanted the standard bacon and eggs, along with pancakes.

When the food arrived, Hannah snagged a bite of his pancake.

She shrugged. "I needed something sweet."

"You need the extra carbs and sugar after that morning cardio workout."

She laughed, then slipped a piece of her frittata onto his plate. He scooped it up and ate it.

"That's good. I'm gonna have to make one."

"Always experimenting, aren't you?"

He shrugged. "I like food. Experimenting with new recipes is fun."

"Maybe I should have you come over and make me dinner on your days off."

He took a sip of his juice. "I'd love to."

"I was joking."

"I wasn't. I'd be happy to cook for you and your family anytime. Just say the word."

She stared at him across the table while she ate.

"What?"

"You're just . . . unique, Kal."

He grinned. "Yeah? That's good. I like being unique. I mean, besides my incredible good looks and all."

Now she rolled her eyes at him. "Never mind. I take it all back."

He laughed, and they went back to eating. But he couldn't deny her compliment felt good.

After their server cleared their plates, she asked, "So what's on the agenda today?"

"What would you like to do? I'm game for anything."

"Actually, there's an exhibit at one of the museums I've been meaning to catch. I know it might not be something you're interested in."

He shrugged. "What kind of exhibit?"

Her phone buzzed, so she held up her hand and looked down at her phone, then frowned. "It's Oliver's school. I need to take this."

He waited while she answered the call.

"Okay, what happened?" she asked. "How badly is he hurt?"

Kal's stomach tightened. He motioned for their server and got up to pay the bill.

When he came back, Hannah was by the door. She looked

pale and really worried, which meant he needed to get in his fire-fighter head and keep her calm.

"Oliver fell playing ball on the playground. They think his arm might be broken. Can you take me home so I can go get him?"

"It'll be faster if I take you right to the school."

She nodded. "Thanks."

They got in his truck, and Hannah gave him directions to Oliver's school. Fortunately, they weren't far away. He pulled into the parking lot, and Hannah shot out of the truck, but Kal caught up with her.

"Hannah." He took her arm. "Before we go in, take a few deep breaths. The last thing Oliver needs to see is you panicking right now."

She breathed in, then out. "You're right. Thanks."

They walked down the sidewalk toward the front entrance.

"I broke my arm when I was six," he said.

She looked over at him and frowned. "You did? I don't think you ever told me that."

He shrugged. "It's because I was stupid. Who tells their girl-friend they did something dumb? Anyway, I was fine. And Oliver will be fine, too. Don't worry."

She nodded, and they went to the front office, then were di-rected to the nurse's office, where Oliver was sitting with his left arm cradled against his chest. The nurse had made a sling for him. When Oliver saw Hannah, he started crying.

"It hurts, Momma."

Hannah came over and sat next to him, cradling him against her. Kal knew from his experiences with his own mom after she'd adopted him that motherly love was the best medicine when you were hurt.

"Are you his father?" the nurse asked.

"No, I'm Mrs. Clark's—" He looked over at Oliver. "Friend. But I'm a firefighter and a paramedic."

She nodded. "It's definitely broken. I can tell from the angle of his arm."

"Got it. We'll take him straight to the ER."

Kal went over and crouched down in front of Oliver. "Roughing it up on the playground, huh, buddy?"

"We were playing kickball, and me and Jose were fighting over the ball. I slipped and held out my hand and then something snapped in my arm. It really hurts, Kal."

Kal ruffled Oliver's hair, then framed his face between his hands. "I know it does. We'll get you to the hospital, and they'll fix it right up."

After thanking the nurse, Kal didn't even bother trying to walk Oliver to the truck. He picked him up, and Hannah walked next to them. Oliver laid his head on Kal's shoulder, and Kal felt such a tug of emotion he didn't know what to do with all these feelings. What he did know was he didn't want Oliver to hurt.

He buckled Oliver in the back seat, and Hannah sat back there with him while they drove to the hospital. They checked into the ER and waited for someone to call them. Fortunately, they didn't have to wait long, and they were put into a room. He was surprised when he saw Carmen come into their room, looking efficient and totally in charge in her nurse's scrubs. Even Hannah's face brightened.

"Oh, hey, Carmen," Hannah said.

"Hey, Hannah. I saw you two when they brought you in, so I thought I'd take your case. This must be Oliver. I'm Carmen Donovan, and I'm going to help take care of you today."

"Nurse Carmen is a friend of ours, Oliver," Kal said. "And she's a very good nurse."

"I fell in the playground and hurt my arm."

"Poor baby. Let's take a look." Carmen untied the sling and examined Oliver's arm. When Oliver winced, Hannah did, too, but Kal kept a smile on his face and nodded at Oliver, letting him know it was all going to be all right.

Kal could tell from the first look at Oliver's awkwardly angled arm that it was broken.

A doctor came in as well and introduced himself as Dr. Lance before examining Oliver's arm.

"Looks like you broke your arm, Oliver," Dr. Lance said. "But we'll need to get some pictures to be sure."

"It hurts," Oliver said.

"I'm sure it does." He said a few things to Carmen, who nodded.

"I'll be back soon to get you fixed up."

After he stepped out, Carmen said, "We'll need to get some pictures of your arm with our X-ray machine."

Oliver looked up at his mom, his eyes wide with delight and pain momentarily forgotten. "I get to have an X-ray!"

"That's very exciting, baby."

Carmen rewrapped Oliver's arm and kept the sling close to his chest. "I'll be right back to get you some medicine for the pain." She handed Oliver the TV remote. "Watch some TV. Would you like something to drink?"

"Can I have a soda?"

Carmen looked at Hannah, who nodded. Oliver took the remote and turned the TV on.

"I'll bring one to you. Hannah, can I talk to you?"

"Sure." She stepped out, and Kal said, "I'll wait in here with Oliver."

She gave him a grateful smile, then walked outside with Carmen.

"So, buddy," Kal said. "Did you know I broke my arm when I was a kid?"

"Nuh-uh. You did? Did it hurt like mine hurts?"

"It hurt bad. I had to get it reset, then had a cast on for two whole months."

"No way. Did all your friends sign your cast?"

"They did. It was pretty cool." Back when he still went to school, when he still lived at home with his mom and stepdad. He could still remember how pissed-off his stepdad had been that day. As if he'd fallen off the top of the slide on purpose. His mother hadn't even stepped in to defend him when, tired and crying after coming home from the hospital, he'd been forced to sit up in bed and listen to his drunken stepfather rail at him for an hour about how now he'd have to pay the hospital bill because Kal had been stupid and careless. Then his stepdad threatened to break his other arm so he couldn't wipe his own ass.

He'd never been happier to get the hell out of that house. Being homeless had been better than living in fear of being beaten all the time. Because those threats of beatings had turned to real beatings. And his mother had done nothing to help him, too afraid of taking her own beatings to defend her little boy.

As he looked at Oliver, who wasn't much older than he'd been when the hitting had started, Kal couldn't comprehend anyone wanting to hurt an innocent child. He'd sworn that one day he'd have kids of his own, and he'd shower them with unconditional love to make up for the painful childhood he'd endured.

He had his adoptive parents to thank for turning around his mindset, for giving him all the love he'd never had during the first decade or so of his life. Because Josh and Laurel Donovan were the best, and he'd been damned lucky to have them as his parents.

And Oliver? He might not have had the best dad, but he sure as hell had a fantastic mom.

Carmen came back in with a soda for Oliver and some liquid meds, which Carmen said was for his pain.

"Where's my mom?" Oliver asked.

"She told me to tell you she was going to go outside to call your grandma and let her know what happened."

"Okay. Thanks for the soda, Nurse Carmen."

Carmen smiled. "You're welcome. And that medicine should make your pain feel better. They should be coming in to take you to X-ray soon."

Not long after Carmen left the room, Hannah came back. "Grandma says to tell you she's really sorry you got hurt, and she's going to fix macaroni and cheese for dinner."

Oliver grinned. "That's my favorite."

"I know," Hannah said with a smile.

"Carmen gave him pain meds. It should dial down his pain pretty quickly, but might make him drowsy," Kal told her.

She nodded. "Thanks."

The techs came in to take Oliver off to X-ray, and Hannah went with him, so Kal had a minute to step out. Carmen was working the desk right near the room. He didn't want to bother her, but she looked up and motioned with her head for him to come over.

"How was the honeymoon?" he asked.

She smiled. "Amazing. I don't think I've been that relaxed in years. Rafe and I laid on the beach, sipped cocktails and napped a lot. We did some water sports and ate so much food I'm going to need to walk miles every day to lose all the weight I gained."

"Bullshit. You look great. I'm glad you had a good time."

"Thanks. Sorry about Oliver. That must have been so scary for Hannah."

"Yeah, it was. But she's handling it."

Carmen tapped her pen on the desk. "She's handling it like a champion. Trust me, I see parents fall apart all the time when they bring their injured kids in here. And it just makes the kid even more scared. Hannah's doing fine."

"I'll let you get back to it because I know you're busy."

"Thanks. We need to all get together and catch up. We'll make plans."

"Okay."

He went back to the room and waited. It wasn't long before Hannah and Oliver came back from the X-ray room. Oliver climbed back into the bed and started watching TV again, but he fell asleep within a few minutes.

"Obviously, the pain meds worked on him," Kal said.

"I'm so glad," Hannah said. "It hurts me to see him in pain."

Kal laid his hand over hers. "He's gonna be okay, Hannah. This is almost a rite of passage for kids."

She laughed. "That's true. It's hard to go through childhood unscathed, without getting a bone broken or having to get stitches."

He leaned back in his chair. "Yeah? What was yours?"

"Bonked my head on the edge of a counter. Concussion. Slid off a teeter-totter, five stitches on the back of my head. Broke my toe tripping over a curb while barefoot."

That one made him cringe. "Ouch."

"Yes, surprisingly, a broken toe hurts a lot."

Despite having a past with her, and all the years in high school they knew each other, Kal was surprised they still had things to learn about each other.

He liked that.

The doctor came in with Carmen after a few minutes.

"His wrist is broken, and I'll need to reset it," Dr. Lance said to Hannah. "We can do a local anesthetic so he won't feel anything."

Hannah exhaled. "That's good. And I can be with him while you do that?"

"Of course. I'll have the staff gather the materials, and I'll be in shortly."

Oliver stirred awake, so Hannah and Carmen helped explain to him what would happen.

"It won't hurt?" Oliver asked.

"We'll give you an injection, and that'll sting a little," Carmen said. "But after that, you won't feel a thing."

"Can I watch?"

Carmen smiled. "Sure."

They had to wait awhile before someone came in, but Oliver fell back asleep, and Kal went up to the dining hall and got Hannah and him something to drink. They watched TV for a while and waited. It wasn't his first trip to an ER, so he was used to waiting it out.

Finally, one of the techs came in with a tray filled with equipment and set it next to Oliver's bed. Kal made sure to stay in the corner of the room, out of the way, while Dr. Lance and Carmen got to work on Oliver. Hannah held Oliver's hand while they numbed the area, and the doctor got to work resetting the bone and splinting it.

Oliver handled everything so well. He didn't even wince when they numbed his wrist area. He seemed more interested in what the doctor was doing, asking a lot of questions through each step. Fortunately, this doc seemed to be a really good guy, patient in answering all of Oliver's questions.

Once the splint was on, the doctor told Oliver how brave he'd been and that he was his favorite patient of the day.

Oliver grinned widely with pride.

After Dr. Lance left the room, Carmen pulled out paperwork and went over it with Hannah. "Here's your at-home care instructions. Minimal activity for Oliver here. No sports, mister," she said to him.

"Aww, really? I can't play soccer?"

"No, I'm sorry, buddy."

Oliver looked crestfallen. Kal felt a lot of sympathy for him. He knew what it was like to have his activities restricted, and it sucked.

"He'll need to see an orthopedist in a week to put a cast on after the swelling goes down," Carmen said. "That information is in the packet, and someone will contact you tomorrow. There's detail on pain management as well. And I've written down my cell, so if you have any questions, call me."

Hannah hugged Carmen. "Thank you."

"Plus, you have an EMT here," she said, looking at Kal, "and he knows how things work, too. He's not entirely useless."

"Hey," Kal said.

Carmen and Hannah grinned at each other.

They gathered the paperwork together, and Kal helped Oliver off the bed. He was still a little out of it from the pain medication, so Kal made sure to keep him close as they headed to the truck.

"Sorry about this," Hannah said as they drove to her house.

"About what?"

"We had a day planned."

"Hey, you have a kid. Life happens. We roll with it, right?"

She reached over and squeezed his arm. "Thank you for understanding."

When they got to the house, Hannah's mom came outside and helped Oliver out of the truck. She kissed Oliver on the top of his head.

"My poor baby boy. What happened to you?"

Oliver filled her in on his day while they walked into the house.

"Well, I should go," Kal said. "I know you want to get him settled in."

She frowned. "Wait. You don't want to stay for macaroni and cheese?"

Kal laughed. "As tempting as that sounds, I think you have enough to handle."

She laced her arm with his. "You don't get away that easily. Come with me."

He thought he'd be in the way, but he had to admit, he was worried about Oliver and wanted to make sure he'd be all right. He was relieved when Hannah dragged him into the house.

When he walked in, Oliver was sitting on the sofa, feet up, his slinged arm propped up on a pillow.

"Grandma made lemonade, Kal," he said.

Kal went to sit next to Oliver. "That's awesome. And I hear you're having mac and cheese for dinner. That's one of my favorites."

"Mine, too."

"I think I'll go get some lemonade, buddy. I'll be back." He went into the kitchen to find Paige and Hannah talking.

"When you called I was so worried," Paige said. "He's okay, then?"

Hannah reached out and smoothed her hand over Paige's arm. "He's going to be fine, Mom. In a week he'll get a cast on. Paperwork with instructions are on the table, so you can read everything."

"Thanks." Paige looked out into the living room where Oliver's feet were rocking back and forth to an action scene on the movie he was watching on TV.

"He seems fine, Paige," Kal said. "Kids break bones. They're pretty resilient, ya know."

"Oh, I know. I went through it with Hannah."

"Yeah, she told me." He reached up into the cabinet to pull out a glass. Paige filled it with ice and lemonade. "I heard all about the stitches and the concussion, and the broken toe."

"Did you tell him about the time you nearly cut your finger off when you decided you wanted to 'help me' in the kitchen?"

"She did not tell me that."

Hannah wiggled all ten of her fingers. "As you can see, I have all my digits, and it wasn't as bad as my mother is about to make it out to be."

"There was blood everywhere. She sliced her finger cutting a tomato. I couldn't tell where the tomato was because of all the blood."

Kal could well imagine, since finger cuts, especially deep ones, tended to bleed a lot.

"Did you get stitches?"

"Two, which were hardly necessary, but Mom panicked."

Paige lifted her chin. "I never panic. It was a deep cut that needed to be closed."

Hannah looked over at Kal and shrugged. "I lived."

He laughed. "Obviously. Were you allowed in the kitchen after that?"

"Not for a very long time," Paige said.

"Whatever. It was a minor slip, and I'm very good with knives now."

"Good to know," Kal said, looking over to see Oliver's feet relaxed on the reclining sofa. He took his lemonade and strolled into the living room to see Oliver had fallen asleep, his head cranked in what looked like a really uncomfortable position. Kal repositioned him, laying him down so that his arm would still be propped up. Oliver had his knees drawn close like he was cold, so Kal dragged the blanket off the top of the sofa and covered him, then patted his shoulder.

"You're gonna be fine, buddy," he whispered.

He grabbed his lemonade off the coffee table and headed back into the kitchen to find both Hannah and Paige staring at him.

"What? He fell asleep and his positioning was awkward."

"It was very sweet of you, Kal," Paige said.

Hannah looked like she might cry, tears glistening in her eyes. "I'll be right back."

She headed down the hall, went to her room and shut the door.

"Did I do something wrong?" he asked Paige.

Paige grasped his arm. "No, honey. You did everything right.

She's done it all by herself for so long that even the smallest things that you do to help are a big deal to her. Thank you for that."

"I'm glad I was around to help today."

She squeezed his arm. "I am, too."

Hannah came down the hall. "Sorry, I had something in my eye. Allergies, probably."

She looked like she'd been crying. After the day she'd had, no one could blame her. As strong as his mom was, he also knew how much she cared about all of them. She'd held it together every time one of them got hurt. And then she'd go to her room, and when she came out later, her eyes would be puffy.

You could be a strong woman and still cry.

He went over to her and folded her in his arms.

"I'm okay, Kal," she said, but she didn't pull away.

"I know you are. I also know that's your baby asleep on the sofa, and he fell and broke his wrist today, and that was some scary shit. So it's okay to be upset about it."

He felt her shuddering sigh as she leaned into him. He rubbed her back, hoping in some way to let her know that she didn't have to go through this alone. He laid his chin on the top of her head and closed his eyes, and just . . . stilled. This moment right here? He could do this forever, could feel her heart beating against him, could feel her arms around him. It made him want to protect her—and Oliver—so that nothing could hurt either of them.

Paige cleared her throat. "So, who's hungry?"

Hannah stepped back, swiped her cheeks where tears had fallen again and smiled up at Kal. "I am. How about you?"

He grinned. "Are you kidding? The only reason I stayed was for the mac and cheese."

She laughed. "Okay, then. Let's get cooking."

Kal offered to help, but Hannah and Paige shooed him out of the kitchen, so he went and sat in the living room. Oliver woke up and said he had to go to the bathroom. Kal went with him and helped him out in there since he was going to have to learn to manage things one armed for a while, at least until the sling came off and he got the cast on. After that, they sat at the table and Oliver drank his lemonade.

"At least you broke your left wrist and you're right-handed," Kal said. "You can still do homework."

Oliver gave Kal a look. "That's good?"

Kal laughed. "Yeah, it's good. And wait 'til you go to school tomorrow. Everyone will want to see your splint with you looking all cool now."

"I look cool?"

"Yeah, you do. Like a bad— Well, you look really awesome."

Oliver beamed a smile.

Dinner was good. The macaroni and cheese was spectacular, and they had chicken tenders with it, along with a green salad and a fruit salad. He was happy to see that Oliver ate well. Typical for kids. No matter what happened, they could still fill their stomachs.

After dinner, Hannah said she was going to give Oliver a bath, which meant a lot of wrapping and maneuvering, so Kal knew it was time for him to leave.

Kal walked over to Oliver. "Get some rest, buddy. I'll be back to check on you soon."

"Okay. Thanks for hanging out today, Kal." Oliver put his one good arm around Kal to hug him.

Kal's heart squeezed as he hugged Oliver back.

"I'll walk you out," Hannah said.

Kal said goodbye to Paige, then walked outside with Hannah. It was a clear night, and humid.

"Looks like a rain shower's coming in soon," she said.

"Yeah." He stopped at his truck and turned around. "He'll be okay."

She nodded. "I know he will. Thank you for being there for me. For Oliver."

He tipped her chin and brushed his lips across hers. "Always will be."

She gave him a look he couldn't figure out. Maybe surprise, maybe disbelief. He wasn't sure. And now wasn't the time to question it, so he got in his truck, waved and backed down the driveway.

What he really wanted to do tonight was stay, to make sure Oliver slept okay, to be there for Hannah because he knew she'd be emotional about what happened today.

He realized on the drive home he had gotten himself deeply involved. Not only with Hannah, but with her son.

And he honestly had no idea how she felt. Which meant he might be in trouble.

"MOMMA, IS KAL YOUR BOYFRIEND?"

Hannah paused as she was tucking Oliver into bed, not knowing how to answer.

Honestly, she supposed. "Yes, I guess he is. What do you think about that?"

He shifted since he was piled up with pillows under his broken wrist. "I like him. He's nice to you. And to me. And he doesn't make you cry."

Her stomach knotted and her heart clenched. "He is nice, and I like him very much. So it doesn't upset you that I'm seeing him?"

"No. You need someone to love. I mean, you got me and Grandma, and we love you and you love us. But it's good that you got Kal now, too. You can never love enough people, right?"

She smoothed her hand over the top of the blanket, then kissed Oliver's forehead.

"Right, baby. Get some rest now. I love you."

"Love you, too, Momma."

She turned out the light and left his door partially open. She went into her room, shut the door and leaned against it, finally releasing the tears she'd been holding in all day.

CHAPTER 20

HANNAH'S MOM HAD TO BOOT HER OUT OF THE HOUSE Thursday night when her friend Veronica invited her to a girls' night out. She initially begged off, claiming she had to stay home and take care of Oliver. Then, when she told her mom about Veronica's call, her mother argued that Oliver was fine, she could take care of him, and that Hannah needed to get out and relax, because she was wound up and hovering over Oliver way too much.

Mom was right, of course. She had been hovering, and it was probably annoying her son. She knew she was irritating her mother. She felt the tension sitting on her shoulders like a boulder. Maybe a night out wouldn't be such a bad idea.

Kal had stopped by this morning before Oliver went to school, and even he'd mentioned that she looked tired. Not exactly the thing she wanted to hear from the guy she was dating. He'd asked her if she wanted to go out tonight, and she'd told him she wanted to stay home and be with Oliver. And then she hadn't even invited him over.

She laid her head in her hands and realized what a hot mess

she was. Her kid had a broken wrist. It wasn't exactly the end of the world. In fact, Oliver was managing his arm just fine, even though he had to work with the sling until he got his cast on next week. To him—no big deal. To her? Huge. She'd been a giant stress ball all week long.

That did it. She was going out tonight. But first she was going to text Kal.

She got out her phone and started typing.

I'm sorry about this morning. My head isn't in the game this week.

He replied back a few minutes later. *You were fine. Don't worry about it.*

She sent another text: *I know you asked me out, and I said no, but I'm going out with my friend Veronica for girls' night. Don't be mad.*

He sent back a laughing emoji. *Not mad. Have a good time. You deserve it.*

What she didn't deserve was a man like Kal in her life. Why was he always so understanding about everything? Didn't anything piss him off?

She typed a return text: *Thanks. Talk soon.*

There was so much more she'd wanted to say to him about how she felt, but she couldn't say it in a text message. She wasn't even sure she could form the words, since they were more emotional than logical.

How *did* she feel? And did she have the right to those feelings? Because she really was a mess right now. How could she bring a man into her life when said life was so unstable? She lived with her mother, she was just starting to make the salon work, and then there was Oliver. No way could she include a relationship in all of that.

In fact, she decided the best course of action was not to think about it. Instead, she got ready to go out. She put on a skirt and top, slid into her heels and kissed both her son and her mom and headed out the door before she changed her mind about that, too.

They met at Veronica's house, which meant she could say hello to Veronica's husband, Eddie, along with their three-year-old daughter, Shay, an adorable strawberry blonde with the cutest curls Hannah had ever seen. Eddie sat patiently on the floor while the toddler clipped small bows onto his hair.

"Best you've ever looked, babe," Veronica said.

"I like the purple one the best," Eddie said, batting his lashes at her. "Brings out my eyes."

"You should wear that to work," Tina, one of their friends, said.

"You think? It would look great with my suit."

"I might have to snatch one of those for Carl," Jess said. "He'd look so cute wearing that when he changes someone's oil or puts in a new engine."

Everyone laughed.

Veronica bent over to kiss her husband and daughter.

"You're a good daddy," Veronica said. "I love you."

"Love you, too, babe," he said. "Have fun tonight."

Hannah felt a well of emotion. There was nothing like seeing two people so obviously in love. She was happy for her friend.

"Bye, Mama," Shay said.

"Bye, my love."

They ordered a car so they could all drink, which sounded perfect to Hannah. She might regret it during her long day at the salon tomorrow, but screw it. She was having a cocktail or two tonight with her girls. She hadn't made time to see them since the reunion, and they had a lot to catch up on.

They went to YOT Bar and Kitchen and got a seat with a view of the water. Hannah took a sip of the mojito she ordered. It was sweet and minty and hit all her relaxation buttons.

"So, Hannah," Veronica asked. "Tell us everything."

She blinked. "What do you mean?"

"I mean your job, Oliver, what you've been doing. Who you've been doing?"

Jess laughed. "Yes, especially the *who* you've been doing."

"Oh." She stirred her drink. "Oliver broke his wrist this week."

"Oh no," Tina said. "What happened?"

She filled them in on Oliver's accident, then they all started talking about their kids, and then about their friend Mary's new baby girl, which gave her a reprieve from discussing her dating life—at least through another cocktail.

"Are you dating anyone, Hannah?" Jess asked.

She inwardly winced, but she knew she was going to have to talk about Kal. These were her high school friends. Plus they all knew Kal.

"I'm sort of seeing Kal Donovan."

Veronica's eyes widened. She laid her palm flat on the table and leaned forward. "Wait. What? You're dating Kal again?"

"Seriously?" Tina asked.

"Tell us everything," Jess said, signaling their server for another round of drinks.

By the time she'd finished her third mojito, she'd spilled the entire story of her and Kal. And her face was numb. She was pretty sure her toes were numb, too.

"Wow," Jess said. "You and Kal Donovan. Who would have ever thought the two of you would hook up again after all these years."

Tina nodded. "It's like you were meant to be. Like Romeo and Juliet."

"Who both ended up dead, Tina," Veronica said.

"Okay, maybe not those two. Like . . . like . . . I don't know. Give me a romantic couple."

"Harry Potter and Ginny Weasley," Hannah said, laying her chin in her hand.

They all looked at her. Hannah shrugged. "Oliver and I are reading *Harry Potter*. And I've seen the movies. They're perfect together. Friends first, and they both stand up for and protect the other through everything."

"Okay, maybe," Veronica said.

"I could definitely see it," Jess said. "You and Kal were always so tight in high school. And now he's back in your life."

"It's like it's meant to be," Tina repeated, a dreamy look on her face. "It's so romantic."

Hannah waved her hand. "We're just having some fun. It's . . . familiar, ya know?"

"Is that all it is, though?" Veronica asked. "Familiar?"

"I . . . I don't know. I feel a lot of things for Kal. I always have. But I don't know if I have the time right now for that kind of relationship. I'm not sure I ever want to have another deep relationship again."

Veronica laid her hand on Hannah's arm. "Of course you don't. You got hurt by someone who was supposed to be your partner in life. No wonder you're anxious about falling in love again."

She wasn't about to tell her friends she had never loved Landon. Not the way she loved . . .

She wasn't going to think about that. She was pretty sure she couldn't put together a coherent thought at all right now.

"I don't know. We're having a good time together. We include Oliver in a lot of the things we do. It's good right now, you know?"

Jess nodded. "And that's enough."

"Exactly," Tina said. "You shouldn't be in a rush. Take things slow. Whatever happens between the two of you will . . . happen. On its own. Organically."

"Right. Organically." Whatever that meant. Her brain went

fuzzy again. The conversation was deep, more than she'd wanted to have tonight. "We should order some food."

"That sounds good," Tina said.

They grabbed their menus, and Hannah tried to focus on the dishes listed. What was in those mojitos anyway? When their server came over, she decided to switch to water. Because she was definitely getting shit-faced, and that hadn't been her intention.

They ordered their food.

"And another round of drinks, too," Veronica said.

Hannah cringed. She hoped she remembered the right address when it was time to go home.

KAL WAS PLAYING A VIDEO GAME, COMPLETELY DESTROY-ing the enemy, when the doorbell rang.

"Dammit." He frowned, paused the game and went to answer the door, surprised to see not only Hannah, but Veronica, Tina and Jess as well.

"Hi, Kal," Veronica said. "Your girlfriend is toasted, but she wanted to come see you. She's all yours now."

Hannah, who was leaning against the doorjamb, gave him a sloppy smile. "I wanted to see you."

"Hi there. Who's driving?"

"Jeff, our friendly Lyft driver. He's taking us all home to-night."

"Okay. Hang on a sec." He walked Hannah over to the sofa and sat her down, then leaned over to whisper to her. "Don't go anywhere, okay?"

She smiled up at him, then tried to pat his face and missed. "You are so hot."

He grinned. "Thanks. Stay here, okay? I'll be right back."

"Okay."

He walked outside where the Lyft driver, Jeff, was sitting in the car. Jeff rolled down the window.

"Handling them all right?"

"They're fine. Tipsy, but they seem to be having a good time. They sang to me. I'll make sure they all get home okay."

"Good. Thanks. I'll call their husbands and let them know you're in the process of safely delivering them."

"You got it."

Kal smiled. Jeff seemed like a good guy, but he wanted to make sure no one was going to take advantage of a group of drunk women.

He held the door open for the women, who slid inside. Veronica grasped his arm.

"Take care of my girl," she said.

"I will. Say hi to Eddie for me."

She kissed his cheek. "I'll do that. Come by and see us sometime."

"I'll definitely do that."

He closed the door and watched as Jeff slowly backed down the driveway, then went inside.

He texted Eddie, Carl and Ray and let them know to expect delivery of their inebriated wives, then went back inside, only to find a path of discarded clothes instead of Hannah.

Like a trail of bread crumbs, he picked up one red high heel in the living room, another one in the kitchen, a blouse at the entrance to the stairs, a bracelet on the landing, a bra hanging over the bannister, a skirt at the top of the stairs and a pair of panties at the entrance to his bedroom.

At least she'd managed to find the right bedroom, so maybe she wasn't as drunk as he'd thought.

He was also thankful that Jackson and Becks were out tonight. Surely, Hannah wouldn't have done her striptease in front of them.

Then again, he'd done some weird shit when he'd been drunk. In front of more people than that.

He opened the door to the bedroom to find Hannah lying on her back on his bed. He laid her clothes on the chair, then approached the bed. Even without the light on he heard her deep, even breathing, and could tell she was asleep.

He shook his head and smiled, then pulled the covers back to tuck the blanket up to her chin. He kissed her forehead.

"I wanted to tell you something," she whispered.

He sat on the side of the bed and smoothed her hair back. "Sure. What is it?"

"Something . . . portant. 'Bout you and me. And stuff."

He waited, but she snuggled into the pillow and that was it. She was out.

He wondered what she'd wanted to talk about. It seemed important enough to have the driver bring her here.

Then again, she was drunk. And who knew what had been in her head?

Either way, he wasn't going to get any answers tonight.

He got up and closed the bedroom door, went downstairs and grabbed his phone and called Paige to let her know where Hannah was, and what condition she was in.

Paige laughed. "How drunk?"

"Pretty drunk, from what I can tell. We only had a short conversation before she went upstairs and passed out cold in my bed."

He heard Paige's sigh. "Poor Hannah. She's been so stressed this week. I told her to relax. I guess she really did."

Kal laughed. "Apparently."

"Her car is at Veronica's, and I think she mentioned she had a ten a.m. hair appointment tomorrow."

"Not a problem. I'm on shift tomorrow anyway, so I have to be up early. I'll drive her to Veronica's to pick up her car."

"Thanks, Kal. I appreciate you taking care of her."

"Sure. I'll talk to you soon, Paige."

He clicked off and laid his phone down, then went into the living room to turn off the game he'd been playing. He headed to the kitchen to fix himself a glass of water, glancing upstairs to his bedroom.

What he really wanted to do was go upstairs, strip off his clothes and wrap his body around the woman in his bed. The woman who was passed out naked in his bed.

Instead, he grabbed his glass, went into the living room and turned on the TV, figuring he'd watch sports for a while until he got tired.

He already knew he wasn't going to get tired for a very long time.

CHAPTER 21

HANNAH WOKE UP TO THE FEEL OF A WARM BODY SUR-
rounding her. That was nice.

She also had a dry mouth and a pounding headache.

Last night came back to her in a rush. All that drinking, and
then getting into the car, and then . . .

And then . . .

Her eyes shot open. Where the hell was she? She tried to get
up, but those arms around her held her still.

"It's okay, Hannah. You're with me."

Her pounding heart settled at the smooth sound of Kal's raspy
voice. She relaxed against him.

"I came here last night."

"Yeah."

"And then what happened?"

"You stripped naked, climbed in my bed and passed out."

She did not remember that part at all. "Really? That was it?"

"That was it."

"Huh." How disappointing. "I need to pee."

He let go of her, and she slid out of bed and went into the bathroom. It was still dark outside, which was a good thing, because she had work today. She used the bathroom, washed her hands, found Kal's toothpaste and rubbed it around her teeth, which helped a little. She went back into the bedroom and sat on the side of the bed.

"There's a glass of water and some acetaminophen on the nightstand."

"Bless you," she said, feeling around in the dark for the glass. She found the tablets and took them, then slid back in bed, positioning her body back against his for warmth. "What time is it?"

"Five thirty."

"Are you on shift today?"

"Yeah. But I've got plenty of time. I called your mom last night and let her know you were with me. She told me she'd take Oliver to school."

"Thank you for doing that. I'm sorry about barging in on you last night."

"You didn't. You know I never mind having you around."

"I can't believe I just popped in like that."

He smoothed his hand down her arm and over her hip. Her body responded with a flash of goose bumps. "You don't need an invitation, Hannah. You're welcome over here anytime."

"I don't want to assume."

His hand stilled. "Assume what?"

"That you're available all the time. You could have had someone else here."

He laughed and nuzzled the back of her neck. "There's no one else but you."

"You mean last night."

"I mean at all."

Her belly fluttered at his words. So powerful and important, making her want to roll over and have a serious conversation with him about where they were in their relationship and what it all meant. But that was a conversation meant for later, when they both had the time to really talk it out.

"And if you hadn't been passed-out drunk, I would have come up here and gotten naked with you."

His erection brushed against her thighs. She was damn sorry she'd missed that. "You're naked now."

He cupped her breast, his thumb teasing lazy circles around her nipple. "Yeah, I am."

He played with her breasts and nipples until her body throbbed, slid his cock between her thighs, stroking back and forth, making her rock back toward him. "I like that."

"You'll like it even more when I'm inside you."

He slipped away long enough to put on a condom, then he was back. He grasped her hip and slid inside of her, making her gasp at the electric contact.

He rolled her over onto her knees. She braced herself on her elbows as he drove deep. The pleasure was so intense, so fiery-hot that she thought she might die from the sensations of his body pressed so intimately to hers. She reached down to rub her clit, to get herself there as he continued to thrust until she was right on the verge of orgasm.

"Oh, fuck yeah, do it," he said, his voice deep and guttural as he dug his fingers into her hips and drove his cock deeply into her. She couldn't take these intense sensations, the way he moved against her, the way her body was so connected to his.

She splintered, feeling as if a thousand stars had exploded within her when she came. Kal pistoned against her and groaned as he climaxed, only enhancing the waves of her own orgasm.

He rolled them to their sides and kissed her shoulder while they both came down from that incredible high. He stroked her all over, and Hannah had to admit she liked the feel of his hands roaming her body. She wished they could stay like this all day.

"Okay, so I meant for that to be a slow and lazy morning lovemaking session," he said.

Her lips curved. "Do you hear me complaining?"

"I heard . . . something. Screaming, maybe?"

She laughed and rolled over to face him. "I did not scream."

He swept her hair away from her face and kissed her. "I definitely heard yelling."

"Okay, stud. Whatever makes you feel good."

"You make me feel good." He rubbed her bottom lip with his thumb, then kissed her again, this time more deeply, until she got lost in the taste of his lips, the feel of his tongue licking along hers.

He rolled on top of her, and their limbs tangled, and this time when he put the condom on, he made love to her slowly, his hand entwined with hers as he rocked in and out of her with deliberate strokes until she broke in a cry that he absorbed with his lips on hers. He released with her, the two of them shuddering together in one epic climax that left her shaken.

Something about the way Kal made love to her shattered her. The way he looked at her when he was inside of her was so much more than sex. It was unnerving. Monumental.

Their legs were still entwined, his heart beating against hers. And she hated that she had to leave him today, when all she wanted to do was explore her feelings, to feel his skin against hers. To do this all day long until these feelings made sense to her.

"I have to go," he said.

"I know. Me, too."

They got up and went into the bathroom to clean up. Hannah got dressed and paused in the middle of putting on her blouse. "Where did I strip last night?"

"You started in the living room, and left me clothing bread crumbs all the way across the house toward my room."

She tilted her head back to stare up at the ceiling in mortification. "Tell me Jackson and Becks weren't home when I did this."

He laughed. "They were out."

"Thank. God. I kind of hope I wouldn't have put on such a public display if they'd been here."

"You wouldn't have."

She shimmied into her skirt. "How do you know?"

He shrugged. "Because I know you."

He had such faith in her.

They got dressed, and after having a quick cup of coffee, he drove her back to Veronica's house, and she fished her keys out of her purse. He walked with her to her car, and she couldn't help but admire how fine he looked in his jeans and T-shirt. Thick clouds were playing with the sun this morning, bathing the sky in a soft orange glow. She wished they had all the time in the world today, to talk, to take a walk, to just be together.

But that wasn't her reality. Or his, either.

"Thank you for taking care of me last night. And this morning."

He leaned into her and laid his hand on her hip. "My pleasure. Twice."

She grinned and wrapped her hand around his neck to pull him toward her for a kiss. "Have a good day."

"You, too."

She got in her car, and Kal pulled away first. She headed toward home, realizing that tension she'd been carrying all week was gone.

The night out with the girls had definitely helped. But the morning with Kal had been what she'd really needed.

She had a smile on her face as she entered the highway toward home.

CHAPTER 22

KAL WASN'T SURE HOW HANNAH WOULD FEEL ABOUT AN invite to his parents' home for Saturday night dinner, but the whole family was going be there, and he wanted Hannah to be there, too.

Surprisingly, when he'd asked her, she'd said yes. His mother said to tell Hannah to bring Oliver along, too, since this was a family barbecue. Hannah had seemed happy that Oliver was included. And Kal was pretty pumped about it, too. He wanted everyone to meet Oliver, and for Oliver to meet his whole family.

And since Oliver finally had his cast on, he was a lot more mobile now. Plus, Kal hadn't seen much of Hannah in the past week because he'd covered a couple of shifts for one of the guys on another TRT who'd been sick, so he'd been working practically nonstop. He was looking forward to spending some time with Hannah today.

He picked up Hannah and Oliver at their house.

"Where's your mom?" he asked Hannah.

"She's out on a date. She left this afternoon, didn't tell me where she was going or with whom, other than she had a date."

"Hmm. Same mystery guy?"

Hannah shrugged. "No idea. I asked, and she told me it's none of my business."

"Secretive, isn't she?"

"Very."

Oliver came running out and threw himself against Kal. "Hi, Kal."

"Hey, buddy. I've missed you." Kal hugged him back, happy to be around Oliver again.

"I missed you, too. We're going to your momma's house today?"

"Yup."

"And your daddy is a fireman, like you?"

"Yup. And so are my two brothers. You remember Jackson from the day we went to the festival, right?"

"Yeah. He's a fireman, too? And you have another brother?"

"I do."

"Wow. You're so lucky."

Kal caught Hannah's sigh. He wondered what that was about, but he didn't have time to ask, because she gathered up a tote bag and handed it to him, and they headed out to the truck. On the way, Oliver asked him tons of questions.

"Are we goin' to the house where you grew up?"

"No, my parents bought a new house a year or so ago. This one has a pool."

"Oh, a pool. Mom, did you pack my swim trunks?"

"I did, but remember, you have the cast so you can't get it wet."

"Aww, man."

Kal smiled.

"Do they have pets?" Oliver asked.

"No, they don't. But they like animals."

"I like dogs. Someday we'll have our own house and then I'm gonna get a dog, right, Momma?"

"That's right."

They turned onto the street and parked in the driveway behind Rafe's truck.

"It's a lovely house, Kal. I can see why your mom wanted this one."

"Yeah," he said as they got out of the truck and he looked at the house. "Mom said it was perfect for her. Just the right size."

"And the landscaping is gorgeous. All the flowers."

He figured Hannah would pick up on that.

He gathered up the bags Hannah had packed, while Hannah picked up the bouquet of flowers she'd brought.

Oliver ran up to the porch and was first at the door. Kal liked that he wasn't shy, which was a good thing in his family. His mom opened the door before Oliver had the chance to ring the bell.

"I saw you pull up." She smiled down at Oliver. "You must be Oliver. I'm Laurel."

Oliver held up his arm. "Hi. I broke my wrist. I have a cast."

"I see that. It must have hurt."

"Yeah, it did."

Kal hugged his mom. "Hey, Momma."

"My sweet baby. How are you?"

"Good."

His mom folded Hannah into a hug, which was her thing. She hugged everyone. If Oliver hadn't dashed inside he'd have been hugged, too. "Good to see you again, Hannah. I'm happy you took me up on my invitation, and that you brought Oliver."

"Thank you for inviting us over today."

"Come on in, you two. I made iced tea and lemonade, and of course there's wine and beer for anyone who wants that. Oh, and I made margaritas. Josh bought me a margarita machine for my birthday. He knows how much I love those."

Hannah and his mom walked in front of him, side by side. "That sounds fun. I'll bet those are great poolside during the hot summer."

"They so are. Would you like one?"

"I'd love one. Fire that machine up."

"Momma, they have the coolest pool out back," Oliver said, tugging on her hand. "Come look."

Hannah had barely gotten to the kitchen and set the flowers down. "Okay. Let's see it."

Oliver dragged her to the door. "That's a pretty great pool, isn't it?"

"Hi, Oliver," Carmen said as she came into the room. "Isn't that an awesome pool?"

"Hi, Nurse Carmen. Did you see my cast?"

"I did. And I thought you might want to go swimming today, so I brought a cover for your cast that'll keep it dry in the pool."

"Really? I can swim today? Can I, Momma?"

"If Nurse Carmen says you can, then you can."

"Cool!"

Kal's dad, Josh, walked over. "Hey, Hannah. Good to see you."

"Mr. Donovan."

He motioned to Oliver. "It's Josh. And come on, Oliver, let's go take a look at the pool. Later we'll go for a swim."

"Okay."

Hannah exhaled now that she'd managed to take a breath. What a whirlwind.

She walked over to the island where she'd set everything down and picked up the flowers she'd brought. "These are for you, Laurel."

"Oh, how sweet of you. They're so pretty. Let me get a vase to put those in."

"I hear we're firing up the margarita machine," Carmen said, sliding into the seat at the kitchen island next to Hannah.

"That's what I hear."

"Momma, Jackson and Becks have their dog!" Oliver ran through the back door, his eyes wide with excitement.

"They do? That's so awesome."

"His name is Edgar and he's a puppy, but he's big. He's German shepherd and . . . somethin' else. I forget."

"Labrador," Kal said, coming up to stand behind Hannah's chair.

"Yeah, that's it. I'm gonna go back out and play with him. After I go to the bathroom."

"Down the hall and it's the first door, Oliver," Laurel said.

Hannah tilted her head back to look at Kal. "You knew about this?"

"The dog? Yeah. Remember the fall festival? The dog they were looking at that day?"

"Oh, right. I remember that puppy."

Kal grinned. "He's a lot bigger now. It took a while for the home inspection and paperwork and vet check and all of that with the foster organization. But he's been at the house for the past few days."

"That's great. How's he doing?"

"He's a lot of energy."

"Oh. So like having a kid around, huh?" Hannah gave him a smile.

"You would know better than me."

Becks came through the door just as Laurel had the machine going. "I'm just in time for margaritas, I see."

"Take a seat," Kal said, grabbing a beer from the fridge. "I'm going out back to hang out with the guys."

Kal left, and Becks slid into one of the chairs.

"You know, it wasn't all that long ago that I was surrounded by nothing but men and boys," Laurel said, filling glasses with margarita mix. "Now look at this room."

"We are pretty awesome, aren't we?" Becks asked.

Laurel slid glasses to Hannah, Carmen and Becks, and lifted her own glass. "Here's to all the amazing women."

"To women," Carmen said.

"Cheers," Hannah said, toasting these women who had become her friends, and Laurel, who she'd known since she was a teenager.

Hannah took a sip. "Mmm, this is very good."

"Thank you."

Hannah turned to Carmen. "So, are you all settled back into work and home life after the honeymoon?"

Carmen nodded. "More or less. Though my head's still on that beach."

"I'll bet it was nice," Becks said.

"So very nice. I was digging in my heels getting on that plane. I thought about a mutiny, but Rafe was the one who insisted on coming home. He's such a practical guy. Wanting us to keep our jobs, pay the mortgage . . ."

Laurel shook her head. "It's one of his biggest faults. I did my best with him, Carmen."

Hannah laughed. "You can always go back on vacation. Or for your first anniversary."

"I'm hoping to be pregnant by our first anniversary."

"That's sweet news to my heart," Laurel said. "Josh and I are so ready for grandbabies."

"Aww," Becks said, chin in her hand. "Babies. I can't wait for babies. Your babies, that is, Carmen."

"Not in any hurry, huh?" Hannah asked.

"Not in the least. I want to get married, run around the house naked with my husband for a year or two. Then we can talk babies."

Laurel gave Becks a smirk.

"Sorry, Laurel," Becks said. "Probably too much information."

Laurel shrugged. "Hey, I still like running around the house naked with my husband."

Hannah laughed.

"Oh my God, Laurel," Becks said, laughing. "Now *that* is too much information."

"Hey, can't I have a sex life, too? I mean, no kids running around my house anymore. What are Josh and I supposed to do around here at night? Watch the news?"

"What are you all talking about?" Kal asked as he walked in to grab a few beers from the fridge.

"Your parents' sex life," Hannah said.

"And, I'm out."

Eyes wide, Kal made a beeline for the back door, causing all the women to burst into wild laughter.

"Can I clear a room or what?" Laurel asked.

"You're the master at it, ma'am," Carmen said.

Laurel shrugged. "Hey, if you can't embarrass your children, you're doing parenting wrong."

"I'm definitely filing that one away for later," Hannah said.

They took their drinks outside and sat at the table on the shaded porch. It was a humid, hot day, and all the guys decided to get into the pool. Carmen fitted Oliver's cast with the airtight waterproof cover, which fit perfectly, but wasn't bulky, so he'd have mobility.

Hannah went over to him. "No roughhousing. No jumping in the pool. You get too rambunctious in the water, I'm pulling you out. Understood?"

He nodded. "Yes."

Josh came over and put his arm around Oliver's shoulders. "You have four firefighters here. And I have very strict pool rules, which I've already told him about. We've got this, don't we, Oliver?"

"Yes, sir." Oliver gave Josh a wide smile.

Hannah could tell Oliver was taking this seriously, so she nodded. "Okay, then. Have fun."

She took a seat and picked up her drink, sipping it while she watched Oliver do his best not to jump headfirst into the water. She'd put him in swimming lessons when he was a baby, wanting to make sure he would always be safe in the water. He knew how to swim, plus, Josh was right—her son was surrounded by the best lifeguards she could ever hope for. She didn't have to worry about him.

The guys batted a ball around in the pool, and Edgar lay at the edge of the pool and barked until Jackson tossed a tennis ball and the dog went to chase it.

Hannah couldn't imagine a more idyllic Saturday evening.

"How's the wedding planning going, Becks?" Hannah asked.

"Good. Got the venue, the caterer, the cake and the invitations ordered. We decided on a deejay instead of a band, so that's taken care of. Now I just have to find a dress."

"Do you have a certain dress in mind?" Laurel asked.

Becks shrugged. "I don't know. Not really. I want to find something I love, but I've had no luck so far. I've tried on several. None of them feel like the right one."

"It can be hard to find a dress," Carmen said. "It's more like a feeling you have when you put a dress on that you know it's your dress. *The* dress."

Becks nodded. "Yes, that's exactly the problem I'm having. Plus going by myself means I don't have anyone to offer opinions."

"Aww, I'd have gone with you, honey," Laurel said. "All you had to do was ask."

"I didn't want to bother you."

Laurel pinned Becks with a look. "We're family. Family is never a bother."

Becks leaned across the table to squeeze Laurel's hand. "Thank you."

"I'd go, too," Carmen said. "I'm loaded with opinions."

Hannah didn't want to insinuate herself in a family thing, so she stayed quiet.

"What about you, Hannah?" Becks asked. "Would you be interested in coming along and offering up your thoughts?"

She internally squealed with delight. "Are you kidding? I'd love to."

"Great." Becks beamed a smile. "Let's figure out a day and time that works for everyone."

It turned out that tomorrow would be the perfect day that worked for everyone. Even though it was a Sunday, the bridal shops were open, and everyone had the day off, so they made plans to have brunch and then shop.

"I'm so excited," Becks said. "Thank you all for agreeing to go with me. There are a few shops I haven't been to yet, so I hope you don't mind doing a circuit with me."

"We're excited, too, Becks," Laurel said. "I'll bet you decide on a dress tomorrow."

"I can't wait," Hannah said. "I love dress shopping, even if it isn't for me."

Becks laughed. "Tomorrow is going to be so much fun."

They decided to change and get into the pool to cool off. Hannah slid into the water and swam over to Oliver, who was obviously having a blast. Josh had given him some goggles, so he dived to the bottom of the pool searching for the items that Jackson, Rafe and Kal had tossed down there. When he surfaced, he grinned at her.

"Can we get a pool, Momma?"

"Maybe someday. When we have a house of our own."

"I like swimming."

"I can tell. Are you having fun?"

"Yeah. And I like this bubble over my cast. Carmen said it . . . uh . . . unflates or somethin'. Anyway, we can take it home and I can have it for the shower."

"Deflates," she corrected. "That was very nice of her."

"Yeah. I'm gonna go play ball, okay?"

She smiled. "Sure."

Hannah swam over to the side and rested her arms on the edge, enjoying the cool water while she watched some of the group play ball.

Kal swam over to her. "Are you okay?"

"I'm fine, why?"

"Because we're all playing and you're over here like you've been excluded." He grabbed her hand. "Come on. Play with us."

She laughed. "Okay."

They ended up stringing a net and playing a game of water volleyball. Oliver was situated on the shallow end of the pool with Laurel, Josh, Becks and Hannah, while Carmen, Jackson, Rafe and Kal had the deep end.

It was so much fun Hannah nearly choked down swallows of pool water laughing. The Donovans definitely played a cutthroat game of water volleyball. No one gave an inch, which Hannah liked. And they treated Oliver like a member of the family. Josh even lifted Oliver out of the water so he could spike a ball over the net.

Jackson shot his father a look. "That's cheating."

"Yeah, show me where in the rule book."

They switched up teams midway, and she and Kal ended up on the same team at the deep end of the pool, which meant that Hannah had to tread water while playing. She noticed Kal stayed close to her, even wrapping his arm around her a few times while they switched locations. It seemed as if he found every opportunity to get close to her, to grab her hand or touch her in some way. And he was always smiling at her and asking if she was okay.

Small gestures, but to her, they meant a lot.

In the end, Hannah had lost count of which team had won the most games. All she knew for sure was that she was utterly exhausted and needed a drink. They all climbed out of the pool and dried off. Hannah went inside with the women, and they made side dishes while the guys started up the grill and cooked pork chops for dinner.

Hannah helped with the mashed potatoes, spinach, collard greens and carrots, along with a delicious fruit salad.

"Kal tells me you don't eat meat, Hannah," Laurel said while they sliced tomatoes and mozzarella to make a caprese salad.

"I'm not a vegetarian. I just don't eat a lot of meat. I'll be digging into those pork chops tonight, though. I think I worked up a meaty appetite in the pool."

Laurel laughed. "Me, too."

Dinner was amazing, and Hannah ate a bit of everything, including a pork chop, which was delicious.

"You ate meat today," Kal said. "Does that mean we've dragged you over to the carnivore side?"

"For today you did. I couldn't resist the pork chops. This barbecue sauce is ridiculous."

"You can thank Kal for that," Josh said. "He made it."

She looked at him. "Really?"

"Yeah."

"Spicy," she said, swiping through a bit of it that remained on her plate. "I like it."

He reached under the table to squeeze her thigh. "You're spicy."

She laughed.

After dinner they wrapped up the leftovers and cleaned the dishes and the kitchen. Hannah made plans to meet up with the women tomorrow morning for brunch, and then, since it was getting late, they said their goodbyes and headed home.

It didn't take five minutes on the road before Oliver was asleep, his head resting against one of Kal's rolled-up jackets.

"He had a busy day," she said. "He'll be out for the rest of the night."

Kal grinned. "He had fun today."

She sighed and leaned back against the seat. "You have such an amazing family, Kal. All of them. Your parents, your brothers, the women. They're all just . . . perfect."

"I don't know about perfect. We have our flaws, Hannah. Just like every other family. But they are pretty awesome."

"They sure are."

He turned the corner, his fingers tapping on the steering wheel. "You know, every damn day I wake up I realize how lucky I was to be adopted by the Donovans."

She looked over at him. "I don't know. I think they were pretty lucky to find you."

His fingers stilled. "What?"

"They're the lucky ones. Look at you, what an amazing man you've become. They must be so proud of you. If Oliver could turn out to be even half the man you are, I would consider myself the luckiest woman in the universe. Parents don't consider themselves to be life givers. We consider ourselves lucky to be given these gifts of children who constantly surprise and challenge us. You were the gift to them, Kal. You and Jackson and Rafe. They were the lucky ones."

He pulled over, parked and leaned over. He cupped her neck and took her mouth in a deep, soul-shattering kiss. When he pulled back, he said, "No one's ever said that to me. That my parents were lucky to have me. I mean, my parents have, because of course they would. But no one else. Until you."

She wound her hand around his wrist. "They should have."

The way he looked at her, the deep emotion in his eyes, made her want to hold him, made her want to wrap her body around him and never let go. But her son was in the back seat and she couldn't. And he knew it, too, because he put the truck back in gear and drove her home.

He carried Oliver inside, and Hannah took over from there, getting him ready for bed. Her kid was like a zombie, nearly sleepwalking through brushing his teeth and getting into his bed, where he fell straight back to sleep.

She came back into the living room. "He's out. Again."

Kal nodded. "I'm taking off."

She pressed her body against his. "I wish you could stay here."

"Me, too." He kissed her, a long, passionate kiss that left her wanting.

But then he stepped back and opened the door. "Night, Hannah."

She shuddered out a sigh. "Good night."

She leaned against the door and watched him walk to his truck. It wasn't until after he'd pulled down the street and disappeared that she closed and locked the front door.

Things were getting so complicated between them. And at the same time, becoming all too clear.

She had feelings. Deep, genuine feelings for Kal.

That's what scared her.

CHAPTER 23

THERE WAS NOTHING MORE FUN THAN A DAY OUT WITH A group of women Hannah really liked. The fact that one of those women was Kal's mother made it even more interesting to her.

They met for brunch at the Alchemist. Laurel had made reservations, so they didn't have to wait long, and they were seated at a table with an amazing view of the quirky gardens. It was fun, and they all ordered coffee and the Alchemosa with champagne and passion fruit.

"So, are you ready for the day?" Hannah asked Becks.

Becks nearly vibrated in her chair. "I am beyond ready to get a dress and check another thing off the list."

Carmen laughed. "You have a book with lists, don't you?"

"Yes. A ridiculous number of things on said list. Who knew that so much went into getting married? We should have eloped."

"Bite your tongue," Laurel said. "I want weddings for each of my boys."

"Just kidding. Mostly."

"What was your first wedding like, Hannah?" Carmen asked.

"Very small. We got married in my parents' backyard. I wore

a short white dress I got on sale at the department store, and I think we had maybe twenty people there. We bought the cake at the local grocery store, and my mom fixed lasagna and salad for dinner. It was very bargain-basement. But I was happy it was over, and then my husband and I moved to Georgia the following week."

Becks blinked. "How romantic."

"Yeah. Not at all. I was young and eager to get away, but my mom insisted on me having a wedding, so . . ."

"But just think," Becks said. "Next time you get married, you can have a big fancy blowout."

Hannah laughed and lifted her glass to take a long swallow. "That is never going to happen."

"Never say never," Carmen said. "I swore I'd never get married again. Now look at me. And I had a big ole wedding, too."

"Okay, fine. I won't say never again. But I just can't see the big fancy dress and a reception and all of that. I mean, I have a kid now."

Three sets of eyes stared at her.

"What?" she asked.

"So because you have a child that precludes you from a celebration of love? A celebration of two people who love each other, that includes your son becoming part of that family?" Laurel pinned her with a look.

Hannah opened her mouth to answer, then closed it. "Okay, fine. I can't speak to the future, because I have no idea what's in store for me. But no foofy white dresses for me."

"I definitely cannot see you in a foofy white dress," Becks said. "For that matter, I can't see me in a foofy white dress, either."

Carmen took a notepad out of her bag. "No foofy white dress. See? We're making progress."

They all laughed.

The food was amazing. They all got something different and shared bites, which was delicious, tasty fun.

After they sat and had a couple more of those amazing mimosas, they paid their bill and headed to the first bridal salon. When they walked in, Hannah could tell from Becks's wide-eyed look that she was nervous. Hannah hooked her arm into Becks's.

"We're going to conquer the wedding dress demon today. Remember, this time you're not going into this alone. We've got you."

Becks smiled. "Right."

The first dress Becks tried on was a strapless silk mermaid style and looked amazing on her, showing off her creamy skin and unique tattoos. When she turned around to face them, they were all grinning at her.

"What?" she asked.

"You look like a bride," Laurel said.

"You don't think the tattoos are too much?"

"I think my son loves you and your tattoos. Do you think he'd want you to hide who you are?"

"Good point, Laurel. And thank you."

"How do you feel in the dress?" Carmen asked.

"Like a summer sausage. How do women dance in these things?"

Hannah snorted. "Okay, so not that one."

Becks tried on two more at that store, but Hannah could tell they weren't the right style, color or fit for her. Her eyes didn't sparkle when she came out, so they gathered up and left. At the next store, Becks couldn't even find a dress she was willing to try on, so they headed to the third store.

Outside the shop, Becks took a deep breath and let it out. "This is so discouraging."

Laurel patted her on the back. "You'll find the one. If not this store, then we'll find another."

Becks nodded, but Hannah felt her tension as they walked inside.

A salesperson named Sally met with Becks and sat down with her, asking her what she was looking for.

"Not too tight, not overdesigned or ball gowns," Becks said. "Something . . . I don't know, me." She sighed. "I've tried on a lot of dresses and just haven't found the right one yet."

Sally nodded. "Sometimes it takes a while. How about you wander for a few minutes and see if something sparks your interest?"

"That sounds good."

They all walked the store with Becks. Hannah saw a lot of dresses she liked, but it wasn't her wedding, and she wasn't choosing a dress for herself. This was Becks's day, so she and Carmen stayed a step behind while Laurel talked with her about some of the dresses.

When Becks stopped at one dress, she looked. She felt. She stared. Hannah could tell that particular dress captured her. And why wouldn't it? It was a porcelain pink, with tulle and just a touch of lace at the waist. It was elegant but not fussy.

Sally came over. "Would you like to try this one on?"

Becks nodded. "Yes, please."

"Let's get you into a dressing room, and I'll go grab one in your size. Ladies, if you'll follow me to the seating area."

They all took seats near the dressing area.

"That dress," Carmen whispered to them, as if afraid to say anything that might jinx it.

"I know," Hannah said.

"And that color," Laurel said. "Could it be more perfect for Becks?"

Hannah sighed. And hoped.

About ten minutes later, Becks walked out, and Hannah swore she was floating as she made her way toward them.

As she stepped up to the three-way mirror and turned, the dress flowed.

And they all gasped.

It was stunning. Becks was stunning. Even without alterations, the dress fit her as if it had been made for her body. And the color—that pale pink porcelain with the ivory overlay—was so unusual, so incredibly beautiful. Hannah didn't know about the rest of them, but she was utterly speechless.

"What?" Becks finally asked.

"Wow," Carmen said. "You glow in that dress, Becks."

"I've never seen anything like it," Hannah said, voicing her thoughts. "It's like it was made for you."

Becks chewed her bottom lip, then looked over at Jackson's mom. "Laurel?"

Hannah saw Laurel batting back tears. "It's so lovely. You are lovely. How do you feel in it?"

Becks sighed. "Like a freakin' princess. I love it."

They all cheered.

Hannah got up and went to Becks. "May I?" She reached for Becks's hair.

"Of course."

She dug out the jeweled hair clip she'd tossed in her bag this morning, just in case, and wound Becks's hair up in it, pulling a few tendrils out to frame her face.

"Okay, now look in the mirror," Hannah said.

Becks turned around, her eyes filled with tears. "I look like a bride."

Hannah wrapped her hands around Becks's arms. "A beautiful bride."

Laurel and Carmen came over.

"Is this the one?" Laurel asked.

Becks nodded. "Yes."

Sally smiled. "Lovely. We'll do some measurements, but we won't have to do much in the way of alterations once your dress comes in. You look incredible."

"Thank you. I'm so happy. And so relieved." She looked at all of them. "I found my dress."

"One more thing to check off your list," Hannah said.

"You're gonna knock Jackson over when he sees you in that dress," Carmen said.

Becks smiled. "I hope so."

They took photos, then Becks changed out of the dress and filled out paperwork. They left the store, hugged and everyone said goodbye. Becks had some errands to do for her tattoo shop, and Carmen was going grocery shopping.

"Where are you headed?" Laurel asked Hannah.

"No plans today," she said.

"Do you have some time to stop for something cold to drink? I'd love an iced tea."

"Sure."

They chose a spot, and Hannah followed her to the sandwich shop.

They went inside, ordered two large raspberry iced teas and grabbed a seat.

"That was so fun today," Laurel said.

"It was. I'm relieved on Becks's behalf that she found a dress. And such a gorgeous one, too."

"It was so pretty. I can't wait for their wedding."

"I can imagine. Two of your sons getting married so close together. That must be a lot for you."

"It's a blessing, really. To see these boys grow up, become such amazing men. Josh and I are so happy."

"I'm sure you are."

"And Kal and you reconnecting. That was unexpected."

She knew this was going to come up. "Yes, it was. I was happy he came to the reunion."

"I know you two didn't have a good parting when he left for college. He was so upset about that."

She took a sip of her tea. "Was he?"

"Yes. He carried a lot of guilt over the breakup."

She shrugged. "We both knew it was the right thing. It just wasn't easy. But we were both so young. Trying to stay together would have been harder."

Laurel's lips curved. "That's the adult in you, looking back on it now. Ten years ago it wasn't so clear."

"No, it wasn't. I cried a lot over him. And then I made a series of really dumb decisions. Like impulsively deciding to get married and moving out of state."

Laurel cast a surprised look. "So you're saying your marriage was a rebound thing?"

She played with the straw. "I don't know. I'd like to think it was more a case of me wanting to get out of Ft. Lauderdale, away from everyone and everything I knew. Carve out a life on my own, you know? My mom was making all these plans for my future, pushing me to go to college when all I ever wanted to do was become a hair stylist. I was desperate to be free to make my own choices and thought if I could just get away, I could breathe, see clearly, do whatever I wanted. The naivete of youth, you know?"

Laurel nodded. "I can understand that. But you did become a hair stylist."

"I did. And I love it. And I had Oliver, and I have zero regrets about him."

"Children are an amazing gift."

"They sure are."

Laurel took another sip of her tea. "So now you're back home. And seeing Kal again."

"Yes." She couldn't help the smile, as if every time she heard his name or thought about him, it made her happy.

And then Laurel sprouted a grin. "My boy put that smile on your face?"

"I can't help it. He makes me giddy. I think about him all the time."

"You used to always smile like that around him."

She sighed. "I know. Some things never change, I guess."

This was so embarrassing. She really had to learn to control her emotions.

"Hey, when you feel it, you feel it. I have to tell you, it makes me happy knowing the two of you are together again. He seems more settled."

"Really?" Hearing that from his mother made her feel even happier.

"Yes. He's been . . . I don't know the right word to describe it . . . searching? Tense?" She waved her hand back and forth. "Whatever it was that's made him feel so unsettled the past couple of years has disappeared. I'm guessing that has a lot to do with you."

She felt her face warm. "Thank you. We're having a good time together." She needed to let Laurel know that it wasn't serious between them. Change tracks in this conversation, because it was heading down a road she didn't want to go. Not with his mother, anyway. "And Kal has matured so much since we were last together. He has an incredible career and seems to know exactly what he wants out of his life. I admire that about him."

"As do you. You already know what you want."

"I guess. Sometimes I feel as if I've taken so many steps backward. I'm not exactly where I want to be. Not yet."

"Where do you want to be?"

"Independent. To know that I can carve out a future for my son and myself—by myself."

Laurel nodded. "I understand. It's important for a woman to know she can do it all on her own. To know she doesn't need anyone's help. Especially not a man's help."

Laurel understood, and Hannah appreciated that.

"Exactly."

"You'll get there. I believe in you, Hannah."

Hannah smiled. "Thank you. Oh, there is one important thing I'd like to discuss with you, if you don't mind."

Laurel tilted her head to the side. "Of course."

"It's about Kal."

"I'm listening."

"You know how he's always doing things for other people, for the community, but he rarely does anything for himself?"

Laurel's lips lifted. "Yes."

"I'd like to do something special for him. You know his birthday is coming up."

"Yes."

"I have an idea."

Laurel smiled. "I'm listening."

Hannah laid out her thoughts, and between her and Laurel, they came up with a very solid plan. A good plan.

Now all they had to do was set said plan in motion.

This was going to be very good. And so much fun.

CHAPTER 24

IT HAD BEEN A WHILE SINCE KAL HAD DONE ANYTHING special for his birthday. Typically, he and his brothers went out for drinks, but now Rafe was married and Jackson was engaged, so he didn't expect to do much today. They'd both said they were busy, but they wished him a happy birthday. His mom had a dinner meeting tonight but said they'd do dinner with him this weekend.

But, hey, at least he'd had the day off today, so he relaxed by the pool since the sun was out, then vacuumed and washed his truck and did laundry. He was even able to grab lunch with one of his high school buddies.

He had a text message from Hannah wishing him a happy birthday, telling him she had a full day at work but asking if he wanted to go out for dinner. He smiled and texted her back, telling her he was game for that. It was a weekday, so he was grateful he'd get to see her at all.

After a quick workout at the gym, he got cleaned up and drove over to pick up Hannah.

When she opened the door, she looked amazing in a flowery red-and-black dress that swung around her legs when she walked.

"You look gorgeous," he said.

"Thank you. And you look so fine. Happy birthday." She lifted up on her toes to press a kiss to his lips.

He stepped inside, noticing right away how quiet it was in the house. "Where's Oliver?"

"He and my mom went out for dinner."

"Oh. I thought maybe he was coming with us."

She shook her head. "He has a lot of homework to do, so they're having a quick bite, then back home."

"Huh. Okay." He masked his disappointment in not being able to see Oliver. "You ready to go?"

She grabbed her bag. "Yes. Starving. How about you?"

"I'm always hungry."

She rubbed his back as they walked out the door. "Of course you are."

They got in the truck, and he started it up.

"I know it's your birthday and all," she said, "but do you mind if I pick the place?"

He looked over at her. "Not at all. What do you have in mind?"

"Becks has told me about Tommy's Fish House. I think it's owned by one of your former firefighter buddies?"

"Yeah, it is."

"She said the food there is really good. She mentioned a few of their dishes, and I've been dying to try it out. If you don't want to go there because you eat there a lot, I understand."

"No, it's fine. I like their food." He'd planned on taking Hannah to a fancy restaurant, but you couldn't beat the food at Tommy Rodriguez's place.

The parking lot was nearly full when they got there, which

was good for a Wednesday night, and great for Tommy and his wife, Estella. Kal was happy to see their restaurant growing.

When they went inside, their hostess, Brenda, smiled.

"Hi, Kal. It's nice to see you."

"You, too, Brenda."

"It'll be just a few minutes if you don't mind waiting. But I'll get a table ready for you."

"Sure. We'll just be in the bar."

Brenda nodded, and Kal led Hannah to the bar.

When the bartender came over, Kal looked at Hannah. "What would you like to drink?"

"I'll have a rosé," she said.

"Beer for me."

The bartender nodded and got their drinks, handed them over, and by that time, Brenda had come back to fetch them. They grabbed their drinks and followed her.

"This way. I'm sorry to have to put you in the back. We're kind of busy tonight."

"Not a problem," Kal said.

"Busy is a good thing," Hannah said, grasping Kal's hand and giving him a smile.

Kal frowned when they passed the dining area and went toward the private room in the back. And when Hannah gave him a wide smile and opened the door, he had no idea what was happening.

Until everyone in the room shouted, "Surprise!"

It took him a few seconds to register that his entire family was in that room. And his friends. Even Hannah's mom and Oliver, too.

He looked over at Hannah, who shrugged and gave him an innocent look, then said, "Happy birthday, Kal. I thought you needed a big birthday surprise."

"Well, I'm damned surprised." He leaned over and kissed her, then walked into the throng of people.

He couldn't believe who was here. Not only Mom and Dad, Jackson and Becks, and Rafe and Carmen, but also Paige and Oliver. And several of his former Station 6 brothers and sisters— Miguel Acosta and Adrienne Smith. Ethan and Penny Pressman. Callie and Aaron Vassar. Tommy, of course, since this was his place. And some of his teammates from the TRT as well. Micah, Meg and Irish had come. Even his lieutenant had shown up. Of course Phil and Dean hadn't showed. He hadn't expected them to. They weren't friends.

He was blown away by the support and the warmth of friendship and family.

"You did this?" he asked Hannah, who had been hovering nearby until he motioned her over.

"With a lot of help from your mom."

He was overwhelmed. He'd had birthday parties as a kid but never expected one as an adult. This was a hell of a surprise. He'd had to admit he'd felt a little abandoned today by his family. Now he knew he'd been a victim of subterfuge. They'd all been damn good at it, too.

And Hannah was the master of it all. He hadn't had a clue.

He watched her as she made her way around the room, either talking to people she knew or introducing herself to people she didn't. She wasn't shy, didn't need to cling to him and wait for an introduction.

There was a tug in the vicinity of his heart that seemed to always be there lately where she was concerned. And every day it was growing stronger.

After he'd greeted and chatted with everyone, they took their seats and dinner was served. Oliver asked if he could sit next to him, which made him feel . . . hell, he didn't know how to feel about that other than really good. Hannah sat next to Oliver.

"This is fun," Oliver said. "I like birthday parties."

"Me, too, buddy. Tell me about your best birthday party."

Oliver looked up at the ceiling to think, then looked over at him. "It was a really long time ago. I think I was three. I had an octopus party, and Momma got me a cake that looked like an octopus because I really liked octopuses."

Kal quirked a smile. "That sounds pretty awesome."

He looked over at Hannah, who shrugged and smiled.

Dinner, of course, was great. Kal had an amazing surf and turf dinner that left him stuffed, but feeling like a king.

He figured everyone would leave after dinner. Instead, he got a few gag gifts and some funny cards, and then the toasts began.

Or maybe he should call them roasts, because it was really bad.

"Remember that time during your rookie year you fell asleep during morning report and the captain made you drag all the hoses up and down the stairs five times?" Ethan shot him a grin.

"Oh." Callie sat up in her chair. "I remember that day. Highly entertaining."

"For you, maybe," Kal said.

"Yeah but you never fell asleep again, did you?" his dad asked.

"No, sir, I did not."

"Or the first time you were on cooking duty," Miguel said. "An hour after we ate, everyone pretended to get sick."

Kal frowned. "That was not funny. You all scared the shi—" He looked down at Oliver. "You all scared me. I thought I had poisoned you."

"We hid his turnout gear on his first day," Micah said. "He spent two hours looking for it when the lieutenant asked him to do a gear check."

His lieutenant smirked.

Kal folded his arms. "You're all very mean."

They laughed, then they shared stories of their own hazing, and he realized what an amazing group of people he got to work with.

And when Estella brought in a huge cake, his eyes widened.

"Cake, too? Come on."

His mom came over and put her hands on his shoulders, then leaned down. "From your favorite bakery."

Damn.

Everyone sang to him, and then they cut the cake and served it up. It was chocolate with vanilla buttercream, and he'd never tasted anything better.

He was one lucky guy.

HANNAH COULDN'T CONTAIN HER HAPPINESS AS SHE watched Kal soak in the love from his family and friends.

This had all come about spur-of-the-moment, but she was so glad it had turned out well. Kal seemed so filled with joy tonight, and she couldn't think of anyone who deserved it more.

That he seemed to appreciate it so much showed the type of man he was.

After dinner, some people left, then everyone else moved to the bar. Her mom was going to take Oliver home since it was already past his bedtime.

"I'll be right back," Kal said to the crowd. "Order me a beer."

Kal walked with her and Paige and Oliver out to the car.

"I wish I could stay," Oliver said, his face crestfallen.

When they got to the car and Oliver climbed in, Kal crouched down. "But you came to my party, and I'm so happy you were there. You know what? When your mom was still keeping the surprise party a secret and told me you weren't coming to dinner with us, I was so sad."

His face immediately brightened. "You were?"

"Yeah. I wanted to spend my birthday with you. You're my best buddy, aren't you?"

"You bet I am." Oliver threw his arms around Kal and hugged him, and Hannah's heart nearly burst with equal feelings of utter joy and abject terror.

It was clear that Oliver loved Kal. But what if things between Kal and her didn't work out? Oliver would be devastated.

This was what she'd been trying to avoid, why she rarely dated, why she never brought men into Oliver's life. Instead, it had happened, and she didn't know what she was going to do about it.

Of course, it was too late now.

Now she just had to hope that she and Kal would continue on the course they were headed, and everything would turn out fine.

But she couldn't ignore the nagging sensation of worry that lived constantly in the vicinity of her heart.

After hugging her mom and Oliver and waiting until they drove away, she and Kal headed back toward the restaurant.

Halfway there, Kal tugged on her hand. "Wait."

She stopped and looked up at him. "What?"

"This." He cupped the side of her neck, wound his other arm around her waist to draw her close and pressed his lips to hers.

He tasted warm and inviting, and she couldn't help but lean into him, to slide her hands along his arms so she could feel the heat of his skin. His hand snaked along her back and farther down to cup her butt, drawing her against the rigid length of his erection.

And here they were, out in public, making out between parked cars, and all she wanted to do was be alone and naked with him.

She pulled back, trying to catch her breath. "Party guests."

He laid his forehead against hers. "Damn." He blew out a breath. "Okay, give me a minute."

"Want me to quote baseball statistics to you?"

He laughed. "Do you know baseball statistics?"

She cocked her head to the side. "Are you really going to ask me that? Who has the highest batting average of all time?"

Now it was his turn to give her a look. "Easy. Ty Cobb."

"Longest home run ever hit?"

"Babe Ruth."

"The longest at bat in history?"

He opened his mouth, then closed it. She smirked.

"I suppose you know the answer."

"San Francisco's Brandon Belt, against the Angels' Jaime Barria. Twenty-one pitches. The at bat lasted twelve minutes and forty-five seconds."

"Damn. And how do you know this shit?"

She shrugged. "I have a thing for statistics."

"And did Belt get a hit?"

"No, he flied out."

He shook his head. "The things I'm still learning about you."

She grinned. "I'm amazing, right? And now your boner is gone, so let's go inside."

He laughed and put his arm around her. "You are magic, Hannah."

She liked the way he said that. She laid her head against his shoulder as they walked. "You just keep remembering that, Kal."

CHAPTER 25

"HEY, DONOVAN. YOU IN DREAMLAND TODAY OR WHAT?" Phil asked. "I'm waiting on slack for that rope."

Kal blinked, realizing he was on the job and needed to get his head on straight. "I'm on it."

He slacked the rope for Phil, who was working in some pretty tight quarters in a pipe where two workers had been stuck after one end caved in. Phil and Meg were currently working the pipe while the rest of the team provided support topside.

"We've got one hooked on to the red rope and ready to pull out," Meg said.

"Roger," Lieutenant Anderson said. "All right, team. Let's do this slow and easy."

Phil had already let the team know that neither of the workers had serious injuries. It was just a matter of pulling them out without causing any injuries—or further damage to the pipe, which could put the workers and their team members in danger.

Phil and Meg had harnessed the workers, so now Kal and Irish were in charge of the red rope, which contained the first worker's harness. They began to pull, slow and easy, since the pipe was tight. Phil fed them verbal instructions on how the ascent was coming along, since the team above had no visual.

"Okay, a little slower, you're getting to a tight spot. Now . . . hold."

Kal and Irish stopped and waited, holding tight to their rope to make sure the worker they had charge of didn't move either higher or lower.

"Okay," Phil said. "Start pulling up again."

It was painstaking work, and it took a while, but after about ten minutes they had the first worker freed from the pipe. He had a few cuts and abrasions, but other than that he looked okay.

Micah and Andy had already started pulling the second worker out. Once he was freed, they retrieved Meg and Phil from the pipe. Their team members were dusty and had a few abrasions of their own.

"It was tight as hell down there," Meg said. "I don't know if we could have gotten them out if that pipe had been any smaller."

"But you did get them out, and that's what counts," the lieutenant said. "Job well done. Let's pack up our equipment and get out of here."

Kal began to roll up the ropes.

"You somewhere else today, Donovan?" Phil asked when he came over.

"No."

"It was like I was talking to myself down there. I need an alert team member, and that wasn't you. Pull your head out of your ass."

"Yeah. Sorry about that. It won't happen again."

Phil pointed his finger at Kal's chest. "See that it doesn't."

Kal put his head down and resumed folding the rope, taking a deep breath and wishing he could have done that rescue over again.

The last thing he needed was to be anything less than perfect on the job, and especially when he was working with either Phil or Dean, the two guys who for some reason he still couldn't fathom seemed to have it out for him. And so what did he do today? He let his mind drift, to think about Hannah, when he should have had his head on work and only work.

But he'd been thinking about the future, playing a game of what-ifs about Hannah and him.

He couldn't let that happen again. His job was too important to him.

He went to the truck to store gear.

"You okay?" Meg asked.

He shook his head. "I let my mind wander, and Phil kicked my ass about it."

"Hey, it happens. And he's not perfect, either. Don't let him kid you into thinking he is. The rescue was textbook. Don't worry about it."

He nodded. "Thanks."

Meg was right, and he should let it go, but it was all he thought about through shift. He'd done nothing but work on high alert the entire time he'd been with the TRT. Mainly to prove to himself that he could do this job that he loved, but also because Phil and Dean had been riding his ass since the first day he'd reported for duty here.

He had something to prove, and he couldn't for one second half-ass his way through any rescue. Today had been a good reminder of that. Focus first on the job, especially when he was on the job. Let everything else slide to days off.

Which was hard to do when Hannah was on his mind all the time. Every day. Every night.

Which was either a really good thing, or maybe a not-so-good thing.

He needed a sounding board.

After shift the next morning, he drove over to his parents'

house. The garage door was open, so he knew his parents were home. There was one of them he needed to talk to.

He knew his mom worked at home today.

He knocked, then went inside. Dad was at the kitchen table drinking coffee and looking at his phone. He smiled when Kal walked in.

"Don't tell me. You came to surprise me and mow the lawn."

"I can do that if you want me to."

"I was joking. I was just about to head to the hardware store. Wanna come with me?"

"Actually, I was hoping to talk with Mom. Is she around?"

He motioned down the hall. "She's in her office."

"If she's working . . ."

His dad cracked a smile. "She'll still be happy to see you. Go on. I'll see you later."

"Okay, Dad. Thanks."

He headed down the hall and stopped at the glass doors in front of his mom's office. She wasn't on the phone, so he lightly tapped. She looked up and smiled, then motioned him inside.

She stood up when he walked in and wrapped him in a hug. That hug alone already helped to relieve some of his stress.

"Hey, baby. What brings you here today?"

"Just thought I'd stop by. How's work going?"

"Pretty good today, actually. I've got a couple of kids placed with amazing foster parents that are looking to make that placement permanent."

He knew kids getting adopted permanently was one of the happiest parts of his mother's job. She'd been instrumental in adopting him, Jackson and Rafe and making them all a family. He didn't know what would have happened to the three of them without having her and his dad come into their lives. "That's great news."

"Yes, it is. Both for the kids and for the parents. Let's go get some coffee. I've been working nonstop since seven. I could use a break and a chat."

And by chat, she meant she'd listen and he'd talk. His mom had always had good insight about her sons, always knew whenever they were happy or sad or upset about something. It's why he loved the only woman he'd ever considered a mother. Not only was she an amazing woman and a fantastic social worker who cared about all the children she worked with, she was also an incredible mom.

Kal had always felt closest to his mother. He'd felt an instant connection to her from the moment she'd come into his life. He'd never felt close to his birth mom, hadn't felt a connection to her because she'd never been affectionate with him, but he never knew why. Her distance hurt him as a child, especially when she hadn't stood up for him when his stepdad had started beating on him.

He'd talked a lot to Laurel about it after they'd all been adopted, had always wondered why his birth mother hadn't loved him enough to protect him. Laurel had told him she didn't have an answer for that, that only his birth mother knew why, but Laurel suggested she'd probably been abused long before Kal showed up, and she'd moved from one abusive man to another. Mom explained that his birth mother had likely been suffering from PTSD and was so afraid for herself that she couldn't show love for him. And that fear for her own safety kept her from intervening when Kal's stepdad had beat him.

Kal could still remember the nights he'd lain huddled in his bed under the covers, trying to muffle the sounds of his mother's screaming while she endured the beatings. It had taken him a long time and a lot of conversations to come to grips with the fact that he'd been relieved that it was her this time and not him. He carried a lot of guilt over that, and that guilt warred with his anger at his mother for not protecting him—for not doing something to protect both of them.

It hadn't been his fault that his stepfather was an abusive monster. None of his circumstances had been his fault. He'd been too young to take care of himself, too young to defend his mother. When he realized she was never going to step up and get them out of the situation, he'd run out of a sense of self-preservation. He'd never been happier than to find Jackson and Rafe on the streets. For the first time in his life, he'd had a family. And then he'd been rescued by Laurel and Josh, and Laurel had been the one to put in the work, to take the time to help him heal.

She had talked to him about his past, had helped him open up about the abuses he'd endured. She'd given him an understanding that he hadn't had as a child, and maybe a little bit of forgiveness for his birth mother. It had allowed him to leave that part of his life in the past and move forward with the adoptive parents he had grown to love so much.

He had never known what it had taken for Laurel and Josh to gain custody of him. Had Laurel tracked down his mother, and had his mother just signed over her rights? Had she died? He'd never asked, hadn't wanted to know.

Some questions were best left unanswered. And the past belonged in the past.

His mom brewed two coffees, and they sat at the kitchen table, evoking memories of so many times they'd sat together and talked things out.

"Did your shift go okay?" she asked.

Kal shrugged. "We had a close-quarters rescue. I was on rope duty."

She waited a beat before asking. "And?"

"My mind drifted, and one of my team members called me on it."

"Okay. So what's on your mind that you couldn't concentrate on your job?"

Kal took a sip of coffee. "Hannah."

She nodded and leaned back in the chair. "I see. Good or bad?"

"I don't know. I mean, I think about her all the time. Normally, when I'm on shift, the only thing I'm thinking about is the job. But lately, thoughts about her are creeping in."

"What kinds of thoughts?" She lifted her lips in a half smile. "Or are those off-limits?"

"No, nothing off-limits. I've been thinking about the future."

"A future with Hannah in it, you mean."

"Yeah."

She took a swallow of coffee, then tapped her fingers on the table while she thought. "So things are serious between the two of you, then?"

"Well, that's the thing. It's not like we've talked about it. It's just in my head right now."

"Maybe you should talk to her about it so it's not in your head."

That seemed easy enough, theoretically. But actually having that conversation with Hannah? Not so easy. "Yeah, maybe I should."

"I sense a 'but' in there."

"She's wary. Just coming off a divorce. She wants to be independent, do things on her timeline. I don't blame her for that."

"And you think what's in your head, what you want to talk to her about, might be rushing her."

"Yeah, maybe. I don't know." He ran his hand over the top of his head. "I didn't expect to run into her again, to start things up with her again after all these years. To feel what I feel for her. And for Oliver."

His mother nodded and continued to sip her coffee without saying anything, which meant she was mulling things over. And probably expecting him to do the same. He knew his mom, knew she wasn't going to solve this problem for him, that she'd expect him to deal with it on his own. She'd always been there for him as a sounding board, but the solution was going to have to come from him.

"I should give her space," he said. "And let things between us play out like they're supposed to."

She gave him a probing look. "Are you in some kind of hurry?"

"I guess not."

"Is she dating some other guy?"

"No."

She laid her hand on top of his. "Then take things slow with her, baby. Do exactly as you said. Give the girl some space and let her breathe. Allow the two of you to come together naturally, like you're supposed to. Love isn't some kind of race that you have to win, Kal. It's a slow, beautiful journey. Take your time getting there. And enjoy it."

He took a deep breath and let it out. "You're right. Thanks, Mom."

She smiled. "Anytime. And just from my personal observations, I think she feels the same way."

His pulse rate spiked at her words. "You do? How?"

"The way her face lights up when you walk into a room. You can read a lot on a woman's face when she looks at a man. The things she does for you that means she cares for you, that she wants what's best for you."

"Like planning the birthday party."

"Yes. And how she trusts you with Oliver—and believe me, that's not easy, especially for a single mother."

"I really like that kid."

"I think you more than like him. Kind of like how you feel about his mother."

"Yeah. Which is why I've been so much in my head." He blew out a breath. "Too much thinking."

She squeezed his hand. "Stop thinking so much and be in the moment more. Things will happen like they're supposed to."

He had to believe that. He had to stop trying to control every situation, to make things happen as he planned.

"Thanks. I needed this conversation to get my head on straight."

"I'm always here for you. And pay attention at work. You know how your dad feels about that."

His lips curved. "Yes, ma'am."

Now he felt better. More focused. His mom was right. He had to get out of his own way and just enjoy what was happening between Hannah and him. Their relationship was going great, and things would happen as they were meant to happen. He didn't need to push it to move along any faster than it was already going.

Knowing that Hannah might be feeling the same way he did helped.

Now he could relax. As much as he was gonna relax about the Hannah situation anyway.

CHAPTER 26

OLIVER'S EXCITEMENT OVER HALLOWEEN WAS INFEC-tious. He'd been practically pacing nonstop since he woke up this morning, waiting for dark. He was driving Hannah crazy.

Fortunately, Kal had the day off, and he'd come over midday, which had been super helpful in distracting Oliver so Hannah could get a few things accomplished. She'd managed to pay a few bills and do two loads of laundry, as well as get dinner put together while Oliver and Kal had kicked the ball around outside, then come in to play some games on the TV. Kal was very adept at keeping a seven-year-old boy occupied. The amazing thing about that was Kal never lost interest or told Oliver he was done playing with him. It was like he could do it all day long. And he seemed genuine in his desire to hang out with Oliver.

A kid always knew when an adult didn't like them. Oliver adored Kal, so she knew Kal's feelings for Oliver were the real deal.

He never failed to surprise her.

She'd made pulled pork sandwiches, along with coleslaw and sliced fruit. At least Oliver could get some food in his stomach before he bombarded it with candy. They sat and ate, though Oliver was squirming in his chair as the sun began to sink below the trees.

"Momma. Kids will be out trick-or-treating soon. Can we go now?"

"Not until dark. Eat your dinner."

"This sandwich is great, Hannah," Kal said as he finished a bite. "I could eat three of them."

Oliver looked over at Kal. "You're not gonna stay and eat three, are ya?"

"I might. You'd wait for me, wouldn't you, buddy?"

Oliver laid his head against his hand. "I guess so."

Hannah resisted the urge to smile.

In the end, Kal only ate one sandwich. They cleaned up the table, and Oliver dashed into his bedroom to change. He'd decided to switch costumes from superhero to firefighter, and fortunately, Hannah had found one in his size. When he came out wearing it, Kal's eyes widened.

"Dude. You're the perfect firefighter."

"I look just like you, don't I, Kal?"

"Just like me." Kal looked over his head at Hannah, who grinned.

Hannah's mom was going to stay behind to hand out candy to the kids who came to the door, so Hannah and Kal headed out with Oliver.

They met up with Becca and Tony, who were taking Jeff trick-or-treating, so Oliver walked along with Jeff, and Hannah and Kal got a chance to talk with Becca and Tony.

Tony was a police officer, so he and Kal bonded immediately and stayed in step with the boys as they went house to house, leaving Hannah and Becca to chat.

"How are you feeling?" Hannah asked Becca.

"Much better now that I'm past the first trimester. Nausea is gone and I have a lot more energy." She rubbed her stomach. "Baby isn't crowding me too much yet, so I'm enjoying these next couple of months before I have to pee every five minutes."

Hannah laughed. "I remember those days."

They walked along, enjoying the boys' glee as they went house to house. They lived in a fantastic neighborhood where almost all the houses participated in Halloween. There were a lot of kids on their block, and Hannah knew almost all her neighbors. She hoped someday she'd find a house nearby since she'd grown up here.

As Kal and Tony walked up to a house with the boys, Becca turned to her. "So . . . Kal seems nice. And incredibly hot and good-looking."

Hannah smiled. "Yes. We went to high school together and reconnected at our ten-year reunion."

"No kidding. That's sweet. How does he get along with Oliver?"

"Pretty great. They have a mutual admiration thing going on."

"That's good, right?"

Hannah waited to answer, since all the boys—both adult and child—met up with them again as they left the house.

"They gave us three candies each!" Oliver said.

"Wow, how awesome is that?"

Tony held up a candy bar. "They gave Kal and me one, too. We may circle around back to this house."

Becca rolled her eyes. "I'm so happy for you. Next time grab one for me."

"Oh, like you aren't going to rifle through Jeff's bag when we get home anyway."

Becca lifted her chin. "For his safety and health."

"And to snatch all the Snickers for yourself."

Hannah and Kal looked at each other and laughed.

"Do you do that?" Kal asked her.

"I plead the Fifth."

"We all do," Becca said as they walked along. "It's a fringe benefit of parenthood."

"I need to borrow a kid every year to go trick-or-treating with," Kal said.

"You can come take Oliver anytime," Hannah said. "I'll stay home and read a book."

"Done deal," Kal said. "As long as I get a percentage of the candy loot."

"You'll have to negotiate that one with Oliver."

The boys headed toward the next porch. Hannah watched as Kal made sure to stay close to Oliver, to keep an eagle eye on what was being put in his bag.

He was acting like a parent, as if the duty came naturally to him. Someday he was going to be an amazing father.

He's already an amazing father, you idiot. He loves your kid; can't you see that?

She pushed aside those unwanted internal thoughts. She had her own life and her own plans for the future. And she still wasn't certain that those plans included Kal.

It was too soon, and all of this was happening too fast. She wasn't ready yet.

Would she ever be?

CHAPTER 27

SINCE KAL HAD SATURDAY OFF, HE WANTED TO TAKE HAN-
nah out. They'd done a lot of family things lately, and he'd enjoyed those, because he sure had fun hanging out with Oliver.

But they both desperately needed some alone time.

Fortunately, she'd said she had an easy day and finished her
last appointment at two. Oliver was spending the night at Jeff's
house, so Hannah was meeting Kal at his house. He told her to
plan for fun afternoon activities and then dinner tonight. She
showed up around three, giving them plenty of time to head out
to their first stop.

Luckily, she had dressed appropriately in workout leggings,
tennis shoes and a T-shirt. The weather was perfect today for
their first outing. It was a cool day, the sun was out and there was
a breeze.

Hannah got out of the truck and stretched, staring out at the
Everglades that lay just beyond the parking lot.

"Wow. This is amazing."

"I thought you might like to take a walk."

"I'd love to."

She put on her baseball cap and so did he. They slipped on their sunglasses, applied sunscreen and started walking.

The trail was amazing, with a path adjacent to the glades.

"Think we'll see alligators?" she asked.

"We might."

She took his hand and he smiled.

"Don't worry. I'll let him eat me so you have time to run."

She laughed. "That's noble of you. How about we both run instead so we both survive?"

"I like your plan better."

They stopped at one point to watch a medium-sized turtle crossing from one side of the road to the other.

"I think we'll name him Alphonso."

Kal cocked his head to the side. "Why?"

She shrugged. "I don't know. It fits him, don't you think?"

"Sure. Why not."

She leaned against him, and he tipped her chin up with his finger and brushed his lips across hers. "But if we ever have kids together, Hannah, I get to name them."

She paused and gave him a look for a few seconds, and he was dying to know what she'd been thinking. Did he go too far? Then she smiled. "Hey. I did okay naming Oliver, didn't I?"

"You sure did."

She gave him a warm smile, and they continued down the path. But that look when he'd mentioned them having kids together. He'd said it just as a random comment in passing. She'd had a scared look on her face though, as if he'd just proposed or something. He wanted to dwell on it, but he reminded himself of his conversation with his mom, about letting things play out like they were supposed to. He needed to let this one go. He was probably overthinking it anyway. It was just a look.

"The colors out here are amazing," she said as they walked

along. "So much greenery, but a mixture of grays and blues and oranges, too. It's like an artist's canvas."

"I thought about taking you to a museum today."

She shook her head. "This is a museum. With fresh air and birds and turtles and, oh, God, there's a snake."

They stopped as the snake slithered along the road. "That's a rat snake. It's not venomous."

"Sure is pretty, now that I see it more closely."

She was right about that. The snake's coral skin was a blast of bright color in the sunlight.

She inched closer, taking her time so as not to spook the snake, then crouched down and took some pictures with her phone. The snake seemed unbothered by her, probably because she didn't make sudden moves. After she got a few shots, she slowly backed away and the snake went about its business, sinking into the marsh.

"Glorious," she said, smiling so brightly at him she dazzled as much as the shining sun.

There were several birds flying around, some sitting on logs and seemingly watching them as they walked by. But then the path started to get crowded with people walking and biking, so they turned and headed back.

They ended up walking a few miles by the time they made it back to the parking lot. Kal didn't want to overtax her, especially since she had already been on her feet all day, but they had water with them and stayed hydrated, and Hannah hadn't once complained.

Then again, she never did.

She leaned against the side of his truck. "That was amazing. I really enjoyed being out here."

"We'll have to come out someday at sunset."

"I'd love to. I'll bet it's incredible."

"You know what I love?" he asked, moving in to slide his hands on her hips.

"No, what?"

He caught the fleeting look of panic in her eyes again, and even though he wasn't intending to say those words to her just yet, he couldn't help but feel disappointed that she wasn't ready to hear them.

Dammit.

He pushed the disappointment aside, not wanting anything to ruin the day he'd planned. "I love the way you're always so happy to dive into anything. Like this nature walk today."

She smiled, and he saw the relief on her face that he hadn't said the L-word to her.

"Oh, hey, this was fun. It was beautiful out there. Who wouldn't enjoy it?"

Let it go, dude. She's not ready.

They drove back to his place. Jackson was outside in the backyard, the puppy Edgar running circles around him.

"Want something to drink?" Kal asked her. "Iced tea or a beer or some water?"

"Iced tea sounds really good."

He fixed them both glasses of tea, then they went out back.

"What's up?" he asked his brother while petting Edgar, who furiously licked his hand.

"Fixing a problem with the pool filter."

"What's wrong with it?"

Jackson frowned and swiped sweat from his brow. "Hell if I know, but the pressure's not working right."

"Should we call someone?"

Jackson craned his head to look up at him. "Why would we do that when I can fix it?"

Typical Jackson response. "Okay, then. What can I do to help?"

"Bring me something cold to drink."

"I'll do that," Hannah said, turning and going back in the house. Kal kneeled down and investigated the problem with his brother.

Within an hour they had the filter problem fixed. There was a major clog causing the filter to slow its process. They cleaned everything out, flushed the system, and now everything was back in working order.

"See?" Jackson said when they both stood and wiped their sweat away with towels. "I knew we could fix it."

"Ever the genius, aren't you?"

"And too cheap to hire help."

Kal laughed. "That, too."

Hannah had disappeared into the house, so while Jackson took a dip into the pool, Kal went inside to find Hannah at the kitchen table talking with Becks, who had come home from work. Edgar lay curled up at Becks's feet, asleep.

"Hey," he said. "You're home early. How was work today?"

"Busy. And I have a hot date, so I didn't schedule any tattoo appointments for tonight."

"Does Jackson know about your hot date?"

"I hope so." She wiggled her brows, then stood. "I'm going upstairs to take a shower."

After Becks disappeared, Edgar along with her, Kal leaned down to kiss Hannah.

She licked her lips. "You taste salty. Did you fix the pool filter?"

"Yeah, all done."

"Good."

"Wanna come upstairs and change for dinner while I take a shower?"

"Sure." She grabbed her bag and followed him up to his room. Kal closed the door and immediately stripped off his shirt, tossing it in the basket, then toed out of his tennis shoes, pulled off his socks and shrugged out of his shorts and underwear.

He turned to say something to Hannah. She was sitting on the bed staring at him.

"What?"

"Oh, nothing. Just admiring you naked."

He laughed. "Come get in the shower with me and you can admire me up close."

"How can I resist?" She pulled her T-shirt over her head, shimmied out of her pants and kicked off her shoes and socks, leaving her in a hot pink lace bra and matching panties.

"Now those are sexy," he said, coming over to reach around her and undo her bra with a flick of his fingers.

"You have such talented hands," she said, smoothing her palms over his chest.

"Get in the shower with me, and I'll show you just how talented my hands are."

"This offer keeps getting better and better."

She shrugged out of her panties and followed him into the bathroom. He turned the shower on and, as soon as the water was hot enough, stepped in, holding his hand out for her.

The water felt good running over his body. The trail had been hot, and it was a relief to wash off some of the sweat.

Hannah felt even better, especially when Kal rubbed his soapy hands all over her skin. Her body prickled with goose bumps as he dug his fingers into her shoulders, trying to massage out some of the stress from her day.

"That feels so good," she said.

He loved when her voice got low like that. Knowing she responded to his touch made his dick hard.

He pulled her under the spray so she could rinse, then let his hands roam over her body. She turned to face him, and he kissed her. It was like being under a waterfall, their lips tangling in a hot spray of water and tongues, a flaming passion that made him want her so fucking bad he couldn't get enough of her.

He pushed her against the wall and palmed her breasts, teasing and rubbing her nipples. She moaned against his mouth and reached between them to circle his cock, stroking him until he responded with a groan. He swept his hand across her pussy, using slow back-and-forth motions until she arched into him, craving more.

He gave her more, slipping his fingers into her as he ground the heel of his hand against her clit. She was hot, wet, everything he needed as she adjusted the position of her hand to tighten her hold around his shaft, the softness of her hand making him push against her. She gave him long, even strokes, guaranteed to make him lose it.

"You're gonna make me come," he whispered against her lips. "I'm gonna explode all over."

"Yes," she said, her body moving against his in frantic motions now as he continued to push his fingers into her. "Make me come, Kal."

And now it was panting and heavy breathing and no more words as they worked each other over with their hands until they both came. He took her mouth with a hungry passion that left him spent.

Kal leaned against her as he caught his breath, and she held on to him, her nails digging into his shoulder. He could feel the frantic pace of her heart beating against his, and he liked knowing he'd been the one to ramp it up.

They washed off and got out of the shower. Hannah hung up her towel and left the bathroom while he finished drying off.

When he walked into the bedroom, she was sitting on the bed.

"Everything okay?" he asked.

"My legs are still shaking."

"Mine, too."

She smiled up at him. "That was a very enjoyable shower. We should do that more often."

He came over to her, swept her damp hair to the side and pressed a kiss to her neck. When he pulled back, he said, "I wouldn't mind that at all."

"I wouldn't mind it, either. Though if we did that, I'd likely be late everywhere I went."

Just the thought of her living here with him made him want things, made him want to hold her hand and pour out his feelings to her. But then he remembered to take things slow, not push, do this at her pace.

"Would that be a bad thing, though?"

She gave him an enigmatic smile, grabbed her makeup bag and blow-dryer and went into the bathroom.

Yeah, still no answers to all of his questions about where they stood.

He knew he wasn't going to get any tonight, so he went to the closet to pick out clothes for dinner.

CHAPTER 28

SIX HOURS. HANNAH HAD BEEN WORKING ON THIS ONE client for six freaking hours. But sometimes that's what it took to get it right.

Abriel wanted to go from a very dark brown to a mermaid bluish green. And the client always got what they wanted, so it was a painstaking procedure that meant Hannah had to strip all the natural color from her hair, which was a slow process so as not to damage it. Once that was finished, Hannah had to apply three different colors to get the correct blend. Often the first application didn't work just right, which meant Hannah would have to brighten the color over several hours. But the client never left the salon unsatisfied, no matter how long it took.

Abriel's hair was processing and Hannah was in the back washing her hands after finishing off her turkey sandwich and enjoying her large glass of iced tea. The front door opened, so she assumed that it was an appointment for one of the other stylists. But Delilah came back looking uncertain.

"Some guy is here asking for you."

Hannah frowned. "Okay, thanks." Delilah knew Kal, so it

couldn't be him. Maybe a client had come in to book an appointment. She walked out and stopped, her heart thudding against her chest as she saw the tall, lanky guy wearing jeans and a button-down western shirt. She'd know that unkempt wild hair anywhere. And that goofy smiling face was one she'd never forget.

"Landon."

"Hey, babe. Bet you're surprised to see me."

Surprised was an understatement. "What are you doing here?"

"I stopped at your house but nobody was there."

Because people actually work for a living. Most people, anyway.

"Yes. I'm at work, as you can see."

"Yeah. Anyway, I came here to talk to you. Found you on the web. Same salon name." He looked around. "Pretty nice place."

She saw all the faces gaping at her. "Let's step outside."

He followed her out the back door where they'd set up a small table and chairs under the awning. Hannah stuck her hands in the pockets of her jeans to keep them from shaking, her mind processing a million things Landon could have shown up here for.

Money. A reconciliation. Their son.

Oh, God. Maybe he was moving here to be closer to Oliver. Or did he want to take him back to Georgia with him?

No, no, no. She had custody. That couldn't happen. Stop panicking.

"What are you doing here, Landon?"

"I came to see my boy. I thought I'd pick him up tomorrow and we could hang out."

She kept her frustration buried deep. "He has school tomorrow."

Landon shrugged. "He can miss a day."

"No, he can't. Oliver needs structure, and that includes making sure he goes to school every day. If you want to see him, we can make arrangements for Saturday."

Landon looked down at his feet. Whenever he avoided eye contact, that typically meant bad news. "Well, that's the thing. You see, I've got this great business opportunity, so I'm moving to North Carolina. I've gotta get going and I don't have a lot of time. Got all my stuff in my truck and I'm joinin' up with a new crew."

Same old story, just a different state.

"Uh-huh. So you thought you'd do a one-day drive by, mess up your son emotionally by saying hi and bye and blowing on out of his life once again? Come on, Landon. Can't you see that's not good for Oliver?"

He gave her a pleading look. "He's my son, too, Hannah."

"I know he is. And I know you love him. And because I know that I also know you want what's best for him. Seeing his dad once or twice a year isn't what's best for him."

She saw the tears well in his eyes. "I miss him. How's he doing?"

She fought back her own tears, refusing to let Landon manipulate her with his emotional pleas. "I know you miss him. He's good. He broke his wrist at school a few weeks ago. But he's got a cast on and he's handling it great."

"He did? Aww, poor kid. I'm sure he's fine. He's always been tough, like his dad."

"Yeah. Anyway, tell me about the job in North Carolina."

"It's an auto repair store. Nothing too fancy or more than I can handle. It's a franchise and these guys that are gonna run it with me are really good. They got a head for business. And I'll handle the mechanical side."

Nothing she hadn't heard before. "And you're sure this one's on the up-and-up? Do you have the capital to invest?"

He nodded. "I've been working for people instead of trying to go out on my own. Got some money saved this time. I'm sure this is gonna work out."

He toed the gravel, then lifted his gaze to hers. "I met a woman, Hannah. She's real nice and has her head on straight. Kind of like you. She keeps me on my toes and makes me save my money and tells me when I'm screwing up. She's finishing up packing her things and she's gonna drive out next week and meet me up there."

A new woman in his life. In theory she sounded good and just what he needed. If it was true. And for Landon's sake, she hoped it was. "Good. I'm happy for you, Landon."

"Thanks. I'm tryin' to do things right this time. And when I get it all lined out, and I'm workin' steady and got money in the bank, maybe I can take some time and come visit Oliver."

This seemed to be a new side to Landon. Thinking things through. Planning for the future instead of just today. Maybe the new woman in his life who was helping him mature had made all the difference.

Maybe. He still had some work to do. And she wouldn't believe anything until he proved he could follow through.

"You can see Oliver anytime you want, Landon. I'm just not pulling him out of school for you to do that. If you want to come over tonight after he gets out of school, you're welcome to stay for dinner. I know he'd love to see you."

He mulled it over, ran his fingers through his hair. "I do wanna see him, but maybe you're right. Maybe just a one-day thing will mess with his head. I wanna see him when I can spend a week with him, where we can go fishin' and we can really hang out, ya know?"

Now he was starting to think like an adult. "He'd really like that."

"Would it be okay if I started calling him, though? After I get up there and get settled?"

"I'm sure he'd love that, too."

"Okay. As soon as I get up there I'll give him a call. By next week for sure."

"You do that."

"Thanks, Hannah. You always knew what was best."

She walked him out, then came back inside to check on her client's color. It was still processing, so she went into the back to take a long swallow of her iced tea while she went over what just happened.

Delilah walked back there. "That your ex?"

"Yes."

"Was it bad?"

"Sort of. He wanted to see Oliver. I talked him out of it."

Delilah leaned a hip against the washing machine and crossed her arms. "Do you have formal custody arrangements?"

She nodded. "I have full custody. But I never stopped him from seeing Oliver and he never put up a fuss about me leaving Georgia after the divorce. He just never made an effort to see Oliver after I moved back here. But maybe things will change. I don't know. We'll see."

"I hope so, for your kid's sake."

"Me, too, Delilah."

She went back to work on her client's hair, but the rest of the day felt like a fog. By the time she got home she was exhausted. Only she couldn't wind down because Kal was coming over for dinner. She got in the shower to rinse off, then climbed into leggings and a T-shirt.

Oliver had finished his homework and was playing in his room, and when her mom got home she had gone to her room, which gave Hannah some quiet time to start dinner prep. When the doorbell rang, Oliver ran to open it and Kal came in.

"Hey, buddy," he said.

"Hi, Kal. I had a pop quiz in math today and I got them all right. Got all my spelling words right, too."

"So, what you're telling me is you're the smartest kid in your class, right?"

Oliver laughed. "Yup. That's me."

Kal came into the kitchen and brushed his lips across hers. "Hi. How was your day?"

"It was fine," she murmured. "Yours?"

"Good. Got some stuff done. Do you need help with anything?"

"No, I'm good, thanks. Fix yourself something to drink."

He did, and then he and Oliver went into the living room, giving her breathing space again. She fixed the turkey burger patties, sliced sweet potatoes for fries, and made a salad. Her mom came in.

"Need help?"

"I've got it."

"You sure?"

"I said I've got it."

She studied Hannah with a look of concern on her face. "Okay, you had a bad day."

"My day was fine. Go sit down and relax."

Her mother shot her another look, but made herself a glass of iced tea and disappeared into the living room.

Hannah knew she was being short with everyone, but she couldn't help herself. Landon's sudden appearance today had reminded her that she wasn't as in control over her life as she'd thought.

Kal took the burgers outside to put them on the grill, while Oliver set the table and her mom made dressing.

"Anything you want to talk about?" her mother asked her.

"Not right now."

"You know I'm here for you, no matter what it is."

"Thanks."

Fortunately, her mom and Oliver and Kal had plenty of topics to discuss over dinner, giving Hannah the time to stay in her head. Kal tried to engage her in conversation, but she only gave him short answers. Thankfully, he didn't press her in front of Oliver.

After dinner, they all cleaned up and Oliver went to take a bath under her mother's supervision, while Hannah put the dishes away.

"Is there something bothering you?"

"No, I'm fine." She didn't want to talk about it, to bring it up again, not when it felt so raw.

But Kal wasn't going to let her sweep it away. He turned her to face him.

"Hannah. Talk to me."

She looked around the corner to make sure the bathroom door was closed. She heard Oliver and her mother chatting away so she knew he couldn't hear her.

"Landon showed up at the salon today."

"Your ex."

"Yes."

He didn't look angry or upset, just concerned. "What did he say?"

She crossed her arms in front of her. "He wanted to see Oliver. At first he wanted to pull him out of school tomorrow to spend the day with him, but I talked him out of that. He's moving to North Carolina. He has a new job, a new girlfriend. He appears to have his life on track, but I don't know. That remains to be seen. He agreed with me that it was best not to see Oliver until he gets his life together. But he did say he'd start calling him on a regular basis."

"Do you believe him?"

She shrugged. "I don't know. He's made a lot of promises in the past that he hasn't kept. All I can do is hope."

"That must have been a tough conversation. I'm sorry, Hannah."

He pulled her into his arms and at first she resisted, but then she realized how comforting it felt to share the burden. And when Kal rubbed her back, some of that tension she'd been holding on to all day eased.

"You're not in this alone, you know," he said. "We'll figure this out."

That was the thing. Her relationship with Landon and Landon's relationship with Oliver wasn't a thing she could share with Kal or with anyone else.

It was a problem she was going to have to deal with on her own. Maybe Landon really had changed. It would be good for Oliver to get to spend some time with his father. But only if it was quality time, and that it happened on a regular basis. The one thing she could count on with Landon was his inability to be dependable.

So as far as him turning his life around and becoming the ideal father?

That remained to be seen.

In the meantime, it would go back to being life as usual for her and for Oliver. And for the next few weeks she'd wait to see if Landon followed through and actually called Oliver. And if not, then she'd deal with it. By herself. Like she'd always done before.

CHAPTER 29

"I WANTED TO TALK TO BOTH OF YOU ABOUT THE HOUSE."

Jackson looked up at Kal. "What house? This one?"

"Yeah."

His brothers had all gotten together to do some painting at the house and had taken a break. They were sitting at the table eating amazing sandwiches that Rafe had brought from their favorite deli, and he figured now was as good a time as any, especially since it was a Saturday and Becks was at work. He wanted this time just with his brothers so they could work this out.

Hannah had been tense and quiet the past few weeks, and Kal wasn't sure what was going on. She kept telling him everything was fine, but he knew there was a lot on her mind. Maybe it was because the holidays were approaching and she was busier than usual at work. He didn't really know, but he felt her tension every time they were together, like there was something she wasn't telling him. They'd go out and she seemed to have a good time, but he knew she was holding back. She wasn't as relaxed.

He needed to fix that, wanted to do whatever he could to help her and Oliver feel more settled in their lives.

It was time for him to make some plans, and the first part of that plan started here.

"What about the house?" Rafe asked, absently petting the pup while they talked.

"I'm trying to make some plans for the future. I was thinking, Jackson, that after you and Becks get married, you'll probably want to stay here in the house."

"Oh." Jackson scratched the side of his nose. "We've actually been talking about that. I was gonna bring it up with you guys."

Rafe leaned back in his chair. "Go ahead."

"Becks and I want to foster older kids, around the ages we were when Mom and Dad found us. We'll probably adopt a few, depending on what the state permits us to do. You know, so kids who wouldn't normally get a chance for a family would get one. Like we did."

Kal grinned. "That's awesome."

Rafe smiled, too. "Love that idea."

"Yeah. So we were thinking this house would be ideal for something like that, with all the extra bedrooms and the pool and now that we have the dog and all."

Kal could already imagine Jackson and Becks being parents to some amazing kids. And he'd been making plans of his own, at least in his head. "This is such a great idea, Jackson. I'll move out."

Jackson shot him a look. "We aren't even married yet. You don't have to leave right away."

"I know, but I'm making some plans of my own."

"Yeah?" Rafe sent him a questioning look. "Wanna share?"

"Not yet. Hopefully soon. In the meantime, we should all talk to Mom about making this house permanently yours and Becks's, Jackson."

"That's not necessary. It's a family house, since it belonged to Grandma."

"I agree with Kal," Rafe said. "If you and Becks are going to raise your family here, then it should be your house."

Jackson shrugged. "Maybe. I don't know. We should all talk to Mom about it. We all put equity into this house with the renovation. If we buy it from Mom, we should all share in that equity. That's what we always talked about."

"Hey, whatever you all decide, I'm good with it," Rafe said.

"Yeah, same here," Kal said.

Jackson nodded. "Like I said, we've got some time. So we'll make a plan. In the meantime, don't go running out of here, okay, Kal?"

"Deal." With that settled, they finished lunch and went back to their paint work. When Kal finished at the house, he showered, then met with a Realtor and told her what he was looking for. She said she'd get some places together for him to look at.

Part one of his plan was coming together. Now all he had to do was wait.

WHILE HANNAH WAITED FOR HER NEXT CLIENT TO ARRIVE, she flipped through her calendar, her irritation growing by the minute as she counted the days. Three weeks had gone by and Landon hadn't called. Not once. Not even a text.

She wasn't at all surprised. But she was so disappointed, more in herself for believing for one second that her ex had changed. He'd sure made it sound as if he'd turned a corner, that he'd grown and matured.

She should have known better.

A leopard did not change its spots. And Landon's were permanently affixed on his sorry ass. She was so grateful she hadn't allowed him to see Oliver. A visit would only have built up his hopes, only to send them crashing down, once again.

Why didn't Landon love their son as much as she did? Oliver was bright and intelligent and fun. She would never understand a father who didn't want to be with his own child. She took a swallow of water and swiped at the tears that welled in her eyes.

Everything had been fine until Landon had showed up. She'd moved on, she had a plan for their future. And with one short visit Landon had totally screwed with her head, made her hope that he'd matured, that he could accept some responsibility.

It proved to her that the only person she could trust was herself.

Now the one thing she knew for sure was that Landon was never going to have contact with Oliver again.

She'd make sure of it.

CHAPTER 30

"THANK YOU FOR CHRISTMAS SHOPPING WITH ME," HAN-nah said as they loaded bags in the back seat of his truck. "It's hard to do this on my own."

Kal and Hannah had spent two hours at one of the large merchandise stores, which hadn't been all that crowded considering it was a Tuesday night and there were still a few weeks until Christmas. He was thankful for that.

"Hey, it was fun. And thanks for helping me pick out gifts for some of the homeless kids."

She leaned against him at the side of the truck. "You're so sweet to do that."

"Jackson and Rafe and Becks and Carmen and I all pitch in. We get toys and games for the kids, then we buy food and bring it out to the camp along with some clothes and necessary items for the adults. They should have a Christmas, too."

She sighed. "They won't go to the shelters or the places that serve meals?"

He shrugged. "Some of them will. Some won't. The ones that

won't are those we want to make sure have a decent meal and a gift."

They climbed in the truck, Kal pausing to check his phone, then headed back toward Hannah's house. Before they reached the block, however, he took a left.

"You made the wrong turn, Kal," she said.

"I know. There's someplace I want to show you."

He pulled to the curb in front of an unfamiliar house. Hannah frowned.

"What's this?"

"It's a house I'm looking at. Want to come with me?"

She gave him a suspicious look, but nodded. "Okay."

The house was a one-story cream-colored stucco with a beautiful front porch and a tile roof.

"This is really nice," she said as they got out.

It was dark out so she wouldn't be able to get the full picture of how pretty it really was. But if she liked it, he'd bring her back during the day. "Come on. Naomi is waiting for us inside."

"Naomi being . . ." she said.

"My Realtor."

"So you're house shopping."

He grinned. "You could say that."

They walked through the front door. Naomi, a mid-forties dynamo who was all of five foot one, waited for them in the entry. She shook his hand. "Hi, Kal."

"Hey, Naomi. This is Hannah."

She held her hand out. "Nice to meet you, Hannah."

"You, too, Naomi. This house is lovely."

"Isn't it? Go ahead and walk through. I'll be waiting outside."

Kal led Hannah through the foyer and into the kitchen.

"Wow," Hannah said. "This is nice."

The kitchen was open to the dining and living area. The kitchen had tons of counter space and lots of cabinets, and the floor was a light travertine, which was amazing during the day. "There's tons of light in here. Look at all the windows."

She walked around, sliding her fingers over the granite countertops. "I can see why you'd like it."

He took her hand and led her through the back door, flipping on the light. "And look at this backyard. Built-in kitchen, fire pit, and plenty of room to build a pool."

She took in the view. "This is really amazing. So spacious."

"Right?" They stepped inside and he flipped the light off, then walked with her down the hall toward the bedrooms. "Four bedrooms, two bathrooms. The master is killer. It's huge."

"It definitely is," she said as they walked through all the rooms. "Nice bathroom, too. It looks like they renovated everything. I like that soaker tub in the master."

He loved that she loved everything. "Yeah. And all the bedrooms are big. Which one do you think Oliver would like?"

She stopped abruptly and spun around to look at him. "Wait. What?"

"Oliver. For his room? Which one do you think he'll choose?"

She held up her hands. "Wait a minute. This house is for you, right?"

"For us. For you and me and for Oliver."

She shook her head. "No."

Now it was his turn to frown. "What do you mean?"

"I mean, no. N-O, Kal. I don't want this."

"You don't like the house?"

"I love the house. The house is great. You should buy it. For yourself. Not for me. I'm not moving in here with you."

Now he was really confused. "I don't get it. So you like the house, but it's not for you?"

"No. When and if I can afford to buy a house, I'll buy one. With my own money. For me and for my son."

What she was saying didn't make any sense to him. "Hannah.

Maybe I didn't make this clear. I want us to move in together. Make plans for a future together. You and me and Oliver. Like a family."

"No, you didn't make that clear, but the fact that you assumed that I'd just ride along on your grand plan without even consulting me about your house-hunting adventure is so typical of the male species it should be written in the 'Dumb Things Men Do' guidebook."

Ouch. "Okay, maybe I thought you were ready to—"

"That's the problem, Kal. You just *thought*. You didn't talk to me at all. No, I'm not ready. I'll never be ready. Not for this. Can you just take me home now?"

"Sure." He didn't know what else to say.

As they walked out, he gave Naomi a tight smile and told her he'd call her later. Fortunately, this house was only a couple of blocks from Hannah's, because the silence in the truck was icy. She got out as soon as he'd parked, then pulled her packages out of the truck.

"Hannah, wait."

She clutched the bags to her chest and turned to face him.

She didn't say anything, so he had to. "I guess . . . I need to know how you feel."

"How do I feel? I don't know how I feel, Kal. Not right now."

He stepped toward her. "Then I'll tell you how I feel. I'm in love with you. And I love Oliver, and I want both of you in my life. But if that's not what you want, then you need to let me know, because I'm invested. My heart is invested, and I thought yours was, too."

She looked at him and he waited.

And waited.

"Like I said, I don't know, Kal. I'm not sure how I feel. I just need some time, okay?"

He gave her a quick nod and watched while she turned her

back on him, walked away and closed the door without once turning around.

It took him a few minutes of standing there in her driveway before he could climb in his truck and drive away.

Okay, so he'd had this all wrong. He figured that this would all turn out like it had for Rafe. That he'd surprise her with his plans to get a house for them. That Hannah would be thrilled and excited to start a new chapter of her life with him.

He'd been dead wrong. He'd been wrong about Hannah.

Maybe this was her way of getting back at him from ten years ago, when he'd made the decision to break them up.

Maybe they hadn't grown and changed.

Maybe nothing had changed at all.

CHAPTER 31

"MOMMA, CAN I HANG UP THIS ORNAMENT THAT DADDY made for me?" Oliver asked, dangling the wooden motorcycle that Landon had made when Oliver was two.

Hannah gritted her teeth and smiled. "Sure."

"Kal said we were gonna go to the Christmas store. And that we'd get a fireman ornament."

"Kal's . . . busy right now, baby."

Oliver looked at her. "I miss him, Momma. Is he gonna come over soon?"

Hannah tensed. "We'll see. How about you find your Spider-Man ornament and hang that on the tree?"

"Okay."

Oliver helped her decorate the tree, then lost interest and asked if he could go play with Jeff. She called Becca, who said Jeff was available, so Oliver dashed over, leaving Hannah and her mother to finish putting up the Christmas decorations.

Great. Just one more task to do today. One more joy-filled thing on her to-do list.

"I don't know who filled this box last, but it's a mess," she said, rummaging through papers and packing material. "I can't find a thing."

"Girl, you've been griping around this house for a week now. Usually the holiday season puts you in your happy place. What's wrong with you?"

Hannah handed her mother one of the decorations to put on the mantel. "Nothing's wrong. I'm fine."

"Right. Snippy, grouchy, grumbly, angry, pouty, sniffly . . ." Her mother paused. "If I could come up with one more, you could be an updated version of the Seven Dwarfs all in one person."

She was not . . . all those things her mom had just said. She reached into the box for the Christmas stockings and hung those up, smoothing her hand over Oliver's. Hanging Oliver's stocking always made her happy. Now it just made her . . . what was one of those words?

Oh, right. Tears welled in her eyes and she sniffled.

Sniffly. That was it.

Nothing was going right. She wasn't all right.

She'd done the right thing in breaking up with Kal. Whatever choices she made were always the best ones for her son. And for herself. Going it alone was for the best. Everything had become so complicated. Now it would be easier. She could concentrate on building up her clientele at the salon and taking care of Oliver, with nothing else to get in the way.

"And where's Kal?" her mom asked.

She stuffed her head in the bottom of the box, but found it empty, so she shoved it aside and opened the next box.

"Did you think by ignoring me I'm not going to ask the question again? Where's Kal?"

"We broke up," she mumbled.

"Oh, honey, no. Why?"

Hannah shrugged, then sat on the floor and looked up at her mom. "I don't know. He wanted to buy a house."

Her mother frowned. "And that's bad, why exactly?"

"He wanted to buy a house that we could all live in."

Her mother gave her the side-eye. "How dreadful. I can see why you dumped him."

"Mom."

"Mom, what? He treated you terribly by wanting to share his life with you? With Oliver?"

"It's more complicated than that."

"Explain it to me."

"It's really complicated."

Her mother moved the boxes aside and took a seat on the sofa, then patted a spot next to her. "And I'm not stupid, so talk to me."

With a sigh, Hannah pushed up from the floor and stood, then sat next to her mother.

"Landon was here a few weeks ago."

Her mother's eyes widened. "He was? What did he want?"

"To see Oliver, of course. On his terms. Like pulling him out of school. He was on his way to North Carolina for a new job. Made all these promises about how he was going to include Oliver in his life, start calling him regularly."

Her mom nodded. "And he never did."

"He never did."

Her mom patted her knee. "I'm sorry. For both of you."

"I'm sorry for Oliver. I was over Landon a long time ago. Fortunately, Oliver doesn't even know Landon was here. I keep hoping he'll change, for Oliver's sake, but I don't think that's ever going to happen."

"You can't make someone be something they're not. And someday Oliver will realize that, honey. You just have to let it go."

"I know I do. I just hurt for Oliver, for the mistakes I made. That I keep making." She let out a long sigh. "And then there's Kal. And me. Mostly me."

"I thought you two were getting along so well."

"We were. But there are things I want for myself. To be able to do by myself. I want to be independent. To save money and to buy a house myself. I don't want to make the same mistake twice."

"Hannah, Kal is nothing like Landon. He's responsible. He has a great job. He loves Oliver. He loves you."

She looked down at her hands. "He told me he loves me."

"And what did you say?"

"Nothing. That I need some space."

"So you don't love him back?"

Tears pricked her eyes. "That's the thing. I do love him. But I'm afraid. I messed up so badly the first time. And this time it's not just my heart that's in the mix. It's Oliver's, too."

"Oh, baby." Her mother folded her into her arms and held her. "Maybe it's time to stop running away. Especially from a good man who loves you."

"I know."

Hannah had to admit that while it wouldn't solve her problems, there was nothing better than being held by your mom while you tried to work out in your head how you were going to fix the mess you'd made.

Because she did love Kal. And maybe they weren't on the same page as far as future planning, but she couldn't just walk away from him.

She missed him so much her heart felt like it was tearing in two.

There had to be a way back from this. And the only way to do that was to talk to him, to figure things out.

She had to stop running away from things that scared her. And loving Kal scared her more than anything had ever scared her before.

It was time to woman up and face it. Face him. Then maybe together they'd figure out what to do.

If he would even speak to her.

CHAPTER 32

THE ENTIRE TRT STOOD ON THE TOP OF THE HIGH RISE, looking down below at the two construction workers hanging on to the scaffolding that had somehow given way and was now tilted at a forty-five-degree angle.

"At least they're tied off," Meg said.

"Which isn't gonna do them much good if that scaffold collapses and plummets them down forty stories," Irish said.

"Okay, let's get ropes and pulleys into action," Lieutenant Anderson said. "Donovan and Starling, I want the two of you rappelling down for rescue."

"Yes, sir," Kal said, immediately climbing into his harness and grabbing the equipment he'd need. Phil and Micah would have the lead on ropes that would hold Kal and Dean. The others would have the ropes and pulleys to bring up the two construction workers.

The top of the high rise was forty-six stories, which meant they'd rappel down six stories. Winds were high, so this wasn't going to be an easy rescue. It also meant the situation below was precarious. They needed to get a move on before that scaffold became even more unstable. They'd have to work quickly, but safely.

A rescue like this meant that Kal and Dean had to put their trust in the team. Phil had hold of Kal's rope. As Phil hooked on and checked everything on Kal's harness, he turned him around.

"I've got you," he said.

Kal nodded and swung over the side, beginning his descent. He kept his focus only on getting down to the stranded workers.

Wind whipped around him, furious and unrelenting. They needed to hurry. He took a quick glance across to see that Dean was struggling, too. The descent seemed to take forever, though he knew only a few minutes had passed before they reached the workers, who were hanging on for dear life.

Scaffolding wasn't all that steady, either.

"Wind just picked up out of nowhere," one of the workers said as Kal reached him. "We never would've been on this thing in high winds. And then the cable suddenly failed."

"It's okay," Kal said. "I've got you."

Dean was working on his guy, too, so Kal could concentrate on doing what needed to be done. He attached a harness and rope to the worker, then radioed to the team to start pulling the worker up.

Dean's guy went up just after Kal's, but then a huge gust of wind blasted the scaffold against the steel frame of the building. Dean got caught up in the rigging and the scaffold shot him sideways, slamming him against one of the beams.

"Dean!" Kal yelled as he saw his team member go limp.

He hustled his way over to Dean to check him out. He was unconscious after that hit and Kal didn't know the extent of his injuries. This was not good.

"What's going on down there, Donovan?" his lieutenant radioed.

"Starling got slammed against a beam. He's unconscious. Injuries unknown. I'm hooking on to him now, sir. Will notify as soon as we're ready to lift up."

"Roger."

He put a c-collar on Dean, then hooked his harness to Dean's and radioed the team to raise them both. They were up on the main floor within a minute, every team member grabbing on to Dean, who by now was starting to regain consciousness. They had already called down for a basket from Station 65, who'd been waiting on the ground, and EMTs were on their way up to attend to Dean.

Kal's pulse raced as they put Dean into the basket and took him downstairs to the waiting ambulance where news crews waited to interview him and the rest of the team. As usual, the TRT was more interested in attending to their jobs than they were in answering questions. They'd let the department PR team handle that. But for some reason cameras had caught his rescue of Dean, so they'd stuck a mic and a camera in his face and asked him tons of questions about how it had all gone down. His lieutenant had told him to answer a few questions so the media would go away.

He wasn't very comfortable being in front of cameras, but he gave a recap of the team's rescue today, giving them a step-by-step of what the team had done and how they had done it. The fact that the media kept coming back to him, personally, irked him, but he kept it on point, making sure to note it was a team effort. Finally they seemed to have enough sound bites and went to interview the construction workers so he could continue doing his job.

Both workers were unharmed, only a little shaky, so EMTs checked them out and released them.

After cleanup, they drove to the hospital to check on Dean. Carmen was working the ER so she came over to them when they arrived.

"He's got some scrapes and maybe a concussion. He's in CT right now, and his wife's in the room if one of you want to go back there and talk to her."

Lieutenant Anderson stepped forward. "I'll go."

Carmen nodded, smiled at Kal and placed her hand on his arm. "He's going to be okay."

Kal nodded. "Thanks."

Phil came over to him. "You know her?"

"She's my sister-in-law. She's the nursing supervisor of the ER. She knows her shit. So if she says Dean's gonna be okay, then he will."

"Thanks." He started to turn away, then stopped. "You acted fast. You saved my partner's life. You did good out there today, Donovan."

Kal nodded.

"I've given you a hard time, thinking you didn't deserve to be on this team. I was wrong."

Kal knew it had taken a lot for Phil to admit that. He also knew how close Phil and Dean were. "We're brothers. All of us. It's what we do for each other."

"Yeah. It is." Phil laid his hand on Kal's shoulder, then walked away.

They all waited, pacing and nervous for an hour and a half until Carmen came out again.

"You can all go in. But just for a minute. And no loud voices and no ruckus. Understood?"

"Yes, ma'am," Irish said, looking to Kal as they walked quietly down the hall. "She's mean."

Kal's lips lifted into a smile. He couldn't wait to tell Carmen that later. She'd love it.

They opened the door to see Dean sitting up in bed. He grinned when the team walked in.

"Well?" Meg asked. "You gonna live?"

"I am. Thanks to Kal."

Kal blinked in surprise.

"Yeah," Phil said, "thanks to Kal, my best friend is going to live to swing on a rope another day."

They all surrounded him, shook his hand, patted him on the shoulder, then made their exit.

"Kal, wait," Dean said.

Kal stayed behind.

"Thank you for what you did out there today. You showed amazing skill and you were damn brave. I was wrong about you. I'm sorry."

Kal laid his hand on his shoulder. "Apology accepted. I'm just really glad you're okay. Get well so we can see you back on the team."

"Thanks, brother."

As he left the room, Kal felt as if a boulder had been lifted off of his shoulders. All he'd ever wanted was to feel a part of the TRT. And he'd only felt partly on the team, because not all the members had accepted him. Now they all did. And it felt great. Out-fucking-standing, actually.

All he had to do was straighten out the rest of his life. And that part wasn't going to be as easy as dangling off of a forty-six-story skyscraper.

Because you couldn't make someone love you who didn't.

And he didn't know how to change that.

CHAPTER 33

HANNAH HAD SPENT THE ENTIRE NIGHT PACING. WORRY-ing. Thinking.

She'd seen the TRT rescue on the news, had seen the way Kal had rappelled over to rescue his fellow firefighter while dangling forty-something stories above the ground. Her heart had leaped into her throat when they'd interviewed Kal and she realized it had been him up there.

All she'd wanted to do was drive over to the fire station, fling herself into his arms and pour her heart out to him, but she couldn't do that. She had to wait and hope that when she went over to his house this morning that he'd be there, that he'd open the door to her. That he'd open his heart to her and listen to what she had to say.

She'd rearranged her appointments so she didn't have to be at work. She dropped Oliver off at school and asked her mom to pick him up today. She needed the entire day, even though she might end up having the door slammed in her face. If that happened, she'd just come home and . . . and . . .

Cry, she supposed. But she'd have no one to blame but herself if that happened.

She pulled into the driveway and her breathing quickened. Kal's truck was parked there. The garage door was open.

Okay, Step One taken care of. He was home.

No other cars were there, so she wasn't sure if Jackson and Becks were home, but she'd deal with that if and when he let her in.

Now all she had to do was actually get out of the car and make her way to the door.

But for some reason her body was frozen and she couldn't seem to make it move.

Grow some courage, Hannah. You got yourself into this mess. Now get yourself out of it.

Nodding to herself, she turned off the ignition, grabbed her keys and got out of the car, forcing herself to walk each step to the door.

When she got there, she sucked in a breath and rang the bell. The sound of the doorbell rang so loud it almost made her turn around and run to the car. But she straightened her spine and threw her shoulders back.

Whatever happened, she'd face it.

The door opened and there was Kal, looking freshly showered and damp and gorgeous in long pants and a long-sleeved shirt.

"Hannah. What are you doing here?"

"I . . . I saw you on TV. That rescue. It was . . . wow, are you okay?"

"I'm fine. You want to come in?"

"Sure. Thanks."

She stepped inside and he closed the door.

"I was making breakfast," he said as he led her through the living room and into the kitchen. A Christmas tree stood by the windows in the living room, and adorable holiday decorations and stockings adorned the mantel. She could see Becks's touch all over. If she hadn't felt so miserable she would have smiled about that.

"You hungry?" he asked.

Her stomach gnawed at her, but it was nerves, not hunger. "A little."

"You can eat with me, then."

He was mixing together eggs and as he laid bacon into another pan, she asked, "Can I help?"

"No, I've got this. So what brings you by?"

She could tell he was tense. So was she.

"I wanted to talk to you. I've been wanting to talk to you. About that day that we . . . that I said some things to you and then I walked away from you."

He gave her a quick look before turning the bacon. "Okay."

If she wanted this to work out, she was going to have to tell him the truth, to pour her heart out. "I was scared, Kal. And upset."

"Upset with me?"

"No. I was upset that Landon hadn't called like he'd promised. And scared about letting you fully in, into thinking about having a future with you when I'd messed up so badly the first time. And I know you're nothing like Landon, but I had all these plans for my future, about how I was going to save money, and buy my own house, and Oliver and I were going to be independent and do everything on our own, you know?"

He put bacon and eggs on a plate, then went to the fridge and grabbed a container that had some melon in it. Then he poured juice into two glasses. "Let's go sit at the table."

They took their plates and glasses to the table.

He ate, and she pushed her fork around the plate and managed to eat a couple of bites of fruit and a forkful of eggs.

"So I came into your life and fucked it all up," he finally said. "Is that what you're saying?"

She shook her head. "No. It's coming out all wrong. I was just scared when you took me to the house. Because the house was perfect. You were perfect, and everything was coming together so well. But it wasn't my dream, you know?"

He laid his fork down. "I know. And I'm sorry about that. I pushed you too hard, too fast, and that was my fault. You weren't ready for everything that I wanted. And that's on me. I'm sorry."

He was apologizing? Why was he saying sorry? This wasn't going like she had thought. "Wait. You have nothing to be sorry about, Kal. I'm the one who screwed up. I'm the one who pushed you away. It wasn't what I wanted."

"It wasn't?"

"No. I'm crazy in love with you. After you left, I was devastated. And angry. With myself, for letting you go. My plans are stupid."

His lips curved. "Being an independent woman is not stupid, Hannah. I admire you for everything you've done to carve out the life you have for you and for Oliver. I didn't mean to get in the way of that, but I can't help that I fell in love with you. That I love Oliver as if he's my own."

Her heart pounded so hard she thought it might burst. "I love you, Kal. I've loved you since I was fourteen years old. I don't know that I ever stopped loving you. Only now it's a different kind of love. It's deeper. The forever kind. I don't want to lose you."

He pushed his chair back and stood, then pulled her out of the chair and kissed her, the kind of kiss that a woman could feel all the way to her soul. When he drew back, he smoothed her hair away from her face. "I love you, Hannah. And whatever plans you want to make for our future, in whatever timetable you want to make them, I'm on board for it."

For the first time in . . . forever, she felt a sense of peace. That this felt right, that she was home in the arms of the man she knew she could spend the rest of her life with.

"How about we make those plans together?" she asked.

He smiled down at her, and she lost herself in that look of warmth and love in his eyes.

"I like that idea a lot."

She laid her head on his chest and knew that right here was all she would ever need.

EPILOGUE

TWO YEARS LATER

KAL SNUCK INTO THE KITCHEN TO GRAB A BEER, THEN turned to watch the melee that was his living room.

This place was a madhouse.

Then again, that's how the Donovans rolled. Especially these days when they all got together as a family. It was general mayhem and he loved it.

Kal was glad that he and Hannah had talked it out and agreed on a bigger house. Not only did they want to have more kids soon, but they knew they were going to need a lot of space whenever the whole family came over. So the oversize family room had been the best choice. Not that they hadn't argued about houses for at least three months before they'd decided on this one. And, okay, this one had been Hannah's favorite. Oliver loved the pool out back, plus there was plenty of yard space for a dog, which they'd gotten almost immediately. Lucy, their golden retriever, was out back running amok with Jackson and Becks's dog, Edgar, the two of them having the best time. And now that the entire

Donovan clan had expanded as much as it had, Kal knew this house had been the best option. He had a feeling there'd be more family gatherings at all their houses over the warmer months.

Plus, Kal really liked having a pool.

It was their turn to host Christmas Eve this year, and as Kal looked around, he realized how much had changed in a couple short years.

Jackson and Becks had added to their family by fostering three kids, all siblings. Jose, Grace and Mirai were now a part of the Donovans. Wild hellions all of them, too, and the whole family adored them. The older two were fourteen and Mirai was eleven, and they kept Jackson and Becks on their toes, but God, it was great to see those kids thriving with foster parents who loved them. He couldn't imagine Jackson and Becks ever giving those kids up. Official adoption plans were already in the works.

Dad was currently carrying eight-month-old James in his arms, showing him all the lights on the tree. James was the spitting image of Rafe, except he had Carmen's eyes. Carmen's grandfather, Jimmy, was here tonight as well, along with his wife, Felicia. Jimmy was doing better than ever these days, which made Kal really happy.

Even Hannah's mom had found love again with Nate Anderson, a local painter, her brunch date who'd turned out to become the second love of her life. They'd gotten married six months ago in a simple garden ceremony. Kal hadn't seen Paige this happy since before Hannah's dad had died. Both he and Hannah were so thrilled for her.

And his parents had become the happiest, most doting grandparents to all the kids, including Oliver. After Kal and Hannah had gotten married last year, and Landon had finally agreed the best thing for Oliver would be for him to legally give up his parental rights, Kal had petitioned to adopt Oliver. It had taken long conversations with Oliver about the whys and hows of it, but he loved that boy, and Oliver loved him, too. Kal wanted to make sure that it was what Oliver wanted as well. But now Oliver was going to be a Donovan forever. His son. Just the thought of it made him smile. It probably always would.

"What are you doing?" Hannah came over and put her arms around him.

"Just admiring the view." He looked out over the family, watching as they all enjoyed one another, the food and drinks, the kids.

"I know. It's like a miracle, isn't it?"

He put his arm around her. "Sure is. Did I mention to you how lucky I am?"

She tilted her head back and smiled. "Every day. But I'm the lucky one."

He turned to look at her. "Yeah? How do you figure that?"

"Because I went to our ten-year high school reunion, and managed to snag the hottest, kindest, smartest guy there. Who ended up loving me, marrying me and becoming the father of my children."

He pulled her close and hugged her. "Aww, babe. Thank you."

Then he drew back. "Wait. You said children."

She smiled wide. "Yes. Children. Plural."

He looked down at her belly, then back up at her. "We're pregnant?"

"Well, I don't know if you are, but I definitely am."

He'd already been filled with so much joy he could hardly contain himself. But this? This was . . . damn. Almost more than he could take. He picked her up in his arms and twirled her around the kitchen.

She laughed. "Put me down."

He did, then he kissed her.

"We have to keep it a secret for now," she said. "Just between us."

He nodded. "Okay. But can I tell you that I love you?"

"Every day. Every hour, if you'd like."

He kissed the tip of her nose. "I'll do that."

He was going to be a father—again. Oliver was going to be an amazing big brother. He was growing up so fast. Becoming smarter, kinder, and utterly amazing every day.

Kal couldn't wait to see the new life he and Hannah had created.

He sighed and smiled and put his arm around his wife as they reentered the family fray.

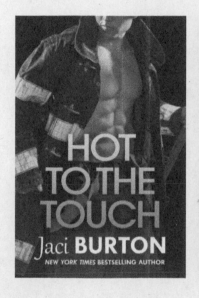

Don't miss *The Best Man Plan!*

Jaci Burton kicks off her dreamy Boots and Bouquets series with a sweep-you-off-your-feet friends-to-lovers romance.

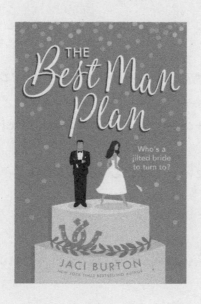

Available from

Jaci Burton's Play-by-Play series

... what's not to love?

Irresistible, ripped sports stars — check ✓

Smart, feisty women — check ✓

Off-the-charts chemistry — check ✓

Intimate, emotional romance — check ✓

Available now from

HEADLINE
ETERNAL

Welcome to Hope, Oklahoma.

*The small town that's sure to warm
your heart.*

*Full of big hearts, fiery
passion and love everlasting . . .*

Jaci's Hope series is available now from

HEADLINE
ETERNAL

HEADLINE
ETERNAL

FIND YOUR HEART'S DESIRE...